Dead
Egotistical
Morons

By Mark Richard Zubro

The Tom and Scott Mysteries

A Simple Suburban Murder
Why Isn't Becky Twitchell Dead?
The Only Good Priest
The Principal Cause of Death
An Echo of Death
Rust on the Razor
Are You Nuts?
One Dead Drag Queen
Here Comes the Corpse

The Paul Turner Mysteries

Sorry Now?
Political Poison
Another Dead Teenager
The Truth Can Get You Killed
Drop Dead
Sex and Murder.com
Dead Egotistical Morons

Dead
Egotistical
Morons

Mark Richard Zubro

St. Martin's Minotaur
New York

Dedicated to the men and women of the executive board of Local 604. Thank you for your kindness and help. And a special thanks to Paula Miller. You made a difference.

www.minotaurbooks.com

Library of Congress Cataloging-in-Publication Data

Zubro, Mark Richard.
    Dead egotistical morons / Mark Richard Zubro.—1st ed.
       p. cm.
    ISBN 0-312-26682-0
       1. Turner, Paul (Fictitious character)—Fiction. 2. Police—Illinois—Chicago—Fiction. 3. Gay police officers—Fiction. 4. Chicago (Ill.)—Fiction. 5. Bands (Music)—Fiction. 6. Gay men—Fiction. I. Title.

PS3576.U225D43 2003
813'.54—dc21

2003043123

First Edition: August 2003

10 9 8 7 6 5 4 3 2 1

Acknowledgments

For their kind help and assistance,
thanks to Jeanne Dams, Barbara D'Amato,
Rick Paul, Kathy Pakeiser-Reed, and Jack Howard.

Dead
Egotistical
Morons

▾ 1 ▾

Detectives Paul Turner and Buck Fenwick waded through the mob of reporters and the crush of shocked concertgoers outside the arena. The corridors leading to the murder scene were packed with police, stadium personnel, and hangers-on.

The detectives arrived in the home locker room of the All-Chicago Sports Arena, newly built just west of McCormick Place. In here muted conversations barely stirred the stunned silence. Turner noted the plush carpet, gilded fixtures, soft lighting, leather couches, comfy chairs, and locker spaces as big as walk-in closets—no crashing metallic lockers here. Hanging from the ceiling and set flush against the wall were ten-foot-high flat video monitors with smaller ones scattered about—all gray and silent. They then moved into the shower area. This looked more like the repose of a millionaire's spa than that of a hard-used stadium locker room. There were ten trapezoidal-shaped shower stalls around a central core. Luxury couches abutted the walls. Stacks and rows of fluffy towels filled a luxurious drying room in one corner. It reminded Turner of a warm-air hand drier gone amuck. There were three other entrances to the room. At the far side from the door they had entered, the detectives found a cluster of police personnel around the entrance to one of the stalls.

Turner and Fenwick waited near the opening for the medical examiner and the crime scene techs to finish their jobs. David McWilliams, a beat cop they'd worked with before, glanced at his notes and recited the events as he knew them. His face was red, and he seemed flustered even though he had been here only half an hour.

"We were on duty outside when the call came in. I got here and the place was nuts. Out in the locker-room area, they'd been having this huge party and there were at least twenty people crowded around the dead guy. I called for backup and then I tried to get everyone the hell away from the crime scene. Everybody was screaming and carrying on. All kinds of people were giving orders and trying to tell us what to do. We had to subdue one of the security guards. After the paramedics finished with the corpse, they had to give medical assistance to my partner. They think he might have a broken jaw. We're waiting to charge the security guard with assault. He's the one who found the corpse."

Turner asked, "Who is the dead guy?"

"Roger Stendar." McWilliams said the name like it should be recognized.

Fenwick sighed. "I'm supposed to know who that is, aren't I?"

Several of the techs gave Fenwick quizzical looks. One of the youngest of them said, "Boys4u? The most popular rock band in the world? He's their biggest star."

Fenwick snorted. "Not anymore. I thought all those guys were a bunch of no-talent, prepackaged, too rich, too young, egotistical morons."

2

Turner said, "This one is a dead egotistical moron."

"Does anybody really listen to that music?" Fenwick asked.

Turner knew for a fact that Fenwick mostly listened to eighteenth-century and earlier classical music. Obscure Renaissance motets were his specialty. Turner also knew he was never to reveal this information.

McWilliams said, "His band, Boys4u, sells one hell of a lot of CDs."

Fenwick said, "My daughters have posters of some boy-band persons in their rooms. Aren't those groups all the same?"

"So far the big difference I see," Turner said, "is this guy is dead. Presumably all the others are alive."

"Of no great import to me," Fenwick said.

The corpse was naked. Turner guessed the dead guy was in his early to mid-twenties, maybe six feet tall and a hundred forty pounds. He lay on his back. Water and rivulets of blood lay near the head. Turner noticed a series of lightning tattoos on both of the boy's arms and a sunburst around his navel. When the ME finished, Turner and Fenwick approached the body.

The wall was pale turquoise marble and sparkling clean. The floor was white marble. The space was maybe five-feet-by-five. Turner and Fenwick squatted next to the body and gently turned it over. In the middle of the back of the head they saw a small black entry wound. No exit wound.

"Small caliber," Fenwick said.

Turner nodded. There were no other signs of violence. "Was the shower still on when he was found?" Turner asked.

"Yeah," McWilliams said.

Turner knew that because of the water and the crush of people who'd been in the room, they were unlikely to find anything helpful in the shower area.

Turner said, "Execution-style murder. Why didn't the killer just leave the gun in here?"

Fenwick said, "We could call *Executioners R Us* and see if they have a special on boy-band killers."

"Executioners run specials?" the ME asked.

"All businesses have slow and fast periods, don't they?" Fenwick asked.

Before they left, Frances Strikal, a representative of the stadium, took them on a tour of the locker area. She was in her late forties and dressed in a gray skirt, white blouse, and gray jacket. The shower room had four entrances. One from the swimming pool, one from the weight room, another from a whirlpool/sauna area, and one back into the locker area itself.

Strikal said, "The band members were permitted full access to these areas. They used the weights and the pool every day."

"All of them?"

"Yeah. Nobody else was allowed back here." She leaned toward them to whisper as if a tabloid reporter were lurking two feet away. "It was kind of a kick. They skinny-dipped."

All the rooms had doors leading to a hallway and entrances leading from one to another. The detectives examined each room. The pool was Olympic-sized. The sauna included luxurious massage tables. The weight room contained five of each kind of the most modern machines. Beyond the pool was a medical facility with more than enough paraphernalia to stock a well-run emergency room. They also found a trainer's room, plus arena and coaches' offices. Strikal left after she showed them around.

Fenwick said, "It's a veritable warren back here, a maze. Maybe nobody is allowed in these private areas, but half the planet could have traipsed through here."

Turner said, "Anybody could have slipped out of the party, come around from any number of ways. Then again, there wouldn't have to be any sneaking around if the last band members who left killed him."

"You could hide a football team and its cheerleaders in here," Fenwick said. "We've got a lot of questions to ask of a lot of people."

Turner and Fenwick did their questioning in a lounge with navy blue walls, a light blue ceiling, white leather couches and chairs, and fixtures covered in gold leaf. Earlier they'd ordered beat cops to keep all the assembled party-goers from leaving and to keep the members of the band separated. Turner doubted if they'd be able to ascertain who left when. A geography of movements would be essential, but he doubted if they'd get anything clear enough from it to be helpful.

As Fenwick settled his bulk onto a deep, plush chair, he asked McWilliams, "How many people were at this party when he got shot?"

"Nearly two hundred in the reception area," McWilliams said. "The shower room was supposedly secure. No one was allowed back there except the guys in the band."

"But there are three other entrances," Turner said.

McWilliams said, "And nobody claims to have heard anything. When we got here, music was blaring from everywhere. You couldn't have heard a gunshot if it had been fired next to your ear. Or if they did hear it, they aren't saying."

Fenwick snorted. "Witnesses, pah! Give me good old-fashioned DNA every time."

After McWilliams left to get the first person to interview, Fenwick glanced around and said, "This place even smells new."

The athletic center had been opened in a grand ceremony by the mayor of Chicago the day before the concerts began. The group Boys4u had opened the venue with a week-long series of performances. All seven concerts had sold out in less than fifteen minutes.

A nearly six-foot-ten man walked into the room. McWilliams said, "This is Jordan Pastern, head of the band's personal security."

Pastern had tears in his eyes. His khaki pants clung to massive hips, his belt cinched around a narrow waist, his black hair was slicked back and oily. A snowy-white T-shirt covered his broad shoulders and well-developed abs. He looked like a two-hundred-forty-pound linebacker in his prime. He might have been in his early thirties. The front of his pants and shirt were still wet. Turner assumed this must have been because he had cradled the dying singer. The security guard had a large bruise on the left side of his face and raw and abraded knuckles.

"This is my fault," he said, "all my fault. I protect these guys as if they were my own kids. How can he be dead? He just gave the concert of his life. All the kids did. They were great. He can't be dead. He was a nice kid. They were all nice kids. Who would do such a thing?" Tears cascaded.

Turner and Fenwick were not inclined to interrupt him. A talking witness was better than a silent witness. They also knew that many killers who knew their victims were eager to talk about the horrific thing they'd just done. The detectives would do nothing to inhibit the possibility of this guy turning from witness to suspect to killer. Eventually, the tears stopped. However, when the man went into his third round of self-recriminations, Turner said, "Mr. Pastern, we understand you found the body."

"I didn't mean to hit the cop. I didn't know who it was. He was in the way. We were trying to help Roger. I'm sorry. This is so screwed up." He pointed to his face. "You guys hit hard."

They'd worry about the assaulting-a-police-officer problem later, if ever. That was minor compared to the dead body.

"What happened tonight after the concert?" Turner asked.

"We had this huge party in the dressing room. It was closing night of their current tour. It was a great tour. Tonight it was wilder than the locker room of a team that had just won the World Series. Lot of relief. Lot of good feelings. Everybody was here to celebrate. Executives from the record company. Hangers-on. The boys all take a shower after each show. They get real sweaty, and even the gel in their hair starts to melt. Roger always got done with his shower last."

"Why was that?"

"After every performance he worked the crowd. He loved it. They all did, but he reveled in it. He let the fans touch him. We had to stick close to him to prevent him from getting mauled. Then he'd throw his shirt to the crowd. Whoever caught it got to meet him. It was kind of a tradition."

"So, he was the last one in from the arena?" Turner asked.

"Well, yeah, but he always took the longest shower as well. Here it was a little different because they each had separate stalls. This place is piss-elegant. So he was taking forever. Everybody wanted him to party. We waited and waited."

"Who was allowed back here?"

"Nobody."

"Was someone guarding the door?"

"I didn't notice anyone go in. I kept an eye on the entrance, but I had lots of distractions. I wasn't worried.

Everyone at the party had been cleared by my security people. Everyone knew better than to try and see these guys naked. These were all professionals, people who'd been around famous groups."

"What about the other entrances?"

"No one was supposed to be back there."

"About how long would he have been in here alone?" Turner asked.

"Maybe fifteen, twenty minutes. I came back to hurry him along. I found him." Great tears flowed down his cheeks. "He was on his back. There was blood. I tried to revive him." His fists clenched. He rubbed them against his eyes. He pulled out a damp hanky and blew his nose. When he was sufficiently composed, he said, "I screamed for help. Nobody came. I left him for a few seconds to get somebody. After that everything went pretty damn fast, too damn fast. It was so horrible. People from the party rushed in. All the rest of the security guys for the band, uniformed guards from the stadium, Chicago cops, everybody. Paramedics showed up pretty quick. There are always some on duty because there's nearly forty thousand people in the arena. I didn't mean to hit the cops. They were trying to drag me away from Roger, and I thought I could help."

"What made you think that?" Fenwick asked.

"I don't know. I figured maybe he just passed out. He couldn't be dead."

"You didn't see the entry wound?"

"Not at first. A little of the water was pinkish red. As soon as I picked him up and held him in my arms, I saw the blood dripping. Then I looked." He drew a deep breath. "I had to do something. I guess I wasn't thinking straight. I couldn't just let him lay there dying."

"Was he breathing at all?" Turner asked.

He spoke very quietly. "No. No, I guess he wasn't. Not at all."

Fenwick asked, "No one heard you yell for help?"

"The party was wilder than usual. They were replaying the concert at top volume on all these video screens."

"Who's in charge of who gets back here?" Turner asked.

"I am. I'm going to be blamed and that's bad. But I'll never forgive myself for this. These boys were friends of mine. I took care of them. I loved them like brothers. If they needed something on the road, I would get it for them."

"Like what?" Fenwick asked.

"Oh, anything."

"Drugs, women?" Fenwick asked.

"I don't pimp for nobody. I don't do drugs."

Turner noted that the answer wasn't as precise as a flat-out no.

"We aren't tabloid reporters," Fenwick said. "Do they do drugs or don't they?"

"If they do, it isn't a problem that I'm aware of. These guys are given anything they want by fans. I don't know what all they've gotten. Security protects them from the fans. We don't protect them from themselves."

"We'll need a list of whoever was here," Turner said.

"We've got a list, even the heads of the company had to give us the names of anyone they wanted to bring back here. Sometimes the boys invite special guests, family, girlfriends, you know. They would have been cleared as well. The publicity people would have the most comprehensive list."

Fenwick said, "Whatever list you've got, we'll take. Did you see a gun?"

"No. But with the chaos of the party anyone would have had a chance to hide it or even leave with it."

"Did Stendar have any enemies?" Turner asked.

"This is the most popular band in the world," Pastern said.

"Which doesn't answer the question," Fenwick said.

"I suppose we all have enemies."

"Any crazed fans?" Fenwick asked.

"There are always those, but that's what security is for. It's pretty tight around the concerts. It's more of a problem when they go back to their hometowns and try to live a normal life. They don't have that anymore. We've got barriers between the boys and the crowd. There are guards at regular intervals stationed all around the stage."

"No problems in the group itself?" Fenwick asked.

"No, the guys really get along. Everybody really cares. It's like a family."

Fenwick said, "Statistically you're more likely to be killed by a member of your family or at least someone you know than you are by a stranger."

"Oh," Pastern said.

"First, we'll need to talk to all the members of the group and the people who were usually backstage," Fenwick said. "Then we'll do the hangers-on. Some of the beat cops will be conducting preliminary interviews."

Pastern left.

2

Jonathan Franklin Zawicki—and he introduced himself using all three names—was tall and slender with a hook nose, gray eyes, and jet black hair that looked dyed. Turner thought he might be in his middle forties. He wore a dark gray suit that looked expensive because it was. He held out his hand to the detectives. Everybody shook hands.

"We understand you're the head of the company," Turner said.

"I've been president of Riveting Records for ten years. I've developed numerous talents in that time. I signed this band to their first contract. Boys4u is the hottest group in the world today. Their latest album sold over three million copies in its first week of release, better than any other album in history."

"Tell us about Roger," Turner said.

"A very fine young man," Zawicki said. "One of the quieter members of the band. Always worked hard. Always on time. Very serious about making music. Loved to sing and perform.

As far as I know, he didn't have an enemy in the world. The fans could be a little crazy, but no one expected this."

"Are you usually at their concerts?"

"I'm rarely on the road with the group, but this was the last stop in a six-month tour. Everyone was here to celebrate. We sold an awful lot of albums on the tour. An awful lot of souvenirs, too. It is hardly an exaggeration to say that a mere mortal could probably retire on the proceeds from the T-shirt sales from this week in this venue alone."

"How did they get picked for the band?" Fenwick asked.

"Several of them knew each other before we put them all together. There's been a big demand to see who would be the next smash-hit boy band. There's a lot of cash to be made from teen and preteen girls."

Turner said, "I don't understand the dynamics of being in a band, going on tour. Could you fill me in from the beginning?"

"Is that important to solving the murder?"

"I need to understand this world," Turner said. "It is totally foreign to me."

"Of course. Well, we have scouts out looking for talent. One of them saw two of these boys singing at a small wedding. They were very good. Very unpolished, of course, but very good. Then we found two others at an open audition. The fifth was in a barbershop quartet at a church fund-raiser. It was serendipitous chance that he got picked. One of my secretaries happened to be there. The chemistry with the five of them clicked. A band works very hard for a very long time. Then, if they are lucky, they open in a few small venues, and they begin their rise. In this case they toured South America and Japan for six months and hit it big there. They came back to the States, and the rest as they say, made millions."

"What about personal relationships between all of them?"

"They were friends. Roger worked hardest of all. Jason

12

Devane was kind of a computer geek. Danny Galyak was a cutup. Dexter Clendenen was sweet and vulnerable. Ivan Pappas was the most mature. For such disparate personalities, they all got along. Remarkably well, for living and working so closely together."

"They lived together?" Fenwick asked.

"On the road and when practicing for a tour. They were wealthy enough in their own rights to afford luxury homes, and they lived in them when they were away from practice and touring obligations."

"Who had access? Who knew them best?"

"Jordan Pastern had the daily access. He was more than a security guard. He was in charge of the detail that took care of the boys' lives on the road and when they were recording. He'll know who was closest to them. I don't really know."

"How about family and friends?" Turner asked.

"We encouraged them to have friends and family as important parts of their lives. Getting a mention of them being out to dinner with their mom in the local gossip columns is like pure gold. It is excellent for their image for them to be seen as normal as possible. At the same time it is very difficult for major celebrities—and these boys were among the biggest—to have normal relationships. The traveling is killer. The hours of work are intense. You don't get to sing and dance in just a day or two. Putting together a two-hour stage show is not easy."

"You'd think they'd have it down pat after doing it for six months," Fenwick said.

"I'm talking about preparation, and even on tour they still practiced often. Plus these boys wrote a great deal of their own music. That was a little unusual. They took great pains with their work. They were very professional young men."

Turner asked, "How often did you see them? How did you get along with them?"

"We got along very well. I saw them before the start of each tour. I was always positive and encouraging."

"Any disgruntled employees?" Turner asked.

"Any boss has to let people go. I don't think anyone was angry enough to kill."

"Drugs," Fenwick said. "These were rock and roll guys. They were young. They were rich. They could have anyone they wanted for sex. They could get any drugs they wanted. Did they?"

"The image of wholesomeness was paramount. Their fan base is girls from six to sixteen. The image we want for this band is for them to appear a little virginal mixed with a lot of sweetness. Knowing them would be equivalent to dating the sexy but nonthreatening, sensitive, big brother of the girl next door. It is a very cultivated image. We allow nothing to get in the way of that."

Fenwick said, "Were they doing drugs or not? Sex, drugs, and rock and roll. You can deny it, but they must have been at least tempted."

"I know nothing about their sex lives. Around the concerts, everything was very controlled. Outside the concerts, they were told to be discreet. We were not called upon to bail them out of jail. Drugs and drug dealers are not permitted near them by us. This isn't some heavy metal band filled with heroin addicts and self-indulgent, crude, low-class, no-talent hacks. These are good kids. If they indulged any negative habits, I don't know about them."

Fenwick said, "The image is pretty well shot to hell with one of them being murdered."

"I am sorry this young man is dead, but the image is magnificent. He will be a martyr. He and the band are victims. In spite of or because of that, their CDs will leap out of the stores."

Fenwick said, "Unless one or some or all of them are the killers."

"They're good kids."

Turner said, "We'll need to talk to them one by one. They each took showers back there. They would be most likely to have seen something."

"Of course."

Turner said, "Do you keep a record of threats against the band? Maybe a list of the crazies who might be stalking them?"

"I'll make sure you get whatever we have on that."

Fenwick said, "If they start to give our people trouble, we'd like your help in making sure they cooperate. They may be young and rich, but they need to understand that they are not free at the moment."

"I will make sure it happens as you say." After that, he left.

"No tears," Fenwick said. "I don't trust him."

"You need tears for innocence?"

"I need grief and emotions to feel confident I'm not being snowed. I didn't say he was lying. I just don't trust him."

Turner said, "Is either one of us in the business of trusting suspects or witnesses?"

"Not this week."

Dexter Clendenen was about five foot six and thin enough to be considered by an anorexia clinic. He wore dark blue jeans, a gray sweatshirt, and white running shoes. He dumped a ratty brown backpack next to his chair. Like Pastern, the front of Clendenen's clothes were wet. He had very pale, almost translucent skin. Turner saw the edge of several tattoos on both wrists. Clendenen had soft brown hair cut short and soulful brown eyes. He spoke in a mellow tenor voice.

Turner realized he was sitting with a young man who half the twelve-year-old girls in the country would trample their own mothers to be in the same stadium with, much less in a private room having a conversation.

"Do you know who killed Roger?" Clendenen asked. He barely looked up at them as he spoke. He wiped away occasional tears with the back of his hand.

"We don't know yet," Turner said. "We're trying to get some information. Tell us about what happened after the concert."

"It was crazy. We did a couple extra encores. Roger always loved doing encores. I just wanted to get the thing over with. I wanted to go home. All of the guys did. Roger insisted on extra encores. He ate them up. He loved getting the crowd riled up."

"Angry?" Turner asked.

"No, nothing like that. Just wildly enthusiastic. Usually, it was great. But tonight, I wanted it to be over with. It's been six months. You don't have a life. I figured I could stay at the after party for maybe thirty minutes and then go home."

"Home to your hotel or home to where you live?" Turner asked.

"Where I live. Eureka, California. I guess I couldn't have really left tonight, but I wanted to. Being on the road is tough. New cities, new interviews, same old questions. New people, same dopey comments. Hiding out, trying to have a few quiet moments. Don't get me wrong, I love this. This is my dream, singing and dancing and being rich. I've wanted to have this since I was little. It really is a dream come true. It's just—after a while anything can get to be too much."

"So Roger kept you guys out there?" Turner asked.

"It seemed like forever. We were sweating like mad. We got back here and then we hurried to take showers. This place is pretty nice. Some of the older venues are a little run-down. We each had an individual stall. That marble was

16

pretty cool. I guess I got done first. That drying room they've got is real nice; soft, warm air. They had thick carpets and warm fluffy towels. Nobody's allowed back there. They don't let anybody see us naked, except maybe Jordan. He's not gay. He doesn't stare. He just makes sure there are towels and stuff and leaves us alone. I finished before the other guys. Roger is always last. I came out here to the party. I didn't hear anything. I was mostly getting something to eat and some champagne. I was really hungry. We always have the best food. The caterers were great. We got anything we wanted. Course the company pays for it."

The guy looked like he could eat hot fudge sundaes for years and not gain an ounce. Turner knew this did not endear the teenager to Fenwick, whose massive bulk had continued to expand over the years.

"How did you guys get along?" Turner asked.

"Little squabbles now and then, but mostly great. We were on top of the pop world. We were the best. Everybody wanted to be us. Everybody wanted to date us."

"What were the little squabbles about?" Turner asked.

"Nothing really. When we're practicing for a tour, we all live together in this big mansion in Cathedral City, California. Nobody bothers us. It's great, but five guys living together, no matter how big the place is, you can get on each other's nerves. Roger could be a little messy, but we had maids to clean things up."

"So everybody pretty much got along?" Turner asked.

"Oh, yeah."

"We heard you wrote your own material."

"Roger did a lot of that."

"That cause any problems?" Turner asked.

"No. There wasn't like a competition to get one guy's music played more than somebody else's. We worked together."

"Did Roger have any enemies?" Turner asked.

"No. He was always patient and friendly."

"No crazed fans?"

"Well, that's what we had security for. Nobody would have been admitted back here who was a crazed fan. They're pretty good about security."

"So someone you know must have killed him," Turner said.

If it was possible, the kid turned even paler. "Who would do that? We're just regular guys."

Not for a long while now, Turner thought, *and probably never again in your lives.*

"Anybody get fired who was close to the group?" Turner asked.

"No, we didn't have anything to do with all that stuff. We just got the best help in the world for everything. The best choreographer, the best video maker, the best makeup people."

Turner asked, "Any of the guys in the band involved with drugs? Any of the hangers-on?"

"No, none of that. Some of us weren't even old enough to buy liquor when we started out."

Turner doubted if that would be an obstacle for a young man who had more money than half the planet and an awful lot of people who would want to please and pamper him.

"A lot of people think we're gay. We're not. I've got a girlfriend."

"Is she here on tour?" Turner asked.

"No. I'm going home to Eureka after this to see her. I miss her."

Someone knocked on the door. McWilliams put his head into the room. "You guys are probably going to want to come see this, now."

▲ 3 ◢

Out in the hallway McWilliams said, "Some of the guys found a gun, and we've got other stuff."

He introduced Ethel Hinkmeyer, the band's publicist. She wore a navy blue outfit with a white, ruffled blouse, and a matching pillbox hat and veil. She carried a thick leather briefcase in her right hand. Frances Strikal, the stadium rep, was with her. Both women promised full cooperation from the groups they represented.

Hinkmeyer took a sheaf of papers out of the briefcase. "This is a list of all the people from the company who were here, all those who had access to the stage area, and the names of all the people who were working here from the Chicago area. We always tape the concerts. I have that for you as well."

Turner took the proffered materials and thanked her.

The four of them followed McWilliams to the floor of the arena, then down lengthy corridors of cinder block painted in rainbow colors. Turner had been to the United Center for professional basketball and hockey games. This place dwarfed that one. The arena was closer to being an indoor stadium than it was to a normal sports palace. Seating rose in vast tiers all around the central core of a playing surface. The sections of seats nearest the ground could be rearranged depending on the needs of the different events.

McWilliams led them under the canopy over the concert stage and the equipment needed for the performance. Even though the lights were all on, beneath the vast stage set everything was dim and shadowed. First McWilliams brought them to a corner near the main entrance. A knot of uniformed cops stood around a pile of black garbage bags jammed with heaps of paper cartons, beer cups, plasticware, and food wrappers. One bag was slightly separated from the rest.

McWilliams used a gloved hand to lift up a corner of the bag. The detectives squatted down and peered inside.

"Small caliber revolver," Fenwick said. Putting on their surgical gloves, they handled it gently. Six empty cartridges in six empty chambers.

"Did they have metal detectors at the entrances?" Turner asked.

"Even if they did, there wasn't one at the entrance for the crew and hangers-on," McWilliams said.

"You found this here?" Fenwick asked.

One of the beat cops said, "We saw the black bag. We were all wearing our gloves like we're supposed to. This looked a little out of place. One of the guys looked inside. As soon as I saw what it was, I stood watch so nobody could touch it, and we sent for you." Turner tagged and labeled the weapon. They would need to do ballistic tests to make certain it was the murder weapon.

"Why is this here?" Fenwick asked. "What is it about this spot that lent itself to concealment? Did the killer toss it here then just walk out of the arena? Or did he or she simply dash out here, desperately fling the gun, and then go back to the party hoping no one would discover the body and notice they were missing?"

Turner said, "My guess is nobody's going to have detailed memories. With over two hundred folks in that space, finding out who was where and when is going to be problematic."

They walked over to the non-cop people. Turner asked, "Who had access to this area?"

Strikal said, "No one was supposed to get back here except authorized personnel."

"Are there metal detectors at the entrances?" Fenwick asked.

"No. Not for this kind of concert," Strikal said. "How many twelve-year-old girls carry weapons?"

"One is all it takes," Fenwick said.

McWilliams said, "There's more."

They ascended a ramp onto the staging area. The vast interior had been turned into an Escheresque warren of ramps and stages. Voices echoed in the empty hall. The fifty-foot-high screens at all four points of the compass stood blank. Turner could see that the ramps and bridges made it possible for the band to move as close to as many segments of the audience as possible. One series of bridges and landings soared nearly fifty feet in the air to a high platform, a precarious perch for singing and dancing. Above the vast stage area was an enormous banner with a swirl of golden circles on a bright red background. The bunting draped along the outside of the balconies had BOYS4U stitched in foot-high letters all around it.

Turner pointed to the banner dangling from the ceiling. "What's that?"

Fenwick said, "You can tell you don't have daughters.

I've seen that thing scrawled on notebooks and drawn on the backs of hands. I'm not supposed to notice. I never knew which band it applied to. I just know it's pervasive, on lunch boxes, three-ring binders, book covers, and probably on their underwear, which I do not want to know about."

McWilliams brought them to center stage. He introduced a short, hefty man as Aaron Davis, the equipment manager for the band.

Davis said, "As soon as we got the word, we stopped taking the set down. We had just gotten started."

"You guys brought all this stuff with you?" Fenwick asked.

"One hundred and eleven trucks' worth of junk. A crew of about fifty permanent members. Union-contracted workers here at the arena help with the load-in."

"How well does anybody know the locals?" Turner asked.

Hinkmeyer said, "We deal with the International Association of Theatrical and Stage Engineers. The union people clear out before a concert. They mostly help with toting things, not with the technical work. That takes expertise. After the locals are done, the members of the band come in for a sound check. They didn't have to do that except for the first night we were here. Our crew does all the final inspections. Only our people."

Davis led them from the center of the stage to a series of coils and ropes that looked like bungee-jumping cords on steroids. Five stagehands in jeans and sweatshirts stood around them. At one end of each cord was a complex harness. The other ends were attached to thick metal wires. Davis said, "The cops said to check everything that didn't look right. One of the guys found this. They reported it to me."

"What am I looking at?" Turner asked.

"Several times during the concert the boys fly over the crowd. Sometimes we lower them close enough to touch a few fans. We even rigged it here so that they could almost touch the highest tier of seats." He held up the ends of several of the ropes. "Someone tried to slice through all of these."

Turner and Fenwick examined each one. Only one of them had been cut very deeply.

"This ever happen before?" Turner asked.

"Never," Davis said.

Fenwick asked, "If someone was trying to sabotage the operation, why not just snip these wires?" He and Turner examined one. It was as big around as the top U of a combination lock. It seemed to be numerous strands of thinner wire braided together.

Davis said, "You don't get that kind of wire at your local hardware store. It's specially made, super-strength. You would need immense tin snips to break through that and even then you'd have to be pretty damn strong."

"Awful hard to conceal that kind of thing, too," Fenwick said. "A hacksaw would take too long."

Hinkmeyer said, "Someone was trying to kill the whole band?"

"Looks that way," Fenwick replied.

Davis said, "We inspect the props every day. All five wires and ropes checked out perfect before the performance."

"Someone examines every inch of every one of these?" Fenwick asked.

"Yes," Davis said, "every day."

Fenwick looked at the stagehands. "You guys checked these?" he asked.

He got a chorus of "Absolutely," "For sure," "Definitely," and "I checked it carefully."

"Only these five had access?" Turner asked.

23

"Yes," Davis said.

"Someone was watching these wires every second?" Turner asked.

"Well, no," Davis said, "but these are the only guys with permission to touch them."

"How long before the concert do you check them?" Turner asked.

Davis said, "We've got five hours of making sure everything works perfectly. These are among the first things we go over. These wires get done early because if something's wrong, we have to fix or replace it right away. None of the crew had looked at the cable for at least an hour before the concert began."

"Has there ever been anything to fix?" Turner asked.

"Sometimes last-minute minor adjustments, but no sabotage, ever."

"Lots of time when they aren't being watched," Fenwick said.

"We would have noticed someone who didn't belong," Davis insisted. "Nobody touches the equipment except us and the guys."

"You would have recognized all the locals after only a few days?" Fenwick asked.

Davis said, "We checked them in each day. They have very specific jobs. Only the professionals handle anything that might possibly be dangerous."

Hinkmeyer added, "We've worked with this Chicago company many times."

Turner said, "If it's not somebody from outside who did this then it's one of the members of the touring company. Members of the band were down here?"

"They all were," Hinkmeyer said, "but really, you can't go around saying these boys could be suspects. This is awful enough. You can't mean to accuse a member of the band."

24

Fenwick said, "We aren't going to accuse anybody until we have evidence. When we get evidence we're going to accuse whomever we have proof against. Fame isn't going to be some kind of goddamn shield if they're a murderer."

Hinkmeyer wrung her hands. "I didn't mean that. You know the problem the press is going to cause. Every cable network is already covering this live. It's going to get crazier."

Turner said, "We're going to follow the clues. We have no desire to smear anyone or hurt anyone. First, I want to know which band member would have used the most cut-through rope?"

"Dexter," Davis said. He held up one of the ropes. "See? They're color-coded. That's so they always go in the same place when we set up. The boys always started and stopped their stunts in the same spot. For something to look spontaneous onstage, it's got to be rigidly organized."

"Would this much cutting have caused one of them to fall?" Fenwick asked.

"Probably not," Davis said. "These things are built stronger than the ones mountain climbers use. Unless you sawed almost all the way through, you couldn't be guaranteed they'd break."

Turner said, "Show us where each of these is supposed to be before the concert."

Davis said, "The wires are always in the same place they're used from, about ten feet apart. Whoever cut them would have to rush from one to the other."

After examining the locations, Turner said, "Maybe the person didn't have time to do a thorough job. Or had to move fast to keep from getting caught. Or wasn't very strong. Or planned poorly."

Davis said, "We've got another thing." He led them back below the stage and under the first tier of seats to a row of

Dumpsters overflowing with garbage. He pointed to a mayonnaise jar filled with amber fluid. "That's not supposed to be here."

With his plastic gloves on, Turner unscrewed the lid. "Gasoline," he said. "Somebody could have lit all this crap on fire."

Strikal, the stadium rep, said, "The sprinklers in this building are state of the art. We have a fire crew on site when there's a performance. Nobody's stupid enough to make the claim that this place could never burn down like they did for the first McCormick Place, but every possible modern precaution was taken. This arena is above code in all areas. No corners were cut."

"They don't have to burn the place down," Turner said. "All you have to do is start a fire and get a panic going. Fear will do the rest."

Hinkmeyer gasped and turned very pale. "Thousands could have been trampled."

Turner felt a shiver at the thought. A lot of innocent people might have died.

Turner and Fenwick stood at center stage. Taped to the floor at all four points of the compass were eight-and-a-half-by-eleven pieces of paper with large dark letters: CHICAGO.

Fenwick prodded one of these with his left foot. "This is in case they forget where they are?"

"Got to be," Turner said.

Fenwick said, "Somebody had to be awful goddamn busy to do all this."

"Maybe it was more than one person."

Fenwick said, "One or all of them would constantly risk being seen where they weren't supposed to be."

"That almost makes it for sure that it has to be an inside job. Which limits us to only a few hundred suspects, including the band members."

"Why not concentrate on just one rope?" Fenwick asked. "Why attempt each one and none of them successfully?"

"We're dealing with an amateur or someone who was planning elaborately but poorly. A young person maybe. Or a nut who couldn't organize themselves out of a paper bag or someone who judges success by how much fear they can spread, death and destruction being an added bonus."

The two detectives walked around the perimeter of the stage. At one end Fenwick pointed. "Those are real drums and guitars, and a violin. These guys had a real band?"

"Did you think they lip-synched all this stuff?"

"Yeah."

One of the uniformed cops hustled over. "You guys need to look at this."

Back under the stage they were led to a dressing room. It was about ten-feet square, set off from the rest of the area by heavy black curtains. Stadium and band personnel clustered around. Davis said, "The guys have a lot of costume changes during the show so they've got a few places around where we keep things. This is the main area."

Turner saw Bulls, Bears, Cubs, and Sox uniform shirts. He pointed, "Why all those?"

Hinkmeyer said, "In each city we have them wear shirts for at least a few minutes with the logos from the different local teams. Fans go crazy for it."

Davis pointed to a box of twenty-four water bottles. He said, "The guys sweat a lot and need to drink during the concert to keep from becoming dehydrated." They looked like ordinary convenience-store containers to Turner. Davis touched the tip of one bottle with the edge of a fingernail on his right index finger. "This is ours." He pointed to the one next to it. "That isn't."

"They look the same to me," Fenwick said.

"The company makes a special brand just for the guys.

It's a little perk. They went from a nothing company in Manitoba, Canada, to the second biggest bottled water distributor in the world because of an ad campaign featuring Boys4u."

Donning his plastic gloves, Fenwick turned the bottle around slowly. Moments later he said, "I still don't see the difference."

"The labels on ours are a slightly darker shade of green." Davis pointed to the bottom. In small print it said, SPECIAL MADE FOR OUR BOYS. "This is missing on the wrong one, and there's no plastic seal on it."

"Where are the bottles they drank from?" Turner asked.

"The used ones are over there." He pointed to a small trash can half filled with empties. "They all have the correct labels."

"Who's in charge of these?" Fenwick asked.

Roger Stendar's personal assistant was summoned. Christopher Abrar was tall and lean. "Yeah, I order all the little personal stuff." He inspected the bottles. "No. We only get the kind with the special label. We keep them frozen then put them out a couple hours before the concert."

There were nearly a dozen empties. "They drink that much?" Fenwick asked.

"It's actually a lot more sometimes, but we lose a lot of bottles. People take them for souvenirs."

"You mean paying customers can get back here?" Fenwick asked.

"No, like custodians and stuff take bottles to give away or make a profit on. The littlest thing these guys touch can become valuable. And they don't just drink this stuff. They do a water-bottle squeeze over the crowd just before intermission."

"A what?" Fenwick asked.

Using one of Fenwick's gloves, Abrar picked up an

unopened bottle, pulled up the pop-up top, and squeezed it. Water poured against the wall. "They aim it at the different parts of the audience. It's supposed to be fun."

"I guess people have different definitions of fun," Fenwick said.

"Are all of them here?" Turner asked.

"At least three are missing," Davis said. "Which is about the same as usual."

"Who could put a fake one here?" Turner asked.

Abrar said, "I guess the crew. The band. Lots of people."

Hinkmeyer said, "I'm not sure who would even know about these. The special ones were a minor perk."

"How did you notice the difference?" Fenwick asked Davis.

"We were going through everything very carefully. The cops said to notice everything. The one with me said he needed to inventory these. I figured it was a waste of time."

"We're inventorying everything," Fenwick said. "It'll take a lot of time. This whole arena is a crime scene. It's not easy, but we're looking for details exactly like this. It's gotta be done. We'll also need pictures of everything like this in its current location."

Turner said, "We'll tag the bottles and send them to the lab." He turned to McWilliams. "David, get back to the members of the band, now. Find out if any of them noticed anything odd about the water. Have the paramedics monitor them for signs of poisoning."

"Hell of a thing," Fenwick said when the two detectives were once again at center stage.

"Lot of failed attempts," Turner said. "Was Stendar a victim of opportunity or was he intentionally killed? Would any one of them have done as a victim? Too many coincidences, which neither you nor I believe in."

Looking at the stage setting from this central vantage

point, Turner could see it was constructed as a vast letter H. He was currently standing at the center crossbar.

A uniformed cop called down from the top platform high above them. "You guys better come look at this."

Fenwick would have grumbled more about the steep climb if he hadn't been out of breath by about the tenth step.

"That doesn't sound good," Turner commented as he waited for his wheezing friend at a landing halfway up.

When Fenwick reached him, he said, "Good thing I'm not a member of a pop group."

"Not a lot of singing and dancing in that picture."

"Got that right."

When they got to the top, a uniformed officer pointed to a side of the platform. The wood had been splintered.

"Son of a bitch," Fenwick said. "Gunshot."

Turner could see every corner of the stadium from this vantage point. He never expected to be in this position in an empty or a full auditorium.

The platform was six-feet-by-six with wide railings at knee level. In the center of the platform a translucent fiberglass center pole with numerous handholds was connected to a steel girder which began about eight feet above the surface. Gossamer-thin thread stretched between the four side posts made of the same material as the center pole. These side posts reached to shoulder height. Turner tugged at several of the threads. They felt as tough as the wires had been. Each was hooked onto the fiberglass corner posts by a snap lock. They had stepped onto the platform between fiberglass sentinels about two feet apart. He undid one with reasonable ease. A killer probably wouldn't risk coming all the way up here. It would be too easy to notice someone in such a public area. Then again, if it was one of the still-living band members, it might be a place to unhook things. Then again, a dangling strand would be very noticeable.

The audience would be unlikely to see these insubstantial barriers, but in effect they were a net to keep the band members from hurtling off if they lost their balance. Turner bounced up and down several times on the balls of his feet. He didn't feel the platform shake or sway. It felt very well constructed. A successful shot up here would have made a spectacular murder. If the handgun they found was the murder weapon, then a fatal shot would have had to have been a pretty random success. Or if it was a sniper with a rifle, maybe he didn't have enough time to take perfect aim. Turner suspected the members of the band didn't spend a lot of time standing still. Or if they did, would a sniper be lucky enough to have an unobserved moment of his own? A rifle would make more sense for this kind of shot, but they hadn't found one of those. And a rifle would have blown a huge hole in the kid's head.

Fenwick said, "Spectacular revenge to have one of them die in the middle of a performance."

Turner said, "Why wasn't the gun loaded? Are we going to find bullet holes in the ceiling, or did the killer shoot off several rounds in some cornfield in the middle of the state? Was the killer blasting away at every loud moment in the concert? The shot or shots must have been fired at the height of the concert. Who did the killer try and hit? With so many thousands in the auditorium, how did the killer miss someone? Why didn't somebody see the shooter?"

Fenwick said, "At least the gun makes some sense. The fire doesn't. A fire hurts more than just the band. In fact, they're in the best position to get off the stage and out."

Turner said, "But the sabotage and the killing have got to be connected. So the killer wasn't aiming just at the kids in the band? Although the bottle and wire things seem pretty specific."

Fenwick said, "I can't imagine that the sabotage and the killing are unconnected."

Davis joined them on the platform. Turner pointed at the railing. "Was it splintered like that before the show?"

"No way. These things are always in pristine condition. Christ, somebody tried to shoot them, while they were performing? That's nuts."

Turner walked the edge of the platform on all four sides. On each side he unhooked the clamps on the translucent knee-high railings. These folded back on hinges onto the platform. Then he lay flat on his stomach and squirmed under the gossamer ropes. He felt them tickle the hair on his head and the shirt on his back. While he didn't lean out far enough to fall off, still he had Fenwick hold his legs as he stretched to the point where he could examine the underside of the platform. On the third side, he beckoned to Davis. A tech held Davis's legs as the equipment man crawled next to him and looked.

"Is that supposed to be like that?" Turner asked. One end of a strut was no longer connected to the rest of the platform.

"Hell, no! And I know it wasn't like that before the concert. I check these platforms myself. We're very careful. They each take off from this perch at least once during the performance. At one point all five of them have to be up here at the same time singing, dancing, jumping."

Turner and Davis scrambled back up.

As Turner had, Davis bounced up and down several times. "See how strong it is with us up here even with one strut broken. There are multiple fail-safe devices. You'd have to work at it to get this thing to fall. You could get a baseball team up here and be safe."

Turner said, "I think one of the shots hit the strut. A very lucky or very good shot."

Fenwick said, "Or the shooter didn't care if he hit anybody or not."

Turner said, "Hell of a risk just to be taking potshots. Anybody could have spotted a gun. Someone was firing rapidly and randomly?" He shook his head and turned to Davis. "Don't take all this down until we've had our people go over it completely."

Fenwick asked, "Is this concert that loud that gunshots could be unheard?"

Davis said, "It sounds like fifty all-fireworks orchestras in here half the time."

"You don't like the music?" Fenwick asked.

"I like the money I make doing this. I work a lot of concerts for a lot of groups. I haven't paid attention to a note in any venue in twenty years."

The sound of someone shouting floated up from below. They all looked over the edge down to center stage. A man stood there. Even from this height Turner could see he was gesticulating wildly.

"Who the hell is that?" Fenwick asked.

Turner shrugged and they descended.

4

As they neared center stage, Turner could see a tall, portly gentleman standing with Pastern, Hinkmeyer, and Strikal. Even at a distance he could hear the voices clearly. Pastern said, "Who let you in?"

"I have a press pass. I have a right to be here."

"Everybody in that mob outside has a press pass," Pastern said. "Only you got in. Whoever let you in is going to get their ass fired."

"Maybe it wasn't one of your people who let me in. Shout as much as you like. You do not have control over the press."

Pastern swore. "You moronic fuck."

Turner and Fenwick arrived.

The new person held out his hand to Turner. "I'm Randall Blundlefitz, the music critic of *Hot Trends* magazine." Turner vaguely recalled the glossy periodical as being a rival to *Chicago* magazine and the *Reader*, two very trendy and popular media outlets in the metropolitan area. Blundlefitz wore an elegant tux, cut well to fit his ample frame. He spoke with practiced suavity. Each gesture seemed timed and planned. Oscar Wilde before he went to seed.

"You must leave," Pastern said.

"I'm here. This is news. Big news. They might not have any talent, but one of them is dead. Of course, none of these bands has much talent, that's not news."

Turner thought if Blundlefitz was this condescending when someone was dead, how insufferable would he be if they were alive?

"No interviews," Pastern snapped.

"Of course not," Blundlefitz said. "I wouldn't dream of attempting to talk to members of the band tonight. What have the police found out so far?"

Turner liked to watch Fenwick at moments like this. His buddy had no patience with the press. He never knew which bit of rudeness or inappropriateness his partner would respond with. Turner kind of liked both the anticipation and the show that followed.

Hinkmeyer stepped in. "Mr. Blundlefitz, I can give you as much information as possible. If you would come with me, I can give you what you need." She took his elbow firmly but gently.

"If you could wait a moment," Fenwick said.

Blundlefitz turned and raised one eyebrow about a fifth of an inch.

Fenwick asked, "Where were you tonight and who can vouch for your movements?"

"I was not permitted into the locker room for the party afterwards. You'll have to leave me off the suspect list. Trust me, no matter how chaotic it was in there—and I assume it was very chaotic—I would have been noticed. When I am in a room, I am always noticed. I suspect much like yourself, Detective." He turned and marched away. All the others left.

"I think I've just been insulted," Fenwick said.

"And about your weight, which the rest of us are too delicate to mention."

"I don't like him," Fenwick said.

"You don't like anybody in the press."

"Your friend Ian isn't odious." Fenwick was referring to Ian Hume, a reporter for the *Gay Tribune* who had been Turner's first lover.

Turner and Fenwick examined the stage area again before they resumed their interrogations. The arena was much quieter and darker now. A few cops and custodians were in the upper tiers hunting for any possible evidence. Turner didn't hold out much hope for that yielding anything helpful.

"Hell of a place," Fenwick said.

Turner scanned the interior. "I wonder which angle those shots came from. With any luck forensics will come up with something. We can also try and narrow the time down from the schedule of when different effects were being used."

Fenwick said, "Maybe someone in the audience was making a tape. They might have a different angle from the one the company made."

"I don't think they allow that, but we can check."

They returned to the lounge.

The next member of the band to be interviewed was Danny Galyak, who Zawicki said was the group's jokester. Turner guessed he was over six feet tall and in his early twenties. His baggy jeans and bulky sweatshirt could not conceal his huge shoulders or his flat stomach. He shook their hands vigorously. He slumped into the chair opposite them. His deep blue eyes met their gazes evenly.

"This is taking forever," Galyak said. "I want to get to the hotel. My clothes are still wet." Turner could see damp spots from the guy's knees to his shoulders.

Turner didn't notice a trace of mist in the boy's eyes or a

hint of sorrow in his tone. He did notice a suggestion of a light Southern accent.

"Somebody died here tonight," Fenwick said. "Maybe you've got blood on your clothes as well as water."

Galyak blanched slightly. "Hey, I'm sad Roger's dead. How come we can't talk to anybody else? Zawicki said you guys wanted us apart."

Fenwick said, "It's customary in an investigation. We try to keep anyone who was near the scene separate."

"Oh."

"How long have you known Roger?" Fenwick asked.

"Like, since forever."

Fenwick said, "I'll need a little more definitiveness than forever."

"We went to the same grade school in Charleston, South Carolina. My family moved there when I was in third grade."

"Someone tried to kill all of you out onstage," Fenwick said.

The boy sat up straighter. "Say what?"

"We found evidence of sabotage," Turner said.

"Is that why they asked us about water bottles? I feel fine. Somebody put something in our water?"

Turner said, "We're having them checked out. Did you guys only drink one brand?"

"Yeah. We had to. We had an endorsement deal with their company. We got all the water we wanted free. We got almost everything we wanted free. People loved to give us stuff, but endorsement deals were the best. We made almost as much money from them as we did from the records. Well, not almost as much, but a lot."

"Did you all drink the water?"

"Sure. You ever sing and dance like we do?" He glanced at Fenwick's bulk. "If you don't drink, you get dehydrated pretty fast. We're pretty careful."

"So whoever planted the stuff knew you'd be drinking the water?" Fenwick asked.

"We always drink it."

Turner asked, "Would each of you notice which bottle you were using? You might have a contract, but it doesn't say which of you drinks from which bottle. Would you really pay attention in the rush of a show?"

"Nobody gets real hyper if you use somebody else's. We kind of keep ours in one place most of the time, but it's pretty frantic during a performance. Things get moved. Clothes get tossed here and there. Wardrobe keeps up pretty well, but we're on the run for nearly two hours. It's hard to tell. You might notice or not."

"When did you leave the shower room?" Turner asked.

"I left a few seconds after Dexter. He's usually done first, me second. The others were still showering when I left. While we were in there, we would have heard a shot. I didn't hear anything. Roger always took those long showers."

"Maybe he died only because he was the last one," Turner said. He told the boy about the gunshots, the cut ropes, and the possible arson.

"No shit," the kid said. "You mean it could have been any of us?"

"Nobody passed you while you were leaving the shower room?"

"Far as I know it was just us back there."

"Did you notice anybody leave the party?"

"No. Who was paying attention? It was a party."

Turner asked, "Do you check your own props, especially those ropes and wires?"

"I go over everything. I didn't notice anything wrong."

"How long before the concert was this?" Turner asked.

"An hour or two."

"Plenty of time for someone to do some damage," Fenwick said.

"There were really gunshots while we were onstage?" Galyak asked.

"We think so."

"I didn't hear anything. I guess we wouldn't. We do a lot of pyrotechnic stuff. Lots of bangs, bells, whistles, and explosions. A couple times fire shoots out all over and then we swing around."

"How did the five of you get along?" Turner asked.

"Great."

"Who was the leader of the group?" Turner asked.

"Me or Roger. They put us up front the most in the videos and things. We're the best looking and in the best shape."

Turner thought, *no self-esteem problems here.*

"That didn't bother the other guys?" Fenwick asked.

"No. We weren't a bunch of jealous fags."

"The proper term is *gay*," Turner said. He didn't often insist on less-insulting terminology, especially if he was getting helpful information. Just lately, he'd been digging in his heels.

"Okay, sorry." He didn't sound terribly sorry to Turner. Galyak continued, "Anyway, we had everything worked out. Everybody was happy. We all sang about the same amount of time. The other guys weren't just backup singers. Some of us sang more on some songs than others. Like we each got to be center stage on a ballad. The girls love that."

Fenwick said, "A death has occurred here. Do you understand that? You don't look sad about it."

"Hey, I'm sad. I don't know what to say. You don't expect this stuff. I'm a little hyper is all. I'm supposed to be the funny one in the group. All our fame and money and then this happens. You'd think being rich would mean this kind of stuff didn't happen."

"Money don't mean shit when it comes to murder," Fenwick said.

Galyak said, "Rich guys get away with all kinds of stuff. We do."

"Like what?" Turner asked.

"Well, like, oh . . ."

Turner said, "We're not interested in harassing you for pranks or parking tickets that got fixed."

Galyak considered for a moment, then said, "Roger liked fast cars. He was going to sponsor a car or a team on a racing circuit. He drove fast all the time. He got up to a hundred sixty once on an interstate outside Houston. That time he got a couple tickets, but they just kind of disappeared. He never had to go to court. The tabloids never got the news. They don't find out anywhere near as much as they think they do. They get all kinds of stuff wrong, too."

"Like what?" Turner asked.

"We don't date most of the people they connect us to. There isn't time in our lives. I never knew famous people were so busy. We get our pick of women, but there's barely time to enjoy the perks. At the same time all the dreams of what it's like to be in the most popular boy band are true. You can have anybody you want."

"And do you?" Fenwick asked.

"I have a normal sex drive."

"Any problems with screwing underage kids?" Fenwick asked.

"Hey, no. Never."

"They must offer."

"Even if you had all the pro football players from every team, they wouldn't be able to keep up with the offers we get. Getting offers isn't a crime. Making it with hundreds of girls isn't a crime."

Turner asked, "Did Stendar ever hurt anybody with his driving? Kill anybody?"

"No. Hell no. Nobody could cover up a murder. How could that happen? Besides, he was careful. He always wore his seat belt. He made us wear ours."

"Pedestrians he hit wouldn't be wearing seat belts," Fenwick pointed out.

"Hey, he never hit anybody, okay? He didn't. Maybe it was luck, but he was careful."

"You were with him when he did this?" Turner asked.

"Sometimes. A few times. Once in a while. Not much."

Distance yourself from suspicion when you don't know if you're going to get caught up in the vortex of responsibility. The kid had a normal reaction about that, Turner thought.

Galyak continued, "People do strange stuff. We could start an underwear company from everything that gets thrown at us onstage or stock a toy store from all the teddy bears. We have people cleaning up one part of the stage while we're on the other. Roger collected all the stuffed bears after the shows. He'd give them to children's hospitals. We'd all go together to give them to the kids. The publicity department loved it." He paused. "I kinda did, too. It's nice to do stuff for little kids."

For a moment he sounded like a sincere, almost likable young man.

"Did he have any enemies?" Turner asked. "Angry ex-girlfriends? Any of the hundreds of girls he made it with unhappy with him?"

"No. Gosh. It really is great being in the band. Everybody always wanted to do stuff for us. Nobody hated us. Everybody thinks all the guys in boy bands are gay, but I don't care if they think that. I'm making a lot of money doing what I like, and I can have any girl I want."

"No friction in the band?" Fenwick asked. "No problems

outside the band? All you guys must have been saints. No ego clashes among the guys?"

"No. We really got along."

"The road crew never got testy?" Fenwick asked.

"How many times do I have to tell you, everybody liked everybody else?"

"Everybody but one," Fenwick said.

⟍ 5 ⟋

The next member of the band was Ivan Pappas. He wore his dyed red hair in complex swirls above a freckled face. He looked like Howdy Doody on steroids. Kind of puffy, but muscular, slightly heftier than the two living and one dead band members they'd met so far. Zawicki had called him the most mature. Pappas wore black jeans and a pale yellow sweatshirt without a logo. Turner thought his worried frown looked genuine. His clothes too were damp. Obviously there'd been a lot of clutching of the dying or lifeless band member.

"What's happening about Roger?" Pappas asked.

"We're talking to as many people as we can," Turner said. "So far everybody in the band claimed you guys got along. Who was best friends with who?"

"We didn't have best friends like a girl group. We were guys. We could all talk to each other. Like, we didn't have group therapy or anything. We just talked guy stuff. You know, sports and junk. We talked about music a lot. About what was happening to us, the concerts, and crowds, and stuff. About girls. Nobody got jealous. Mr. Zawicki treated us all equal. We all got those super-thin televisions as presents from Riveting Records for Christmas last year."

"Did you hear anything in the locker room?" Turner asked.

"There wasn't no gunshot when I was there. I just showered and got the hell out. I wanted to party. I was hungry. I called to Roger as I was leaving to hurry up."

"Did he answer?"

"He yelled okay or something. He was always so slow."

"That bug you?" Turner asked.

"No. Not in a serious way. We were just guys getting along. Sometimes the press would print stories about one of us pursuing a solo career, but that was all fake. Even if we wanted to, the contracts we signed were pretty ironclad. They were making us rich. Nobody was unhappy about them."

"Did you see anyone leave the party area?"

"No. I was talking to a bunch of girls the whole time."

"Did Roger have any enemies?" Turner asked. "Fights with anybody? Old girlfriends who were jealous?"

"Nah. We've got girlfriends and then we don't. Besides Roger, a couple of us were dating, but nobody had anyone special. We're not really home in one spot for much of the time. Most girls like it if you're around. Even if they come with us on the tour, they get pretty ignored. People might want to have this life, but most of them don't realize all the sacrifices you have to make."

They asked about the water bottles. He hadn't noticed anything. "It was just a big, fast concert. The time goes quick. Who notices much of anything? Was somebody really trying to kill us all?"

"We're checking out everything," Fenwick said.

"While we've been waiting to talk to you, they wouldn't let us talk to anybody," he said. "How come? Do we get to go soon?"

"Pretty soon. We've got one band member left to talk to."

Before the last member of the band walked in Fenwick asked, "Why do so many people think these guys are gay?"

Turner said, "I never thought about it much. My boys don't listen to their music. They're into rap or bits of heavy metal or some crap I'd rather not listen to. Before tonight I wouldn't have recognized the guys in this band if they walked past me on the street."

Fenwick said, "What about those heavy metal bands that wear all the makeup? Why don't people think they're gay?"

"My gay ID card didn't come with a list of who is and who isn't gay, nor the secrets of how to tell who is and who isn't."

Fenwick said, "I don't know why you didn't get the gay-dar gene."

"Lucky I guess," Turner said.

The last member of the band, Jason Devane, was tall and willowy with very light blond hair. He trembled noticeably. He wore a muscle T-shirt, a leather jacket, and black leather pants slung low on his narrow hips. Whether he didn't hold the dead or dying Roger Stendar or the leather didn't absorb dampness, his clothes were dry. He sat very straight in the chair. He looked from one to the other of the detectives then said, "This is the most awful thing that's ever happened to me. I've never known somebody who died. I liked Roger. I can't believe this. He was so alive. The concert was so great. We sparkled and now all of a sudden he isn't there." Tears cascaded for several moments. He didn't seem ashamed of them. After using and discarding a tissue, he wrung his hands. "Is there something I can do? There's gotta be something. How can he be dead? Just gone. I don't believe it."

Turner thought he had the deepest of any of the voices of the members of the band. He guessed Devane might be twenty-two. The kid rambled for over five minutes while wringing his hands, rubbing at his face, crossing and uncrossing his legs, brushing at his buzz-cut hair. When he asked, "Can I do something?" for a second time, Turner said, "We've got a few questions."

"Anything."

"Did you hear a gunshot in the locker room?"

"No. Ivan and me walked out together. We were last except for Roger."

"As you left, did you see anybody going toward Roger or hanging around the entrance?"

"No, we just went to the party. I was hungry. I always am after concerts."

"Did you notice anybody walking out during the party?"

"Everybody was in and out. I don't remember who was where."

Turner explained about the sabotage they found.

"Somebody was trying to kill all of us?"

Turner said, "Or trying to make it look like they were."

"I coulda been dead."

The detectives nodded.

"Are you saying that whichever one of us was last in that shower, we'd be dead?"

"We aren't sure," Turner said.

The boy shook his head. "This is gonna be the end of the band, isn't it?"

Turner wondered how much of the angst about the murder was really a cover for this question, which all of them had to be asking themselves. Great tragedies can affect us, he knew, but how much they affected us personally was usually the unspoken main agenda.

"You guys have a lot of casual sex?" Fenwick asked.

Devane shook his head. "That sounds like a question from one of the tabloid reporters."

Turner said, "We have no desire to involve the press. It could be important if one of the casual relationships had gone sour."

"We're straight guys with the world at our fingertips. It would be abnormal if we didn't have sex. It was offered to us. Thrown at us. I never thought I'd have sex with so many girls. I only dated one girl in high school. This is like being in a candy store that automatically refills itself. We could keep a condom company in business all by ourselves."

"Was there heavy drug use?" Fenwick asked.

"No, man. We had to keep a clean image. If any of the guys was doing drugs, he kept it quiet. Really quiet. I wasn't. This isn't a heavy metal band where the more outrageous you are the more the fans like it. We understood the image we had to portray."

He knew nothing else helpful.

They had a conference with the beat cops who'd been interviewing the other people at the party and the members of the crew. No one at the party had heard anything suspicious or unusual. The cops had no suggestions for people the detectives might interview.

Outside it was cold. The temperature on this February night was supposed to get to five below zero. It felt like it. Despite the frigid air, about a hundred people had gathered across the street from the arena's main entrance. A sea of candles surrounded heaps of flowers and mounds of teddy bears which leaned against a crowd-retention fence. It would take several thousand of the tiny votive candles to add the slightest bit of warmth in the shivering mass of humanity. Most of the crowd were young girls, with a scattering of parents. Turner figured most of the rest of the oldsters were in their cars in the nearby parking lot with the heaters on full blast. A few television crews made occasional forays among the teenagers for tear-filled interviews designed to escalate any possible frenzy. Things wouldn't pick up with that until the morning news shows. It was nearly three in the morning. The two detectives hurried to their car. Standing next to it was a huge, well-muffled figure. When they got close, Turner realized it was Randall Blundlefitz, the critic.

"I've got to talk to you guys. Now."

"Somebody dead nearby?" Fenwick asked.

Blundlefitz look confused. "No."

"Are you the murderer?" Fenwick asked.

"No."

"Do you have the killer in your car?" Fenwick asked.

"I don't know who did it," Blundlefitz said.

"Then it can wait until we get back to the station," Fenwick said. "Meet us there." He bulled past him.

6

Fenwick's first question after he started the car was, "What the fuck does that moron want?"

"The pleasure of your glorious presence?"

"Are we wasting time with this asshole? We've got a million things to do before we can go home."

"He's taking too much interest," Turner said. "Does his interest mean he's a meddling creep, or a killer trying to stay close to an investigation and find out what we've got? I'm not sure. His claim that he wasn't at the party is probably true, but anybody could have gotten in from the pool or the weight room or the sauna. I think we should give him a lot of rope. If we're lucky, he'll hang himself with it."

The short trip to Area Ten headquarters took only a few minutes. The station was little more than a brick-encased landfill. It was the ugliest, most hideous, most rundown police station in the city. You could wash and wax the floors every day and repaint it inside and out weekly, but it would do no good. Fenwick was convinced if they held a national competition for worst police station, this one would win.

Turner agreed. No one bothered to complain anymore about things that didn't work. Nothing changed. When the building collapsed, with or without the cops in it at the time, they might get a new one. Even then they weren't sure.

The detectives arrived ahead of Blundlefitz. At the station the lieutenant on duty, Fred Falcoli, shuffled over. Falcoli walked and talked slower than almost anyone Turner knew. He was also excellent at making sure the police work done on his shift met every bureaucratic requirement. His superiors appreciated his efficiency. His underlings, depending on their willingness to get paperwork done right the first time, either hated him or tolerated him. Turner and Fenwick were closer to the tolerating end than the hating end of the spectrum, although on a bad day, Fenwick could be convinced to strangle all the bureaucrats in the system. Turner wanted to be present when he did. Falcoli got his update then said, "Lots of press on this."

"Got to be," Turner said.

"Get started on the paperwork," Falcoli said and left. He spoke mostly in platitudes, rarely gave out praise or criticism unless your paperwork was wrong.

The detectives began to organize the forms they knew they'd have to fill out after they were done with the rest of the interviews and visits for the night. Moments later Blundlefitz strutted into the third-floor squad room. He marched over to where they sat. He flung his coat, hat, and gloves on an empty desk. He grabbed a swivel chair from ten feet away and pulled it over. After seating himself, Blundlefitz announced, "I have been investigating."

Turner watched Fenwick's expression. His partner's face resembled the gapes of the audience members in the movie *The Producers* at the beginning of opening night of *Springtime for Hitler*.

After a more than comfortable pause, Fenwick asked, "You what?" His voice was far softer than usual. Turner knew this was a bad sign for whoever Fenwick was addressing. Loud, Fenwick was intimidating. Soft, he could be dangerous. Even more so because the object of his ire was usually unaware that the quietness did not denote benignity.

"I've been Jessica Fletcher and Miss Marple combined. I've been busy, as you should have been."

This opening gambit pissed Turner off. Anyone with any sense never mentioned an amateur sleuth to a working detective. The grumbly but benevolent, patient and kindly detectives of television lore were a joke. The bumbling, wise, and kindly interferers—a pleasant fiction. The concept underlying them being that anyone with a modicum of sense and determination could solve a crime. An unpleasantly untrue concept. Turner had never considered the possibility that he'd actually run into someone who claimed to be an amateur sleuth.

Turner and Fenwick watched Blundlefitz in silence.

"I went to their hotel. Why haven't you been to their hotel? I was there. I'm used to getting in where I want when I want. Bluffs or bribes or both."

"Oh my," Fenwick said.

Blundlefitz glared.

Turner said, "Please, continue." He didn't want the guy to stop talking. A killer or a clown or something in between, he might talk himself into an admission of guilt. Although Turner doubted if he actually knew anything that might lead to an arrest in the case.

Blundlefitz said, "I think Jonathan Zawicki is a perfect suspect. I found out stuff that is going to make the tabloids ring. It's going to make headlines around the world. I already have calls in to all the trade papers. I'm going to have an exclusive. This is going to rip the lid off the music industry."

More silence from the two detectives. If Blundlefitz cared about their lack of reaction, he didn't show it.

"I found notes from a meeting. I found out the band was going to break up. I found everything. They didn't get back from the concert for hours. They had to wait so long for you. In Stendar's clothes I found all kinds of things. I found condoms. You know what that means?"

Fenwick answered, "He practiced safe sex?"

"It means he was screwing somebody. You'd think a girl-friend would be using birth control, so he was either making it with guys or picking up women. I know you're thinking it can't be unusual that these guys could have anybody they wanted. You need to find out who he picked up during this past week. That's more suspects. I found out who Stendar was screwing on a regular basis. He got a call while I was there. I've been to visit her. I've got her name. Sherri Haupmin. She left the party early. She didn't know about the murder. She had the private number to his room. She's another possible suspect. Where did she go and why? She's the lead singer for one of the opening acts. She knew things. Why haven't you interviewed her? She said the guys in the band barely ever talked to each other. She said Roger wanted to get away from the band. She claimed they all had to have sex with Zawicki and Pastern."

"Pardon?" Turner asked.

"To get into the band they had to agree to have sex with their bosses. They had to be at the beck and call of all the executives. She said they didn't get any respect as' musicians, which is true. They were just raw meat to be ground up in this big money-making machine." He drew a deep breath. "But I don't trust her. I went through some of the other boys' things."

"You interfered in an investigation?" Fenwick's voice was barely audible in the large squad room.

"No one said not to. There was no crime-scene tape. I've checked with the magazine's lawyers already. I'm going to be bigger than any amateur sleuth has ever been. I don't have much time to keep talking to you guys. I've got to get to the morning news shows. I found evidence of drugs. Bottles of pills."

"Give them to me," Fenwick said.

"I sent them out to be analyzed."

"You're not going to be on the morning news shows," Fenwick said. "You are going to go get those pills, and you're going to do it now. We are going with you."

Blundlefitz said, "Are you trying to save their pristine little reputations? Are the police covering up? I won't let you bully me."

Fenwick said, "We either arrest you this minute, or we go get those pills. They are part of a murder investigation. They are part of a dead person's belongings. They are certainly not yours."

"I get a phone call."

Turner suspected the ego of the man had blinded him to the simple expedient of bringing one of the lawyers with him or waiting until one was available. He'd made a mistake. Turner didn't believe in trampling people's rights. Unfortunately for Blundlefitz, it was no longer a question of his rights. The reporter had acted precipitately and committed several crimes.

"Here's how it works," Fenwick said. "We find a nice cell for you, and we forget you're there for as long as we can. No phone calls. No communication with anybody."

"That's illegal. You can't deny me my rights. I'll yell brutality."

Fenwick stood up. "You mother-fucking moron!" His bellow was at full roar. "You stupid fucking shit!" Bang, went his fist down on his desk. Blundlefitz jumped. "Do you take stupid pills?" Fenwick demanded. "Who the fuck do you think you are? Fucking amateur sleuths don't exist in the real world, and you aren't some great untouchable journalist looking for truth and light. You work for some third-rate rag that specializes in gossip, speculation, and innuendo. You think you're going to tell the police how to do their job? And you're going to fuck with my investigation? And you're going to tell me that I can't fuck with you? That you have fucking rights? You do not have a right to fuck with an investigation. What kind of asshole are you? Certainly the moronically stupid kind. Do you take asshole pills *and* stupid pills? You can't have been born this way." Fenwick's fist banged again. Turner noticed several of the uniformed cops from downstairs appear at the top of the stairs. They saw Fenwick in full roar and immediately retreated. Someday Turner half expected to see steam coming out of Fenwick's ears just like Yosemite Sam at the height of his anger and frustration.

Fenwick continued at full volume. "All three of us are going down to our unmarked car, and we are going to drive to wherever the fuck you took those pills. We're going now or you are going nowhere for twenty-four to thirty-six hours and with the slightest bit of luck, over forty-eight hours. And believe me, my superiors will back me up on this. A famous kid is dead and you broke into his room. Don't tell me I don't know a story that will hurt somebody when I hear one. Your name will be synonymous with shit when I finish with you. You think we haven't dealt with reporters before? You think we don't know how to plant things that will help us? Let's go."

Blundlefitz didn't move. Whether in awe at this spectacular display of genuine anger or in fear for his own safety, or for some other reason, Turner wasn't sure.

Fenwick banged his fist down harder than before. The desk shook. Fenwick pointed a finger at Blundlefitz. "Defy me, you dumb motherfucker. I dare you to defy me."

Blundlefitz looked at Turner, who was glad to see the

reporter was very pale. Blundlefitz mumbled, "I didn't have time to take the pills anywhere."

"Where are they?"

"In my car."

The three of them marched into the cold. Blundlefitz opened the glove compartment and extracted two bottles of pills. Turner placed the containers in evidence bags. Fenwick reached past Blundlefitz and pulled out a handful of crumpled-up men's underwear.

"Why are these here?" Fenwick asked. Turner checked the sizes, either twenty-eight or thirty.

Blundlefitz said, "I took those, too."

Back at their desks Turner held up the evidence bag with the pill bottles in them. "Your fingerprints have probably obliterated any possible clue." Turner examined the labels. "These look like ordinary prescription drug containers. It says 'Take for pain as needed.'" One container looked nearly full, the other half full.

"What better way to hide drugs?" Blundlefitz said. "And being addicted to prescription drugs is just as much an addiction as any other."

Turner examined the underwear. There were three pairs of white briefs, Calvin Klein, Hanes, and 2Xist as well as two pairs of boxers, one pink, one black. Blundlefitz looked frustrated. "You can't humiliate me," he said.

Turner realized they didn't have to. He'd done a good enough job on his own. He also suspected that Blundlefitz would hope they wouldn't report his theft to the press or to his superiors. The break-in was bad, but you could rationalize it under an umbrella of twisted journalistic logic. The underwear was a killer.

"You stole a dead guy's underwear?" Fenwick asked. His tone had changed from attack mode to stunned disbelief.

"He wasn't going to need them anymore." A touch of Blundlefitz's old bravado crept into his voice. "The others wouldn't miss them."

"I bet you took them from the dirty clothes piles," Fenwick said. "Did you take them for kicks or are you planning to sell them as souvenirs?"

Blundlefitz raised his head and glared at Fenwick. "I did wrong. It's sleazy, and you could try and smear me. There are people in this town who would like to see me taken down. Fine, be a party to that. Arrest me if you can, but I'm not sure I have to listen to you berating me."

Turner asked, "Did you steal anything else?"

"No. Just that stuff. And I wrote notes. That's not a crime. And I took pictures. That's not illegal, either. The tabloids would pay huge amounts of money for them."

"We need to look at the pictures," Turner said. He could demand the camera, but he wanted Blundlefitz to give it up voluntarily. The reporter took a one-use camera out of the inner pocket of his overcoat and placed it on Turner's desk. Turner noted that while completing the movement, Blundlefitz caused his chair to move farther away from Fenwick. If Blundlefitz had enough stuff hidden, he might be sitting in Turner's lap before long. Turner grimaced at the thought.

"Did you talk to anyone else?" Turner asked.

"Other than Ms. Haupmin, no."

"Where is Ms. Haupmin now?" Turner asked.

"She's staying in the same hotel as the rest of the road crew. Only the members of the band and some security people were staying at the Hotel Chicago." Turner knew it was the newest, most exclusive, and most expensive hotel in Chicago. "She and the rest of them are at the Plaza Mart Inn just past Halsted on Madison."

"We'll go see her," Turner said.

Fenwick said, "Mr. Blundlefitz, you will go home and you

will do nothing to interfere with this investigation. You will not talk to anyone. I will not see you again. No one will report to me that you bothered them."

"Okay." The agreement was just a little too quick to suit Turner. He couldn't read Blundlefitz's expression. Turner wasn't one of those who thought you could read volumes from the look on someone's face. Still, he thought there might be defiance or the beginning of a smirk just below the surface. Blundlefitz certainly didn't come across as sufficiently chagrined. Turner couldn't prove the man was going to keep interfering, and Blundlefitz had said okay. Nothing to be done about it now. Turner didn't trust him but if they had to, they could arrest him later. At the moment it wasn't worth the hassle to lock him up. So far as he could tell, Blundlefitz had given them all the information he had and told them all he'd done. They would let him dangle for a while.

Before Blundlefitz left they sent him to get his fingerprints recorded. They'd have to eliminate them from the others in the suite. Fenwick told the beat cop in charge to take his time with the process.

Joe Roosevelt and Judy Wilson, two other detectives on the squad, sauntered over with one of the new Area Ten detectives, Arnie Krempe. Joe was red-nosed and short, with brush-cut gray hair and bad teeth. Judy was a fiercely competitive African-American woman. They were as good at clearing cases as Turner and Fenwick, but they argued a lot more. About everything. Constantly. Arnie looked like a kid compared to the old veterans.

Roosevelt clapped his hands. "That was your greatest performance ever," he said.

"Nope," Wilson said. "Remember the killer who used gallon containers of ice cream to bash his victims? He figured he could eat the evidence? He didn't realize he needed to eat the containers as well. Remember when he attacked Fenwick with a gallon of rocky road that had been thawing on the counter for an hour and a half? That was classic. And a mess. If the eating fiasco didn't prove he was stupider than most, attacking Fenwick would."

"Wasn't a performance," Fenwick stated. This stopped the incipient debate. The four of them looked at Fenwick. "A lot of these music people are moronic creeps," Fenwick said. "They think they are the most important people on the planet. They're rich and famous. Or they deal with the rich and famous, the presumption of status based upon proximity. Big fucking deal."

"Upon proximity?" Wilson said. "You swallow a thesaurus?"

"You ever been rich or famous?" Roosevelt asked.

"Not likely," Fenwick said.

"Then how would you know how big a deal it is?" Roosevelt asked.

Fenwick said, "My shrewd detective sense. My brilliant powers of observation. My—"

"Stop," Wilson said. "I can only take so much of this at four in the morning."

Krempe said, "As far as I've seen these past couple weeks, Fenwick does bombastic at half the witnesses and most of the suspects. With us he attempts humor and tells the dumbest jokes. What difference does it make what time of the day or night he dishes it out?"

"Night shifts amplify our faults," Wilson said. She held up a hand to Fenwick. "For those of us who have faults," she corrected.

"Thank you," Fenwick said.

"How do you do that?" Krempe asked. "You get so angry but don't have a stroke or a heart attack."

"Practice," Fenwick said.

Krempe said, "I don't mean to get personal, but why is there a stack of underwear on your desk?"

Turner said, "Blundlefitz, the guy who Fenwick was unhappy with, stole them from the Boys4u suite."

"You could make yourself rich auctioning them off on the Internet," Krempe said.

"Ugh, others people's underwear," Wilson said. "That is disgusting."

"I do believe they were very likely used underwear," Fenwick said.

Wilson said, "Double ugh. That is the most disgusting thing."

Roosevelt said, "I can think of something more disgusting. There was this Dumpster . . ."

Ignoring this new debate, Turner and Fenwick left to continue their interviews. On the way out they logged in the underwear and the pills, sending all of it to be analyzed by the crime lab. They didn't expect much from the underwear and even the pills had only an off-chance of being anything useful in catching the killer. Confirming salacious bits of gossip about the band members' private lives wasn't likely to give them much evidence. An addiction could raise numerous questions, but they had no proof yet that any of them were involved in drugs.

.7.

In the car they shivered while waiting for the heater to reach full strength. The new heater that had been installed the year before was only slightly less temperamental than the last. This one kept the car consistently almost warm enough.

Fenwick and Turner drifted over to the Plaza Mart Inn. In some cities cops drive places, in Chicago they drift. The Plaza Mart was a twenty-story mass of lesser priced rooms. It had all the charm of concrete blocks. The 4 A.M. darkness hid much of what Turner thought of as its greatest flaw, its deep-puce-colored exterior. While the rooms cost less than they would have in the Loop itself or on the near north side, still they weren't cheap.

The detectives asked for Sherri Haupmin at the front desk. The woman on duty pointed to a crowd on the far side of the lobby. The detectives found a group from the touring company huddled together. Turner thought he vaguely recognized a few of them from the arena. The color scheme in the lobby was pale cream and puce. The furniture was a step-above-plastic ultramodern. When they asked for Haupmin, a woman about five foot two held up her hand. She had blond hair and wore jeans and a winter coat. Turner guessed she was in her early twenties. Neither she nor anyone else in the group looked like they'd been to bed.

"Ms. Haupmin, we need to talk to you," Turner said. They held out their identifications.

"I can't talk to anyone else," she said. "I've talked enough. This has got to stop."

Fenwick repeated the cop mantra that they'd used a zillion times. "The early hours of an investigation are the most important. We know you're grieving, but it would help us a great deal."

"I'm too overwhelmed. I loved him."

"Who did you talk to already?" Turner asked.

"All the major news outlets and that odious fat, local man. I probably told him too much."

"Like what?" Turner asked.

"I don't know. Everything. Nothing really."

Turner said, "If you could talk to us, it could make a difference in finding Roger's killer."

She shrugged.

They sat in three chairs grouped far from the others. Turner found that the chrome and vinyl seats were as uncomfortable as they looked.

Haupmin shivered. "I can't wait to get out of this cold. This city is awful. I'm going to hate it forever."

"We understand you were Roger's girlfriend," Turner said.

"Yes, oh my, yes." She wiped at tears with a crumpled tissue she took from her coat pocket.

"Did Roger have any enemies that you know of?" Turner asked.

"Every single member of that band. Every single employee of that company. The other members of the band hated him. They were jealous of his talent."

Turner heard Fenwick's sigh of satisfaction. The best thing to do was find the local gossip and/or someone who had an ax to grind. Haupmin might have a negative view of all these people, but what she said might give the detectives better information than the others.

Haupmin said, "Half an hour ago, Zawicki was here. He told us all not to tell anybody anything. He didn't talk to us until after I spoke with the national press and that local reporter. I can't imagine giving an interview to some nobody from a nothing rag would make much of a difference. I can talk to the police, can't I? I think I have to."

"Why did they dislike Roger?" Turner asked.

"They didn't dislike him. I said *hate*. He had more talent than the rest of them combined. That Ralph Eudace, their agent and manager, he was a pig. Pastern was a vicious prude. I protected Roger more than he did. I saved him from grasping women. I kept him on an even keel. And that Murial Arane, their choreographer! She was trying to hold them back. Her position was precarious. She should have been fired long ago. Roger could plan their choreography better than anyone. He deserved to be out front all the time. I practically had to tear her hair out to get her to listen."

"Did she and Roger fight?"

"She was so far behind him in talent. She should have stood aside and let him create."

Turner asked, "Can you remember their last public fight?"

"They didn't have to use words," she said. "I could see her jealousy and her spite in her eyes."

Turner always doubted those whose insight came from interpretations of eye movements. He wondered how much of what she said was an exaggeration or a product of her imagination rather than her having witnessed actual events. He asked, "How was his relationship with Riveting Records?"

"Roger should have had a better contract. He should have been paid more money. Eudace wasn't protecting his interests. All the boys had the same agent. That was stupid. Roger should have gotten his own years ago. Those weren't rumors about him trying to have a solo career. He wanted to. Boy, he wanted to. He wanted to be free to sing with whoever he chose to."

Turner assumed she was referring to herself. He asked, "Riveting Records was keeping the two of you from having a career together?"

"And trying to stop our relationship. That Zawicki was such an asshole. He would never listen. Roger had to put his foot down for them to let me be one of the opening acts on this tour."

"What exactly did he have to do to get you to be the opening act?" Turner asked.

"The band has its own production company. They can't take that from them. I'm one of their discoveries. Roger discovered me himself. They like to bring some of the talent from their own company along as opening acts. Gives them lots of exposure."

Turner said, "We understand you told Mr. Blundlefitz that Mr. Zawicki required sex from the boys before they could be in the band. Maybe one or some of them were required to perform sex acts for Mr. Zawicki as a trade for letting you sing."

"Roger would never do that."

"Was performing sexually required of you?" Turner asked.

"Hell, no. Zawicki was sick. I would never let anybody do that to me."

"But Roger was required to have sex with Zawicki to get into the band."

"Roger wasn't gay. I told Roger to file suit. I told him he could make millions from what that shit did."

"Why didn't he?" Turner asked.

"He said it wasn't a big deal. How can it not be a big deal? He was raped."

"Did Roger use the word *rape*?" Turner asked.

"Well, that's what it was."

"Who told you Roger had to have sex with Zawicki?"

"Roger did. He told me Zawicki made him do it every month or so. Roger hated it."

"But not bad enough to put a stop to it."

"He had his own reputation. All those no-talent males who hate boy bands think the guys are gay. Believe me, I know. Roger Stendar was not gay. No way."

"Was Roger planning to go public with what he was forced to do for Zawicki?"

"No. Definitely not. Zawicki is really powerful in the industry. Roger might be rich, but Zawicki has a lot of friends and a lot of power. Being a talent in this industry is really tenuous. If you're very lucky, you're in the right place at the right time, and if you get all the breaks, you wind up on top. Roger couldn't risk jeopardizing that. The fall from the top is pretty steep."

"Why not just leak the information to some reporter?" Fenwick asked.

"There were only a few people who knew. Zawicki would be able to figure out who told. And Roger had to protect his own reputation."

"Did Roger tell you the other guys had to have sex with Mr. Zawicki?"

"I'm not stupid. I could tell."

Fenwick asked, "Did you start having sex with Roger Stendar before or after you were part of their production company?"

"We were lovers way before I got hired."

Fenwick asked, "Was going to bed with him part of your plan for getting signed by the production company?"

"No, hey, no."

"Did the two of you use condoms?" Fenwick asked.

"These questions are awfully personal. Do I have to answer them?"

Fenwick said, "Condoms were found in his luggage. If he didn't use them with you, presumably they were there to be used with someone else. Unless he has a condom collection or used them when he was entertaining himself."

"Roger wasn't a pervert." She glared at Fenwick. "Are you making this up to trick me?"

"No," Fenwick said.

"One of the other guys must have put them there or they were left from before he and I got together. He didn't use them with me. We didn't need them because I'm on the pill. I'm sure there's a simple explanation. We loved each other. I know he wasn't cheating. I bet Zawicki killed him."

"Why do you say that?" Turner asked.

"He was so creepy to be around."

"What happened tonight?"

"I sang for about half an hour. There were two opening acts. I watched their show and Roger's."

"Did you notice anything unusual?"

"No. It was a great show. The guys were perfect. They could perform together, but they didn't get along. I know they all have this image, but I would tell Roger over and over, he had to move on for his own good. He could be among the greats."

"Were the two of you planning to get married?"

"Not yet. We had our careers."

"Did you stay with him on the road?"

"That was impossible. Pastern was a son of a bitch. He was worse than a constipated nanny. Pastern should have protected him from Zawicki. Instead he concentrated on protecting Roger from me. Asshole. It was always their goddamn image that they had to be careful of. They even brainwashed

Roger into believing that. We were discreet. We'd find time to be together at odd moments before concerts. A lot of times when he claimed he was checking props, he and I would get together. We did a lot of sneaking around. The tour bus was the best. It was like home."

"Did he check the props last night?" Turner asked.

"I suppose. I didn't ask. I wasn't interested in that. We met in that big locker room area. It was great. Lots of privacy. We got into all kinds of places. We did it in the hot tub. I've never seen a bigger one. Sex before a concert relaxed him, improved his performance." She didn't seem to notice the double meanings. "I wasn't the only one dating a guy in the band or having sex with one. The other guys had sex with lots of girls. That Danny Galyak screwed anything with a twat. If a girl was breathing, he was interested. They couldn't keep the girls away from them. Either the guys or the fans or both always found a way."

"But Roger was faithful to you?"

"Of course."

Turner couldn't tell if she was doing heavy-duty wish fulfillment, or if she was as close to Stendar as she claimed. Maybe she was just another lay for the dead band member, although she did know about Zawicki's sexual escapades, which implied that Roger had felt close enough to confide in her. Turner still wasn't sure how much credibility to give her claims.

Fenwick said, "You told this to the local reporter, but not to the beat cops when they questioned you at the arena?"

"They were cops, strangers."

"Wasn't Blundlefitz a stranger?" Turner asked.

"He was a critic. A reviewer. I knew that much. He said I could trust him."

Whether she was terminally stupid, moronically naïve or rapturously self-centered, Turner couldn't tell.

"What time did you leave?"

"Before Roger was killed. I don't like to be around Zawicki. I had to get back to do some packing."

"Did the guys fight a lot in other people's presence?" Turner asked.

"Nobody ever saw them fighting. They were too clever for that. And that publicist Hinkmeyer is a snake. She covered for everybody. And Eudace is a bigger snake. And Pastern is a certifiable Nazi. Roger confided in me. I knew."

"How was Hinkmeyer a snake?" Turner asked.

"She's a shill for the company. She'd tell any lie to keep the guys in the band passive and quiet."

"And Eudace?"

"He was in league with Pastern in trying to keep Roger and me apart. As if they could. Puke on them both."

"Did Roger get any direct threats that you know about?" Turner asked.

"You get those crazed fans, but that's what security is for."

"Nothing specific?"

"Not that I know of."

In the car, Fenwick said, "I don't think she was as close as she thought she was. And it's convenient to have somebody on the tour who happens to be your fuck buddy. I bet Stendar was using her the way Zawicki was using him."

"Wouldn't be surprised," Turner said. "Haupmin is the only one who admits to leaving the party early. She could have gotten into that warren of interconnected rooms down there. She'd been there with Roger. She knew her way around."

"She's on my suspect list," Fenwick said.

*   *   *

The Hotel Chicago was luxury personified, everything that the Plaza Mart Inn was not. The carpets were plush, the chandeliers cut crystal, the woodwork imported teak.

They were led to the boys' suite by the head of hotel security, Herb Gibbons. Two beat cops were on duty at the door. The band had half the top floor of the hotel to themselves. Floor-to-ceiling windows opened to the spectacle of the lights of the Loop and Chicago's near north side. Turner could see the Ferris wheel on Navy Pier and traffic heading north and south on Lake Shore Drive. Overstuffed chairs predominated. Sectional seating. A fully stocked bar.

"Where's the band staying at the moment?" Turner asked Gibbons.

"I heard there was some big-deal meeting. I have no information if it is over or not. I can find out where they are if you wish."

"Not just yet," Fenwick said.

Turner and Fenwick roamed through the suite. In an unused bedroom they found an enormous Harley motorcycle. "How'd they get this up here?" Fenwick asked.

Turner said, "I think why'd they get it up here is a better question. Did they need it for races up on the rooftop?"

"With only one bike?" Fenwick snorted. "Self-indulgent rich kids."

Their inspection took half an hour. They found the mounds of dirty clothes that Blundlefitz must have taken his souvenirs from.

They could only tell which boy was in which room by the labels on the luggage. In Stendar's room they found a paperback copy of *The Proof of Nothing* by Fredrick Schermer. A wide variety of teddy bears was mounded in the middle of the floor of his room. Each boy had his own bathroom. They found deodorant, shampoo, razors, toothbrushes, and toothpaste. The members didn't have a lot of clothes. Turner figured they learned to pack light. Dragging tons of luggage from venue to venue had to be a hassle. Or did these guys have to carry their own luggage? Devane and Pappas had portable CD players with earphones connected to them. Galyak and Clendenen had condoms in their personal packs, as had Stendar. In all this Turner and Fenwick found nothing unusual.

"I can picture it," Fenwick said. "The most famous boy band in the world doing a condom commercial. They'd sell a zillion and their name would be mud. The Religious Right would make sure of that. They'd rather have a mythical virginal band and more babies."

"Things don't change much," Turner said.

"Where are the notes Blundlefitz found?" Fenwick asked. "Either someone else was in here or he wasn't quite as intimidated as we'd hoped. I can't believe I'm losing my delicate, suave touch."

"Hard to lose something I've never seen."

They returned to the station. There was already a mob of reporters crammed into the first floor and spilling outside the station. Fenwick glowered at them as they approached the mass of humanity. "Famous dead people depress me."

"Why?" Turner asked.

"I think a whole lot of people who don't know them indulge in cheap emotions."

Turner said, "You don't have to know someone to feel sad that they're dead."

"Yeah, but you see so many nearly hysterical people who didn't know them."

"Maybe that's mostly television. They prefer to show the heavily weeping over the rationally dealing."

"I guess you're right."

It was near the end of their shift, but they put in an hour and a half on the paperwork. Before they left, Turner and Fenwick reported to the commander, Drew Molton, on their progress. Everyone knew the kind of pressure that accompanied the death of someone famous. They would do their best, just as they always did.

8

Paul Turner pulled into his driveway about a quarter to seven. The first light of dawn was barely touching the neighborhood. He could see the lamplight in Mrs. Talucci's front room. She'd have been up for at least an hour and a half by this time. She arose before dawn every day of the year. He knew she was getting ready to go to New Orleans for Mardi Gras. Mrs. Talucci was in her nineties and determined not to spend her days waiting to die. She'd found a place to rent right on Bourbon Street, a block and a half off Canal. She was permitting one of her grandnieces to accompany her. Paul's own family wouldn't be awake for another hour or so. They'd have a large breakfast and walk to church. Paul would stay up long enough to accompany them and then get some sleep. He knew he'd have to go in to work early tonight. Paul rubbed his hand across his face and tried to clear his mind. When you worked nights, you never did feel like you got enough sleep.

Paul saw the curtains twitch in Mrs. Talucci's parlor window. She beckoned to him. Tired as he was, he hustled through the cold. He was not about to refuse a summons from Mrs. Talucci. She'd been more than a help to his sons, Ben, and himself over the years.

Paul entered the front room. Mrs. Talucci said, "You have a visitor. I checked his coat pockets. He's not armed."

"Why did you check his pockets?"

"You investigating the Boys4u murder?"

"Yeah."

"Well, one of the band members is here. Kid named Clendenen. He may or may not have killed somebody, but I don't take chances. If he's got a gun in the tight clothes he's wearing, it's smaller than a pea shooter. I inspected his winter coat and his backpack. Nothing more dangerous than a harmonica."

"You know him?"

"I watch all the news." Paul knew this was true. She also read three newspapers a day. She said it helped keep her mind sharp. Mrs. Talucci said, "The band was interviewed on three different local channels during the last week. They seemed like perfectly ordinary boys. They could use a little feeding. I gave him some nice ravioli. That stopped the tears for a little while. He doesn't look like he eats much, but he managed three helpings along with meatballs and some sausage and some good garlic bread. I think they must abuse these children on the road. You've got to feed people properly." Mrs. Talucci belonged to the fill-them-up-until-they're-too-stuffed-to-worry-or-complain school of psychotherapy. To Turner her method seemed to work as well as many others and better than most.

Turner said, "All the teenage girls in the neighborhood would be outside if they knew he was here."

"He doesn't need teenage girls. He needs help. Adult help. I feel sorry for him. I found him sitting on your porch. I was out for my morning walk. I think he'd have waited until he froze to death." Mrs. Talucci walked to the store every day to buy her newspapers. If there was a glaze of ice on the sidewalk, she was on the phone to the alderman making sure it would be gotten rid of. She had his home number. If there was deep snow, she had a crew of relatives and neighbors, led by Paul, Ben, and their sons to help clear paths.

Mrs. Talucci led Paul into the kitchen. Elbows propped on the table, head resting on the palms of his hands, a pile of used tissues next to his arm, Dexter Clendenen raised swollen eyes and looked at Turner.

"I can't go to the hotel. I can't sleep. I came here." He shook his head and moaned.

Clendenen wore only a thin yellow T-shirt, tight faded jeans, and athletic shoes. Even if the kid had the best winter coat, he'd get awfully cold very quickly in that outfit.

Mrs. Talucci asked, "Is there anything else I can get for you, young man?"

"No, thanks," he muttered. She patted Dexter's shoulder, then left the room.

"Why didn't you knock on my door?" Paul asked.

"I knew you were still at work. I called the station. They said you'd be back, so I knew you hadn't gone home."

"How'd you find out where I lived?"

"Zawicki knew. He always knows stuff."

"How'd you get here?" Turner asked.

"I had our limo guy bring me. I can't stay with the other guys. I need help. I know I need help." Clendenen's head swayed from side to side. Paul thought the boy might be close to a total nervous breakdown. He took off his winter coat, pulled up a chair, and sat down next to him.

"The limo didn't stay?"

"I had him stop at the corner and told him to go."

"How can I help you?" Paul asked. He wouldn't have been surprised to get a confession to a murder.

"I'm scared," the kid said and stopped.

"Of what?" Paul prompted.

"Of everything." Paul waited. "Of the other guys in the band. Of Zawicki." Silence.

"We were told there were notes from a meeting about the band breaking up."

"I don't know about any such meeting. We weren't breaking up."

"We were told that each of you had sex with Mr. Zawicki."

"What? Well. Who told you that? All of us?"

Paul evaded the questions. "That was a cruel thing for him to do."

"Zawicki made me have sex with him. He said nobody would ever know. Do the other guys know about me? He made each of them? Nobody ever talked about it. He said I couldn't be part of the band if I didn't. It was either bend over or get out."

"Why didn't you just leave?"

"This was my dream. Sometimes you have to make sacrifices. I just wish he'd have stopped. Do I really have to talk about that? It's embarrassing. It can't have anything to do with Roger."

"Maybe Roger resented it. Maybe he threatened to go public with what Zawicki was doing."

"Roger never talked to me about it."

"Did any of the other executives make you service them?" Paul asked.

"No, none of them. Zawicki screwed me lots of times. I hated it. It hurt so much."

"Couldn't you tell anyone? Mr. Pastern was your security guard."

"I liked it when Jordan took care of me. He was gentle. He never let anybody hurt me, but there was nothing he could do. He was an employee just like me. I never told anyone."

"How about your agent, Eudace?"

"All he cared about was money. He's our agent, not a friend. The company picked him for us. It was in our contracts that he had to be our agent."

"Were you afraid of him?"

"No. He was just a corporate asshole."

"Are you afraid of anyone else?" Paul asked.

"The guys in the band. They make fun of me. I get the fewest parts in the songs, but I get big play in the videos because I'm the sad-eyed baby. The other guys didn't like that. As if they had that much more talent than me. I can sing. I'm good." He burst into song.

Turner thought the voice seemed a little thin and high, but was generally pleasing. Turner didn't think of himself as a music critic. He'd gotten stuck in the era between Elvis and the Beatles. His friend Ian claimed that Paul had never gotten over the Great Folk Music Scare of the early sixties. Paul thought this was probably true, although he did like old time rock and roll.

"Was Roger afraid of anything?" Paul asked.

"No, he was always brave, and now he's dead, and there's nothing I can do about it." Clendenen began to cry. Turner put an arm around his shoulder. The boy put his head on Paul's chest and practically crawled into his lap. The kid's knee pressed awkwardly on Paul's left thigh and the boy's elbow poked uncomfortably into his side. He let the kid cry and held him gently.

After a minute or so, Paul twisted as best he could. He didn't want to dislodge the boy, but he wasn't comfortable with this level of intimacy with a possible murder suspect. Obviously, there was something very wrong here. He had no doubt the boy had numerous people he could have cried with about Roger Stendar dying. This might be genuine grief, but if it was, it seemed woefully misplaced genuine grief.

Paul knew he was basically a stranger to the kid. Why come to him? A killer feeling great remorse? Maybe, but totally unsubstantiated. A gay kid who was reaching out was possible. Galyak might have caught on that Turner was gay and not just being politically correct during their interview and could have told the others. Clendenen must know other gay people he could go to. Dependence on the kindness of strangers was more cliché than truth. None of this made sense yet. His detective instincts didn't prevent him from comforting the boy, but he remained wary.

After several minutes he heard the boy say, "I feel safe here in this house with you. The only safe place we really had was the tour bus. I felt protected there. Roger was good to me. The other guys weren't. Roger was nice." The voice was muffled against his chest. Paul gently disengaged himself and got the boy sitting back on his own chair. The kid took several tissues and wiped his nose and eyes. "Roger never made fun of me. He always helped me with my dancing. The other guys were more coordinated than I was, but I worked harder. In the beginning sometimes they'd say I was holding them back. But I practiced more than they did. I needed it. Roger spent lots of extra time with me. He was like the big brother I never had. I can't believe he's dead. I thought we'd all just go on singing together forever."

"We talked to Sherri Haupmin. She said Roger wanted to leave the band."

"I hate her." No tears now. He'd turned from sadness to red-hot anger in an instant. "She should be the one who's dead. She's the one who put ideas into his head. She's the one who said he wasn't getting enough respect. She was like Yoko Ono who ruined the Beatles. She was always pushing for things to change. Why? Things were perfect. We got along perfect until she showed up. We laughed a lot. We had good times. I don't know why Roger liked her. Maybe she was good sex. He never threw her in my face but I couldn't say anything to him about her."

"Did you try?"

"Not really. She always hung around. She got to perform because our production company signed her. We have a couple of opening acts, a different one every month. After the tour we were going to drop whoever the kids in the arenas didn't respond to. She was gonna get dropped. She didn't have any talent. Roger protected her, but it was getting obvious even to him."

"Did he protect her like he protected you?" Paul asked.

"Hey, that was different. Roger was my friend. We were close."

"Were you lovers?"

"No. No way. I'm not gay. Neither was he." If this kid wasn't gay, Paul was ready to turn in his ID card and return the toaster. "We just cared for each other. It's okay for guys to care for each other. The other kids in high school used to laugh at me because I was in chorus and band. Called me a band fag. I went back to my hometown last year for a reunion. I didn't see a lot of my tormentors, but I know they all saw my pictures in the paper. My going back was the biggest thing that town had ever seen. They even had a parade for me."

"You must have been pretty young when you joined the band if you guys spent time in South America and Asia before you hit it big here."

"I joined when I was seventeen. Just enough over the age of consent for Zawicki to take advantage of."

"That bothers you?"

"Yeah."

"I've got a few more questions about last night."

"Sure."

"Did you see anybody leave the party?"

"No. Why?"

"We found the gun some distance away. We're trying to figure out if anyone saw somebody leaving."

"I didn't notice. I was kneeling next to Roger the whole time until the paramedics got there. Then I was talking to Jordan. I wasn't near the door."

Turner said, "Who else at the company do you think would actually try to harm you?"

"Can you not ask me questions about Roger for a while, please?"

"Is there anyone I can call? Someone you're close to? Is there anybody from Riveting Records who could help you out?"

"No. I'd rather stay here."

"I'm worried about you. I could call your parents or a friend you're close to."

"I don't want to be near any of those people from the band. They aren't good for me. I should never have been in this band. I get so depressed."

"About what?" Paul felt too tired to be turning into this kid's therapist. Was this a needy boy, just barely out of his teens who'd grown up too fast and been given too much, or was he a manipulative and devious killer?

"I'm scared somebody might kill me next."

"Did someone threaten you?"

"Not directly. Jordan told me you found all that sabotage."

"Tell me about the water bottles."

"Usually, we kept them in our own little places, but it wasn't like real set. Kind of just the usual spot."

"Did you check your own props?"

"One of us could have fallen. All we had keeping us up were those harnesses. In the beginning I was afraid of heights. They told me I could go up or leave. I pissed my pants the first time we practiced. I was so embarrassed. But Roger saw and he managed to get me away from the other guys without anyone seeing me. He never mentioned it. Not once. He was nice. I got used to it, and I did all the stunts, but I was scared every time. What if one of those wires broke? I even hired a therapist. I'm better as long as I remember what he taught me. Then tonight Jordan said one of the wires was almost cut through. We were way up high. One of us would have died right in the middle of the concert. I could have died."

While his fear was understandable and in a lot of ways justified, Paul was concerned that his terror was close to paralyzing the kid. He was also aware that the kid hadn't answered his question. "Who checked your props?" he asked.

"The road crew and then Roger and everybody checked everything. I didn't know how any of that stuff worked."

Turner glanced at the silver-framed kitchen clock. Nearly eight. Ben would see his car in the driveway and wonder where he was. He said, "Let's go over to my house, and we can talk more over there. I want to check in with my family."

"I'm afraid of meeting new people."

"You must meet hundreds every day."

"No, not really. Only those we want to meet. The company filters everybody out and security keeps the crazies away."

"Well, my lover and my boys are perfectly nice. I need to do this. You don't have to come. We could call your limousine service and have them come get you and take you back to the hotel."

The boy fidgeted. Paul got up, put on his coat, and handed Clendenen his own. The boy shuffled to his feet. Mrs. Talucci met them in the hall. She placed a calming hand on Clendenen's arm. "Are you feeling better?" she asked.

Clendenen shrugged. "A little."

Paul said, "We're going to go next door. I want to see Ben and the boys. Thanks for helping out."

Clendenen caught the cue and mumbled, "Yeah, thanks for the food. It was the best."

She patted his arm. "You take care, young man. You have a lovely voice. Good luck."

9

Paul walked into the house. As he hung up their coats, he heard sounds from the kitchen. Ben appeared in the doorway. Paul kissed and hugged his lover. He didn't bother to worry about what Clendenen might think. He didn't particularly care. This was his home and what some famous twinky thought, gay or straight, wasn't going to influence him. He introduced Ben to Clendenen.

Paul added, "He's involved in a case I'm working on. Mrs. Talucci fed him earlier. He needs a haven, and I'd like to provide it for a while." Ben nodded.

The three of them moved into the kitchen. Ben was beginning Sunday breakfast. After Ben had moved in, he'd become the official Sunday breakfast maker. Paul and his two sons alternated weeks cooking the family's daily breakfast, a meal Paul insisted they all have together. As each of their individual schedules was so hectic, it was often the only meal all of them were present for. More than half the time, dinner was eaten in shifts. Even working nights, Paul made it home for breakfast.

Clendenen said, "I need to use the washroom."

Paul pointed. "Down the hall on the left."

Ben said, "Father Flanagan brings home lost boy, or do we have a serial killer among us?"

"He's one of the guys from the band Boys4u."

"It's all over the news. Worse than when Princess Di was in the car crash." As they talked, Ben began frying bacon and chopping vegetables.

"Fenwick and I have the case. This kid showed up on our doorstep, and Mrs. Talucci noticed him on her morning walk. He claims he's afraid to be with the rest of the group."

"What's he afraid of?"

"I'm not sure. What he really needs is a good therapist. I'd like to make a call or two and get someone I trust to come over."

Ben said, "At least you can be thankful that neither of your kids has expressed a desire to be a rock star."

"Somebody gave Brian a drum for his third birthday. Dumbest thing he ever got. Fortunately it never took, and I was never the kind of parent who insisted on a kid taking music lessons."

Paul heard thumping that could only mean one thing. His overactive older son was pounding down the stairs. He wondered if the steps would last until the boy went to college. Brian breezed into the kitchen. He wore red boxer shorts, white athletic socks, and nothing else.

"Good morning," Paul said. "Is that the same pair of boxers you've had on for the last several days?"

His son tended to parade around the house in his underwear. Brian pulled a gallon bottle of orange juice out of the refrigerator. He yanked off the cap and began to raise the container to his lips. Silently Ben handed him a glass. Paul knew the kid probably guzzled half the liquids in the refrigerator from the bottle when the adults weren't present. Brian took the glass and filled it. After finishing it off, Brian said, "I have fourteen pairs of these. All the same color." He began refilling his glass. Sometimes Paul felt half his salary was spent to keep his sons in provender.

"And the reason you have fourteen of the same?" Paul asked.

"I like the color."

Ben said, "With so many the same, he doesn't have to sort his clothes as much. In there somewhere is probably part of a scheme to do less laundry, although I'm not real sure about that. If he has all the same color, maybe he'll stop borrowing yours. One hesitates to say his girlfriend might like them."

The seventeen-year-old turned slightly pink. "Mandy has opinions about everything. I'm probably gonna drop her." Brian continued to sift through a passel of girlfriends. Most often now, he and a mixed male/female group attended events in a clump.

Clendenen reentered the kitchen. Paul introduced them. Brian gave no sign of recognizing the name. Paul noticed that Clendenen took careful note of his son's state of undress. Brian played numerous sports and had made all-state in football. He worked out for several hours a day. Clendenen averted his eyes quickly when he realized Paul was watching. It wasn't gaydar, but it was the first overt hint that Clendenen might not be heterosexual.

Paul said, "Dexter is going to join us for breakfast. You need to shave, shower, get dressed, and get ready for church before you finish depleting the supplies in the house."

"Got it covered." Brian thumped back up the stairs.

Paul heard his youngest son Jeff's wheelchair. The twelve-year-old had been refusing help lately in getting dressed. For years he'd been doing okay on his own, with just a little help. The younger boy had insisted on being more independent. He made himself get up half an hour earlier so he could accomplish this. Paul admired his determination and stamina.

Jeff wheeled into the kitchen. "Morning Dad, Ben." He looked at Clendenen. "You're in Boys4u," Jeff said. He went to the refrigerator and got out the same gallon of orange juice as Brian. He began imitating his older brother's from-the-bottle guzzle. Silently Ben handed him a glass.

Jeff finished pouring his juice and wheeled over to Clendenen. "On the Internet this morning, I saw about one of the guys dying. I'm sorry your friend died. Are you okay?"

Tears started down Clendenen's face.

"Hey, I'm sorry. I didn't mean to make you cry." He looked at his father. "I didn't mean anything."

His father reassured him. "You expressed your concern. You did right."

Clendenen said, "It's okay, thanks."

While waiting for Brian to finish in the bathroom, Paul used the upstairs phone to call Robert Grannett, a psychologist he knew. Grannett and Guy Moriville were a couple that Paul and Ben occasionally spent an evening with at the movies or a play.

On the phone Paul explained the situation. "I don't know what to do with this kid."

"Want me to come over?"

"I think I'm going to drag him to church with us."

"Probably nothing harmful in that as long as the kid isn't recognized."

"I don't want to leave him alone in the house."

"I think that's a good idea."

"Do you think he's suicidal?" Paul asked.

"I'd have to talk to him. Anything is possible. From what you describe, there's little question that he's very fragile right now. He might be that way all the time. I can be over later this morning and give you a hand."

"That would help. I have no reason to mistrust him, except for normal cop precautions. I don't think he's a killer."

Brian finished in the bathroom and Paul showered and changed. The water revived him a little. What he really needed was sleep.

Breakfast conversation consisted mostly of Jeff asking Clendenen reasonably innocuous questions about what it was like being in a boy band. Clendenen was reserved at first, but the down-home atmosphere seemed to put him at ease. Since he'd dined sumptuously at Mrs. Talucci's little more than an hour ago, he only sipped from a glass of orange juice.

Brian said, "I'd like to be as rich as you are when I'm your age, but I can't sing, and I can't dance."

"We have lots of coaches, and we practice for hours every day."

"Gotta have talent," Brian said. "That kind of talent, I don't have."

Paul announced, "We're going to church." They still attended the local Catholic mass every Sunday. Paul hated the Catholic Church's stance on gay people and he wasn't sure how he felt about the reality of a supreme being running the universe. Brian attended the Catholic high school connected with the parish, one of the few left in the city that was still active, and Paul had decided years ago that church attendance would probably be good for the kids. To his surprise Brian hadn't begun rebelling about the Sunday ritual. Paul figured attending the local school must have a lot to do with it. It also gave Brian a chance to socialize with his buddies and the girls in the neighborhood. The high school hadn't become coed yet.

"I can't be recognized," Clendenen said. "You don't know

what it's like. It's a madhouse. A swarm. It only takes one."

"We can disguise you," Paul said. "Dark glasses, a high turtleneck sweater. A hat might be out of place in church, but a knit stocking cap on such a cold morning wouldn't get you thrown out. You can leave it on. We'll sit in the back. The boys know enough not to say anything."

"I've got some stuff that will be too big for you," Brian said. "It would be perfect for a disguise."

Clendenen almost smiled. "I'd kind of like to be in a public place without a million people recognizing me. If we want to shop at a grocery store, we have to do it at two in the morning." He thought for a minute. Turner saw a bit of a fleeting smile. "Okay, I'll go." The kid had showered immediately after the concert so he probably didn't need to clean up much. Paul doubted if he shaved more than two or three times a week. He actually thought Jeff's clothes might fit Clendenen better—the band member's figure was so slight—but he was afraid the twenty-something guy might take it as an insult.

Brian led him upstairs. Ben and Paul filled the dishwasher. Jeff headed for his computer to check the Internet for the latest news.

When all the kids were gone, Ben said, "You look like you could use some sleep."

"Yeah. Soon. I hope. I've got Robert Grannett coming over. He should be here just after we get back from church. I want a therapist with this kid. He's unstable. I'd like to get him back to his own people."

"Do you think he might have done it?" Ben asked.

"I don't know. I doubt it right now, but you know me, I never rule anybody out. Mrs. Talucci checked in his coat and backpack for weapons. He's not armed. The kid's so frail, he wouldn't take much to subdue."

Brian came down the stairs with Clendenen. The white

fisherman's turtleneck sweater swallowed the boy, covering nearly the entire bottom part of his face and hanging to mid thigh. He wore dark glasses and a navy blue, knit cap. "Perfect," Paul said.

Church went off without a hitch.

About ten minutes after they got home, Robert Grannett arrived. Clendenen had gone upstairs with Brian to change.

Grannett said, "What's the deal?"

"He doesn't want to go back to the band. I'm not a therapist, but something seems to be really wrong. Why would he come to me, an almost total stranger?"

"It's that fatherly thing you do and the deep voice. Makes everybody feel safe. You should try and package it and sell it."

"I wish it worked on more criminals."

"Who knows with this kid? Maybe he desperately needs a father figure. Fame could have destroyed his ego instead of building it up. You and Fenwick interviewed him?"

"Yeah."

"Almost anything could have clicked in his head while you were talking. And with his friend dead, that could push a fragile ego way over the edge. You've seen it in the people you bring bad news to. They react to stress in all kinds of ways. We don't know what his life is like. He could have been abused. He could be a pathological nut. He could be a killer. Or he could be a sad young man who just lost his only friend."

"Dad!" Brian called from upstairs. It was a voice of urgency parents recognize. Paul bounded up the stairs. Grannett followed. Ben rushed up from the basement. Jeff wheeled himself to the bottom of the stairs. Brian was at the open door of his room. Paul looked over his shoulder.

Clendenen sat against the far wall, between Brian's desk

and his bed. He was rocking back and forth clutching his backpack. When the motion brought him upright against the wall, he would softly pound his head against it three or four times, then he would resume rocking.

"What the hell?" Paul said. He sat on the bed next to the boy. He reached out a hand to touch him. No reaction. He propped a pillow behind the boy's head so he wouldn't hurt himself. "Dexter. Dex," he said softly. The boy gave no sign of recognition. Paul returned to Brian and Grannett near the doorway.

Brian said, "We were talking. I was showing him some of my football stuff. I didn't think he was real interested. I tried talking with him about the band."

Grannett asked, "Do you remember exactly what either of you said just before he started doing that?"

Brian shut his eyes. "We were talking about sports." He opened his eyes. "Then I asked what it was like being in the band. He said something like, 'okay.' Nothing real expressive. I asked if it was anything like metal or rock bands, the kind I listen to. Did the guys in this band have to deal with all the girls and drugs like heavy metal bands are supposed to? Seemed like an okay question. You know, kind of a guy thing. He said that nobody knew what his life was like. That's it."

"Was he doing anything special, touching anything?" Grannett asked.

"He took a couple things down from the shelf above my desk, not like he was interested, just maybe something to hold onto. All of a sudden he got real creepy, like he turned pale."

"What did he touch exactly?" Grannett asked.

Brian turned red. "Well. Um."

"Brian keeps his condoms up there," Paul said. "It's been the same box since he was fifteen. He doesn't think we know about it."

"Dad!"

"Son?"

Clendenen continued rocking but had stopped banging his head against the wall.

Grannett asked, "Then what?"

Brian said, "He kind of sagged against the wall and started the rocking and banging. Nobody freaks at a box of condoms, do they?"

They might if they've had a negative sexual experience connected with them, Turner thought.

"You did nothing wrong," Grannett said. He knelt in front of the boy who began a high-pitched keening. Grannett spoke very softly. "Dexter."

The boy continued to rock but as Grannett reached to touch him, he began to bang his head again. The psychologist backed off immediately. They decided they had better get him to an emergency room to check for physical problems and get him some meds.

Turner approached the boy carefully. "It's okay, Dexter," he murmured. The boy's eyes followed Turner's hand as he rested it on Clendenen's forearm. Turner helped him to his feet. When Clendenen was upright, he began to sob and cling to Paul as if he were his last hope before drowning. Paul held him and patted his back. Dexter clung more tightly.

Grannett retrieved Dexter's coat, hat, and gloves. They had to pry his arms away from Turner's body one at a time to get his coat on. When Paul let go to put on his own outer gear, the kid sank in a heap to the floor. They got him on his feet again, but he didn't seem capable of standing on his own.

Grannett said, "I wish I believed in the slap-him-till-he-snaps-out-of-it school of helping clients."

Paul had no notion of what would work with Dexter. He doubted if there were enough meatballs in Mrs. Talucci's feed 'em psychology to help this kid. Maybe not enough meatballs on the planet.

Paul said, "I can carry him downstairs." Paul used a fireman's carry. Grannett went in front of him and Brian behind so that they could help if there was any problem on the stairs. Paul carried Clendenen out to their jeep and buckled him into the backseat. The boy looked at him with tear-filled eyes. Paul patted his arm and smoothed back the hair on his head. Clendenen didn't look like a famous rock star. He looked like a pathetic young man who could use a lot of help.

Paul and Grannett drove him to the nearest emergency room. Paul left him in Grannett's charge. He also made sure a beat cop was on duty. As he left, he could hear the nurses murmuring Clendenen's name. His whereabouts wouldn't be secret for long.

Turner went home to bed. He woke up around five. Ben was folding laundry and placing it in their dresser. Ben wore black jeans on his lean hips and a gray T-shirt that hugged his torso. Paul rolled over. Ben glanced at him.

"Sorry," Ben said. "I didn't mean to wake you."

"I need to get up anyway."

Ben sat on the edge of the bed and placed his hand on his lover's shoulder. "You didn't get enough sleep. The boys are out. Jeff's at his Harry Potter club meeting. Brian is escorting a damsel home from the library where I have no doubt they have been doing nothing but studying all afternoon."

"I should get to work."

Ben leaned down, nuzzled the fur on Paul's chest. Nuzzling proceeded to passion and after several moments Paul said, "The mountains of paperwork won't notice how early I am for work." More than a few minutes later he was feeling very much better but hardly less tired.

Paul phoned Robert Grannett.

"How's Dexter?" Paul asked.

"They sedated him. He's been asleep most of the afternoon."

"Any way to know a prognosis?"

"Not yet. Sometimes these things happen simply because someone is exhausted. Six months of touring is tough. I've talked to his parents for a few minutes. They're heading for the airport even as we speak. They were as concerned as you'd expect parents to be. I sensed confusion and hostility, but I'm not sure if it's directed at their kid or Riveting Records, or somewhere else. We'll have to see after they get here. You know, Dexter's presence in a hospital isn't going to be kept quiet long."

"Can't be helped," Paul said.

Brian and Jeff came in and the four of them ate together. As Paul was leaving, Brian cornered him in the living room. The boy asked, "I didn't drive him nuts, did I, Dad?"

"He was near a breakdown. You were not the cause of all that led up to that moment. You are not responsible for his reaction to your question or your condoms."

Jeff said, "'Famous Rock Singer Driven Nuts by Simple Questions.' You could be famous."

Paul said, "You are not to talk about him. The poor kid needs help, not cheap gossip."

"Dad." Lately Jeff had added an unattractive whine to his repertoire. "How come he's got condoms in his room?"

"You and I have talked about condoms. You may ask your brother about his. If he wants, he can answer your questions. First, you might want to check with him about the success of adding whining to his list of ways to get me to agree to something. Whining will also not prevent my comments about the need for changes in your behavior."

"Doesn't work," Brian said, "and I am among the best. The more you whine, the more likely he is to make long boring comments like that last one."

Paul added, "Editorials from teenagers about parental behavior are also frowned upon."

"See?" Brian said.

Paul frowned.

"Sorry," Brian said.

With a last admonition to keep quiet about their recent visitor and a kiss for Ben, Paul drove to work.

⹂10⹂

Thirty or forty reporters and four camera crews clustered in the frigid air outside Area Ten headquarters. It was supposed to get to seven below tonight. Paul parked down the street and used a side entrance. Fenwick would have pushed straight through them. Turner didn't feel the need.

As prearranged, Turner met Fenwick at about seven. They were hours early for their shift.

Dan O'Leary, one of the cops on duty at the admitting desk said, "Fenwick, you got a call from someone who claimed to be a lawyer for Riveting Records. He said you're to call no matter when you get in."

Fenwick crumpled up the note and tossed it into a trash can. "I don't respond to lawyer's directives outside of a courtroom."

The acting commander, Drew Molton, met with them. Turner told them about Clendenen's visit. Turner didn't believe his actions in helping Clendenen compromised his position as an investigator, but once the Zawickis and Blundlefitzes of the world started twisting things, even the most unassailable act of kindness was unlikely to escape unscathed.

Molton said, "Don't worry about his visit. It's all over the media that he's in the hospital. It's a good thing you had your therapist friend check him in. Otherwise we'd have even more questions from the press. We've got intense pressure. Ignore it as you usually do. Our media people will handle any direct questions. We are having a problem with these music people trying to leave town. This Zawicki guy must know somebody."

"We've got a cure for the Zawicki problem," Fenwick said. "He's been screwing the boys in the band. We'll threaten to reveal that to the press. He'll back off."

"Screwing them?" Molton asked. "As in he's a rotten, cheating businessman or as in he had his dick up their butts?"

Turner said, "I don't have details of specific physical acts. It certainly wasn't just figuratively. I'm pretty sure it was very literally."

"Amazing," Molton said, "but believable. Underage?"

"No."

Molton said, "Still, I think that kind of threat should work. I got a call from a guy saying he was a lawyer from *Hot Trends* magazine. I am to tell you both that you are evil, awful people for threatening his client."

"I know the drill," Fenwick said. "He has rights and they're going to be really pissed if we bug him again."

"No, they're really pissed now. If they could find any kind of witness, I think they'd be in front of the cameras already."

"He interfered in an investigation," Fenwick protested.

"I know that. You know that. The lawyers know that. When you're a cop, it makes no difference whether you're right or wrong. A smear in the press, an accusation that takes forever to disprove, those often do enough damage. There's a lot of folks who don't like us."

"We didn't hit him or shoot at him or kill him or profile him," Fenwick said.

"You bruised his ego," Molton said.

"Fucking egotistical moron," Fenwick said. "Wish he was dead."

"Be careful what you wish for," Molton said.

First Turner called the evidence techs and asked if they'd had time to examine the underwear. "Nothing much," was the reply. "The guy in the pink boxers beat off a lot or he used that one pair of shorts as a cum towel."

"Not a lot of help," Turner said.

"Did you really expect much from these? If we find out anything, we'll call."

They did paperwork for nearly an hour and also set up a meeting at the murder scene.

Turner and Fenwick stopped at the medical examiner's office on the way over. There were reporters camped out in the lobby.

The ME had Roger Stendar open on the slab. Turner thought even the staunchest fan might be inclined to puke at that sight.

"What have you got so far?" Fenwick asked.

"Gunshot wound. Rattled around in there. Killed instantly. No bruises. No other wounds. No signs of fighting back."

"Have you had time for drug screening?"

"Sent that out a few hours ago. Whether he was killed because he was a drug-addicted rock star or not is something you guys will have to figure out. I've got no obvious track marks or anything else that says this kid was doped up."

"Not much," Fenwick said.

The ME said, "He's got the largest flaccid prick of any corpse I've ever measured. Five inches."

"That's important?" Fenwick asked.

"Not to me. I just give out information. The other bit of major news I have is that he was anally penetrated within an hour of his death. No semen. A little bit of tearing around the anus. Whoever did it either used a condom, or didn't have an orgasm, or used an artificial device."

Fenwick said, "Could it have happened after he was dead?"

"No. He was alive for it."

"But no marks of having fought back?" Turner said.

"Nope. If he wasn't willing, I've got no evidence that he tried to do something about it."

Fenwick said, "We'd never be able to get DNA samples until we get a suspect."

Turner said, "If the person who screwed him is also the person who killed him."

"Can't tell that from what I've got," the ME said. "Might not be able to. I'll keep everything from the cavity, but it's possible he was using a dildo on himself."

Turner said, "Buck, if you say this is truly fucked up you may find an unpleasantly large artificial device in places you never imagined."

"I can image a lot," Fenwick said.

Turner said, "Presumably, only the killer knows Stendar was penetrated before he died. If that's true, we need to keep that little bit of information quiet."

The detectives drove to the All-Chicago Sports Arena. The shrine outside had grown larger along with the crowd. Turner estimated well over two thousand people huddled against the frigid temperature. They had to have a lot of fervor to be out in the bitter cold. The sea of votive candles was threatening to become a flood. Even with this vast amount, the flames barely held their own against the rising northeast wind.

They met Aaron Davis, Frances Strikal, Ethel Hinkmeyer, David McWilliams the beat cop, and Simon Pomfret, an evidence technician.

McWilliams said, "I talked to all the officers on duty. They confirmed that nothing else was found."

Fenwick asked, "Would the gunshots have caused the platform to fall?"

"No," Pomfret said. "Everything was too well put together and designed. You'd need a rocket launcher." He handed them a sheaf of papers. "You'll see in there that I've got a general idea where the gunshots came from."

Turner and Fenwick examined the diagram of the gunshot trajectories. "Where is this?" Turner asked. Pomfret led them to a spot under the vast stage complex. The dressing room was about ten feet away. The evidence techs had found a bullet embedded in the bottom of the platform, one in a strut twenty feet above it, and the original one Turner had found. The general area they had come from was an exit to the washrooms and concession stands.

Fenwick said, "Do you have an outline or chart or schedule of everything the boys did during the concert?"

Hinkmeyer said, "Yes, and I have the list of their songs. I can also tell you which people in the crew should have been where or the general area they were assigned to work in. There's another list that shows at what times the boys sing or dance. The choreography was pretty rigidly set."

As they eyed likely hiding places, Fenwick said, "You wait for a moment of big explosions, everybody watches the pyrotechnics, and you fire away. Wrap the gun in your coat, and you've got it concealed. You just look like you're raising your hand to point at what's going on. As long as your coat doesn't slip, you've got perfect cover."

"And little real chance of hitting one of them," Turner said. "We've got personal attempts like the water bottles, large attempts like the fire, and random attempts like these shots. I don't get it." He checked the crew list then asked Davis, "If the band isn't changing, who is down here?"

Davis said, "One or two costume people are usually around. Mostly they take what the boys are done with and get it out of the way. Their clothes are set out pretty carefully. The crew is well trained. They've been doing the same basic thing for six months."

"We'll have to check the beat cops' reports for who talked to the costume people," Fenwick said. "And we'll have to talk with them. Who else?"

"None of the pyrotechnics originated from this area. That's all controlled by computers and the stuff that looks like flames comes out of gas pipes or sometimes it's just computer-screen images."

"When is the concert loudest?"

"I've got a list from special effects," Davis said. "They check it before each concert, make sure all the computers are synchronized."

"Are there ever any foul-ups, computer glitches?" Turner asked.

"Nothing went wrong with them last night. I can't remember a glitch this tour. And every system has at least three backups, none of which are connected to each other."

"Who has access to these lists?" Turner asked.

"They aren't secret or anything," Davis said. "The guys in the band, most of the work crews."

"Are they ever handed out to critics?"

"There'd be no reason to seek them out to give one to them. Wouldn't really be any reason not to. No critic requested these here."

"But a fan couldn't just randomly pick one up?" Turner asked.

Aaron Davis said, "They aren't just sitting out in the open, but I guess somebody could get one. No one had a reason to keep these particularly secret."

"What happens if the boys decide to banter with the audience or each other?" Fenwick asked. "Wouldn't that throw off the timing?"

"There is really very little variation from performance to performance. What you see as casual banter may not be perfectly scripted, but the time allotted for it is. For example, Galyak might vary his jokes slightly. If there are any alterations, we've got people working the computers on-site. We've got pause buttons."

"The band's set started at exactly what time?" Turner asked.

"Nine-fifteen."

"So we can come pretty close to exact times of loudest moments. It makes sense the shots coincided with those moments, or they would have been heard." The group worked together several minutes to attach approximate real-times next to each noise high-point.

"Are the guys in the band onstage all the time?" Turner asked.

"No. Sometimes one or two change while someone is singing a solo, or some effect is going on and they all rush down here."

"Anything else?" Fenwick asked.

Everybody shook their heads no.

"Can we start packing this stuff up for shipping?" Davis asked.

"No," Fenwick said. "We'd like to leave it for a day or so more."

"One odd thing," McWilliams said.

"What?" Fenwick asked.

"All the towels from the shower area are missing."

"Who was in charge of that?" Fenwick asked.

Davis said, "We were. When we went to collect them, they were gone."

"Souvenirs," Hinkmeyer said. "I don't think it's anything sinister. I've seen it happen before. Anything these guys touched would be valuable. A towel with the water on it from one of these guy's bodies would be worth a small fortune."

Turner asked, "But how could anybody prove it had been used by one of them?"

Hinkmeyer said, "I suppose someone who was there would have to vouch for it, or someone would have to be extremely gullible."

In the car Fenwick said, "I'm looking forward to talking to all of them again about Haupmin's claims of dissension and Clendenen's claims of being picked on, and about Roger getting screwed in the shower."

Turner said, "Disparate data depresses me."

"If I'm forbidden from quoting poetry, you can't say things like that."

"I'm pro-poetry. I'm anti-listening to it while I work. I'm anti-listening to it when it is not of my own choosing."

"Philistine."

The largest crowd of reporters up to this point in the case was in the lobby of the Hotel Chicago. Turner and Fenwick could see Zawicki at the podium answering questions. He was flanked by Ralph Eudace, Ivan Pappas, and Danny Galyak.

"No, we don't know how long Dexter is going to be in the hospital. We are monitoring his situation. We are flying in his parents from Midland, Kansas, as we speak. We are all very concerned."

"Where's the other band guy, Jason Devane?" Fenwick whispered.

"I don't know," Turner said. "I just got here myself."

A reporter asked, "Is someone out to get this band? We've heard there's a conspiracy. That there was sabotage."

"I don't know where you guys get this stuff," Zawicki said.

"I do." The voice was next to Turner's ear. Randall Blundlefitz parked himself in front of the detectives. "That was some performance this morning." All his bravado was back. "I let my ego get in the way of my common sense. I should have brought the magazine's lawyers with me. You bullied me into submission. That won't happen again."

"The lawyers are here now?" Fenwick asked.

"I don't need them now. This whole thing is going to blow up in your faces."

"What's that supposed to mean?" Fenwick demanded.

"Fuck you and the horse you rode in on." Blundlefitz stomped over to the mob of reporters and shoved his way into the middle of them. He stuck his hand up and was called upon immediately.

"Are the police acting properly?" he asked.

Zawicki said, "We have many questions about how this case is being handled. Remember the detectives in the Ramsey and Simpson cases?"

Fenwick said, "Zawicki's in it with Blundlefitz. They've made a deal."

Turner knew the hazards of a job that involved interacting with the public. Whether a dogcatcher or president, when you're a public figure, you either have to get used to people going after you or you get out. Most people had no training or professional spin doctors to help them. Turner and Fenwick were used to pressure, as all detectives had to be.

Ethel Hinkmeyer, the publicist, rushed up to them. "Thank God," she said. "I just got back a few minutes ago."

"What's wrong?" Turner asked.

"No one can find Jason Devane. They postponed the press conference for an hour then decided they couldn't put it off. The press was in a frenzy. Everybody's out looking for him."

Turner said, "Everybody except all the people at the press conference."

Hinkmeyer shook her head. "This is bad."

Fenwick asked, "None of these reporters knows he's missing?"

"Not yet."

"How long has he been gone?" Turner asked.

"No one's seen him all afternoon."

Turner knew they could step in and stop the proceedings, but that might only add to the frenzy. Being missing for an afternoon was not usually a cause for concern for an adult, but nothing was usual today.

Fenwick said, "We have to talk to these people right now. You've got to get them to end the press conference."

"That's what I was going to try to do. This is out of hand. Jordan Pastern is up in Mr. Zawicki's room. He's going nuts. Maybe you should talk to him. The rest of us will join you up there as quickly as we can." The detectives agreed, and she hurried away.

"She's not part of the Blundlefitz-Zawicki axis?" Fenwick asked.

"She didn't act hostile. Of course, she's a publicist. They're paid not to be assholes to outsiders."

In the suite Pastern paced. The band may have lost their luxury lodgings, but Zawicki hadn't lost his. The room they were in might have been as large as the entire square

106

footage, including the basement, of Turner's home. White walls made a stark contrast with massive cubes, squares, and triangles of burnished bronze.

Pastern said, "Thank God you're here."

"Hinkmeyer told us Jason Devane is missing. What happened?"

"When we checked his room late this afternoon, he was gone. We had a huge meeting after everybody got back last night. Mr. Zawicki assured everyone that the band would go on. That our jobs would go on. I know he's going to fire me. I know he thinks that this is my fault. I'm head of security, so actually he's right. It was my job to protect them."

"Was Devane registered under his own name?" Turner asked.

"No. There wasn't another suite available, so we got whatever rooms we could. Jason was on the tenth floor. Nobody else from the band was. The rooms were all under the same name. Elvis Presley. It was as good a code as anyone could come up with. I haven't been able to sleep. I picture the guys laughing and being silly on the bus. All the good times. They were great kids. That's gone. All gone." He sighed deeply. "Nobody saw Jason all day today. Late this afternoon, I went to his room. I knocked. There was no answer. I got worried. Hotel security let me in. His bed had been slept in. Why would he walk out without telling anyone? The guys know better than to go out alone. They know the problems with crazed fans. Once they're recognized, it's a mob scene. Nobody's reported anything like that. And Jason wouldn't run away. He couldn't. Where can one of the most famous people on the planet run to? Where the hell do you look in a metropolitan area of millions of people? We've checked all the airlines, the bus station, the rental car companies, the trains, nothing. Unless he walked back to California. I feel like I should be out there, but what good would it do for me to be walking the streets? We're supposed to have another meeting after the press conference."

"Are they telling the press he's missing?"

"They decided not to. He's only been gone a short time."

Turner said, "He's disappeared and they hold a press conference to attack the cops? Nobody even thinks to call the police?" Fenwick glanced at his friend. The words contained more than a hint of anger which Turner rarely showed to suspects, witnesses, or arrestees. Fenwick had heard that underlying, steely tone only a few times in their years as partners. But a moment later Turner asked in a voice only slightly quieter than usual, "Did anyone see Dexter Clendenen leave?"

"He went to his room earlier than everybody else. No one knows how he got to this psychologist. Probably someone trying to take advantage of the rich, make himself a name."

Turner said, "Clendenen claimed that the guys in the band picked on him. That only Roger protected him."

"You talked to him?"

"Yes."

"In the hospital? How is he?"

Turner said, "Getting some help. Did he seem depressed to you or unstable?"

"These are emotional guys. It's a hell of a life. You're always on the edge."

"Downstairs it sounded like Mr. Blundlefitz and Mr. Zawicki had some questions set up."

"Yeah, I don't get that. I'm going to be fired, but I want to help these boys. I'm not sure they do. Those two guys met for a couple hours early this afternoon. I don't know what they decided. Something is up, and I don't like it."

Hinkmeyer entered. "The rest of them should be up in a few minutes." She carried several thick three-ring binders with her.

Turner said, "We heard the rumor that Mr. Zawicki and other executives were having sex with the boys."

"Absolutely not true," Hinkmeyer said.

"Zawicki was," Pastern said. "I don't know about any others. I think I'd know."

"Jordan, how can you say such a thing?" Hinkmeyer asked.

"How often was he having sex with them?" Turner asked.

"I'm not sure. No one told me, but I figured it out over time. Who got to do things and who didn't seemed pretty arbitrary until I realized a late-night visit to Zawicki's home usually ended with something good happening for the visitor."

Hinkmeyer said, "Maybe they just talked."

Pastern said, "Maybe, but I doubt it."

"You have any proof?" Turner asked.

"I don't have pictures," Pastern said, "but I think it's time for some truth around here."

"Are you making any progress?" Hinkmeyer asked.

"Not as much as we'd like," Fenwick said.

Turner said, "We're getting reports that there was dissension in the band. That Roger was thinking of leaving."

Hinkmeyer said, "You get all kinds of tabloid rumors. Most of the ones about problems originated with Sherri Haupmin. I know Mr. Zawicki was trying to get rid of her. It was complicated because she wasn't directly under contract to us. She was a bit of a problem, but the band was not going to break up."

Fenwick said, "Blundlefitz mentioned that he found some notes about a meeting where breaking up the band was discussed."

Neither of them admitted to having heard of such a meeting.

"Dexter told me he was afraid of heights," Turner said. "That he was forced to do all those stunts."

Pastern said, "I had to help him out a lot at first. We all did. It took some time before he got used to them. I didn't think he was still afraid."

Hinkmeyer said, "I hadn't heard anything lately. Jordan did a marvelous job with the boys making them feel at ease."

"What about Murial Arane, the choreographer?" Turner asked. "We were told she and Roger had disagreements."

"Murial?" Hinkmeyer said. "I'll get her up here right now. She worked wonders with these boys." She picked up a hotel phone and placed a call.

While they waited for the choreographer, Fenwick asked, "Could you line up these kids' personal assistants for interviews for when we're done with Mr. Zawicki?"

"Certainly. I'll have them available for whenever you need them."

A few minutes later Murial Arane entered the room. She was Asian, slender and muscular, maybe in her mid-thirties, and stood about five foot two. She spoke in a soft voice.

They sat across the room from Hinkmeyer and Pastern, out of earshot. Not hard to do in such a huge room.

"Ms. Arane," Turner said, "we're wondering about your relationship with the members of the band."

She sighed. "I knew it would come to this. I worked with these guys for years. At first it was great. Then Roger would have a few questions. He did have some very good suggestions, but I'm paid to be the creative director. Every step in their first videos was mine. Every one. What was so wrong with success?"

"What happened?" Turner asked.

"Haupmin. That woman is evil incarnate. She knows nothing about dancing. Nothing. But no, she had to have everything changed. She barged into rehearsals. I finally talked to Mr. Zawicki, and he ordered her to be kept out. It wasn't so bad after that."

"Did the guys get along?" Turner asked.

"I worked with them, I didn't judge them."

"We're interested in your observations," Turner said.

"There were no fights that would cause murder. Galyak told stupid jokes, but that's not a crime. Dex was a little shy about a lot of things. The guys kind of teased him, but guys tease about a lot of things. They teased me. There was a lot of back and forth. You dance for hours a day, you get close. I had a creative team second to none. We had a budget beyond that of any other group."

"We were told you were going to be fired," Fenwick said.

"I was not in danger of losing my job."

"Tell us about Roger," Turner said.

"A nice enough guy. Smart. You've heard about or at least seen the whole teddy bear thing."

"Yeah."

"He couldn't have cared less about teddy bears or kids' charities. He saw a couple other bands doing charity work. He decided it would be good for their image. That shirt-throwing thing? It was fake. The person was picked in advance. He knew who he was supposed to throw it to. It was always somebody connected with the band or the company or friends of someone with influence, maybe the kids of one of the employees, or like here, the winner of some contest. Don't get me wrong. Roger was a nice guy, but he was a shrewd businessman first. That whole teddy bear thing got him and the band huge amounts of positive publicity."

"What about the other guys?" Turner asked. "How'd they feel about the charity?"

"I'm not sure they cared a lot. If Roger suggested something, they usually went along. They weren't a hard bunch to get along with."

She knew nothing else and left.

Turner said, "Kind of blows the sweetness and light concept out of the water."

"I'm for that," Fenwick said.

.11.

The door to the room swung open. Blundlefitz, Eudace, and Zawicki walked in. Eudace marched straight up to Pastern and said, "You lost another one."

"No one, *no one*, cares more about these boys than I do," Pastern said. "They make a lot of money for the corporation and you people care about that, but no one cares about them the way I do. How dare you make such an accusation?"

Eudace said, "I just made an observation." He turned to the detectives. "We also need to reveal that before this tragedy, Jordan Pastern was going to be fired."

Pastern stood up. "What the hell?"

Turner visualized rats deserting a sinking ship or turning on each other in desperation.

Zawicki said, "That's correct. Mr. Pastern had reason to harm me."

"This is bullshit," Pastern said. "I knew nothing of this. I would never hurt these guys. You mother-fucking son of a bitch."

Everybody froze.

Turner said, "Mr. Zawicki, you told us in our first interview that there were no disgruntled employees."

Zawicki licked his lips. "Jordan didn't raise a fuss when we told him. He was going to go quietly. He would get a large severance package."

"You're trying to frame me, you mother-fucking asshole." Pastern lunged toward him. Eudace and Zawicki leapt back. Turner and Fenwick grabbed him before he could get far. Pastern was big and strong, but Turner was strong as well and Fenwick was certainly bigger.

When Pastern was calm enough to be subdued, Fenwick said, "Someone is not telling the truth."

All three said, "I'm telling the truth."

Nasty glares all around. Turner didn't think they were going to find out who was telling the truth at the moment. He said, "Mr. Blundlefitz told us he found notes from a meeting that talked about the band breaking up."

Zawicki said, "We make scenarios for what could happen, what might happen. He misunderstood what he found. He sees it differently now. I try to make sure my company has all contingencies covered. If it could happen, we'd like to plan for what we would do."

"Including the death of one of the band members?" Fenwick asked.

"Yes," Zawicki said. "I believe in dealing with reality. It can happen. I cannot leave my company in the lurch."

"That seems awfully cold," Fenwick said.

"This is a business," Zawicki said. "Because I am good at business does not mean I am heartless." He deigned to honor each of the detectives with a cold smile. "You should be talking to your boss right about now. I'm sure he's trying to get in touch with you. This investigation is totally screwed up."

Blundlefitz pointed at the detectives. "You fucked with

me last night. Now another one of the boys is missing. You're going to be nothing in this town."

Fenwick said, "I wasn't much interested in becoming 'something' in this town before I met you. Meeting you has not inspired me to want to be more than I am."

"You know what I mean."

"I may know what you mean, but I certainly don't care if you know what I understand."

Everybody glowered at everybody for a few moments.

Turner said, "We need to talk to Mr. Zawicki alone, please." It was barely a whisper but carried more steel than all the skyscrapers in the city.

Eudace, Hinkmeyer, and Pastern inched toward the door. Blundlefitz said, "Don't let them threaten you."

Zawicki had his back to Blundlefitz so the reporter didn't see the businessman's sneer of contempt. Turner slowly walked toward Blundlefitz and stopped two feet away. "Get. Out." Quieter than a zephyr. Harder than titanium. Turner fixed his eyes on Blundlefitz's until the reporter lowered his and turned away.

"Yes, go," Zawicki said. "I can handle this."

The four others left. Zawicki sat down on a chair of red leather and teak. Fenwick remained in the background. Turner stepped slowly toward Zawicki and stood over him.

"What?" Zawicki demanded.

Turner let the silence lengthen beyond the comfortable. Then he leaned in even closer and said, "I spent some time with a young man today." His voice was so soft Fenwick could barely hear him from fifteen feet away. "A very frightened young man. Dexter Clendenen came to my house early this morning."

"So that's where he was."

"How'd you get my home address?" Turner asked.

"I had my people do some basic research. We didn't find

out he was missing until the hospital called, and it was on the news. It's interesting that he was at your house. Were you keeping that information . . ."

Turner interrupted. "I'm going to talk now and you're going to be very, very quiet." Deadly soft. Fenwick might rage, and shift from volcanic to ice-cold arctic to impress or intimidate, but Turner had the ability to command those he wanted to listen to him. With Fenwick there was always an explosion waiting just underneath. The tension came in wondering when, not if, the explosion would come. Turner relied on his sense of himself, a sense of presence, a confidence, a self-assurance. His quietness was without pretense. He didn't need a podium and a microphone to make a point. Turner pulled over a metal-frame chair with a chrome bottom. He sat so that his knees almost touched Zawicki's.

"Dexter confirmed what we already knew," Turner said. "You screwed every member of the band. Why didn't you tell us this important fact?"

"Who told you this besides poor deluded Dexter?"

"We have other sources as well," Fenwick said. "We were also told that the other executives had sex with the guys in the band."

"I don't know about that. I doubt it. Feel free to ask them. They, as well as I, get to confront any accuser. My having sex with them is important only in terms of what they were required to do for the band. It has nothing to do with the murder. If they wouldn't let me have sex with them, they couldn't be in the group. So what? That was years ago."

"They're all gay?" Fenwick asked.

"I assume they're all straight. I never asked. They never told. I don't care. Their public image had to stay intact, and they had to be willing to service me."

Fenwick said, "They have to be fucked by you to get into

116

the band, or they have to keep fucking you any time you want, or both?"

"Definitely to get in. I didn't push them too much after that. Once I had them, that was usually enough. And there's always a group that wants to form another band."

"It's a requirement for all the guys in all the bands in your company?" Fenwick asked.

"It's less than fifty people. These guys know you have to pay a high price for fame. Most of them are nice, middle-class boys who have a lot of ambition. I'm willing to help them fulfill that. I believe I deserve some fulfillment in return. They were perfectly free to say no and leave. They had to have sex with me before they were added to the group. I made it clear that they would need to continue servicing me if I wished. After the first time, I seldom asked."

"This didn't piss them off?" Fenwick asked. "None of them said they resented it? None of them tried to stop it?"

"I'm the gravy train. A great, big, huge gravy train. The largest and longest gravy train they were ever going to be on. I've made these young men very, very rich."

Fenwick said, "Yeah, but these groups can go to different companies. They can make other deals."

"Not with the contracts my lawyers draw up."

"You put a clause saying sex was required with the company owner into their contracts?" Fenwick asked.

"No, of course not, but to make this kind of money, they had to obey the rules. We didn't try to cheat them like some of the labels do. They signed. A contract is a contract."

"Fucking somebody against their will seems like a violation to me," Fenwick said.

"Are you a lawyer?" Zawicki asked.

"I'm as close to one as you're going to see for the moment."

"Which is not good enough for an indictment."

"No, it isn't," Fenwick admitted.

"I'm not some politician that the right-wing wants to smear to death. I'm just a business owner."

"Nobody in their families got upset about your sexual relationship with them?" Fenwick asked.

"I don't know who they told, if anybody. I don't think it makes sense to look there for a motive for murder. If a friend or relative was angry about what I was doing to their little darlings, you would think they would want to kill me, not their son, or brother, or best friend."

This last statement made sense to Turner. If you're being abused, you don't murder the one getting abused. Unless.

"Was one of the boys angry about having to service you and threatening to expose you?" Turner asked. "That might give you a motive."

"Blackmail? No. If they accuse me, they are implicitly part of the sexual activity. They have as much invested in their image as I. They may be able to besmirch me, if they were able to prove they actually had sex with me. Believe me, there is no pair of underwear with my DNA on it in their possession. They might score points against me, but once a whiff of scandal was associated with the band, all those pre-pubescent girls would begin drooling over someone else. There would be no more rides to attend Boys4u concerts from doting parents."

"Maybe one of the guys was willing to risk it?" Turner asked.

"I'm sure you will investigate the possibility. No one was trying to blackmail me. You will find no record of threatening notes because there aren't any. Ask the boys. They won't say they were if they weren't."

"We can ask all but one," Turner said. "Maybe he was the one."

"There is no proof, because none exists," Zawicki reiterated. "By all means, check with them."

Fenwick asked, "What if a guy who wanted to be in a band didn't go along and told?"

Zawicki sighed. "If I told someone it was a condition for me hiring them, in reality, I'd already decided to do so. It was a bluff that never failed. Plus I have power. Real power in the music industry. A threat by me to destroy any possible career for any of them was very real. Everyone knew I could and would do it. I've done it before for other reasons. I'm sure I'll do it again."

Turner felt like he did when he stood in front of the deadly reptile cage at the zoo.

"Did they have sex with each other?" Fenwick asked.

"If they did, I don't know about it."

Turner had had enough. He said, "You had power and control over them. You took advantage. That they were of age is not my concern. Your ability to harm them is. You may have made them rich, but a young man, a very troubled young man, was at my house this morning. He's had a breakdown. I imagine before he got to you, he may have been a mess, but you are a big part of what is wrong with him. We'll find out about his home life. We'll try to pinpoint what went wrong. Maybe no one will ever know. What you did to him so that you could make a profit is unconscionable."

Zawicki didn't meet Turner's eyes. He squirmed in the chair as if trying to put more space between himself and the angry detective.

"Do you even care that Roger Stendar died?" Turner asked.

"Of course I care. So I'm not weeping like a fourteen-year-old girl. That is not a crime. I learned long ago not to weep. I'll have time for tears later. I want his killer found. No one more than I. I'm doing whatever I can to make that happen."

Turner said, "Then we get here, and you're having a

press conference spewing blame while another one of your band members is missing. How dare you? The boy could be dead."

"He could just be out walking," Zawicki said.

Turner said, "You lost the right to justify yourself when you screwed the first boy for your first band. One of the members of this band has been murdered. For all we know someone could be after the others as well. Instead you're having a press conference blathering bullshit to the world."

"You're not a therapist or a priest. You're just a cop. You have no moral authority over me."

Turner said, "For now, you are in my jurisdiction. While you are here, you are going to concentrate on helping us deal with four boys who you've helped to fuck up. Yes, they're rich beyond their wildest dreams. You're right, I'm not a therapist, but I've been a cop for a long time. I know ill health when I see it. I saw it this morning in this poor kid. Don't you understand there's depth here? Don't you realize the effect you are having on these boys' lives? And you want to blame us for investigating poorly. Are you nuts? If there is someone to blame, look to yourself, and not just for sexual activity with them. Something is wrong here. One of them has been murdered. Another is missing. There is going to be a price to be paid for what's happened. I'm going to make sure you pay your share of that price."

Zawicki licked his lips and glanced to Fenwick and back to Turner. Finally he muttered, "I didn't kill anybody."

"Don't say one more word of justification. Not one."

Zawicki shrugged.

Fenwick asked, "Did Roger Stendar trade sexual favors so you would permit Sherri Haupmin to be one of the opening acts?"

"I knew she was trouble. I did everything in my power to minimize her influence. Roger thought he was in love.

What a mistake. I thought I'd try keeping her close, the better to keep her under observation. She could barely sing two consecutive notes and was an even worse dancer. The best packaging in the world can't cause there to be talent."

Turner said, "I think you lied to us a few minutes ago when you said you had sex with them once and that was about it."

"Sex has nothing to do with this murder."

"How often did you have sex with the members of the band?" Turner demanded.

"I didn't mark it on a calendar or carve notches in a gun."

"How often?"

"Roger more than the others. He was the most independent of the bunch, the hardest to control, so the most fun for me to force to submit, but he was the most passive during sex."

Turner said, "This morning Dexter told me you had sexual relations with him almost continuously."

"With the other three, just the once. With Dexter once in a while. At times I find his type alluring. He seemed to enjoy it more than the others."

Turner said, "That's more than harassment, that's sick. Forcing a presumably straight boy to continue servicing you. Doing it to anyone male or female, gay or straight from a power position is loathsome. Here's what you're going to do. You are going to hold another press conference in which you say you are retiring from your job as chairman of Riveting Records. That you are donating your severance package to charity. We'll find one that specializes in helping abused children. If you do not do that tomorrow morning first thing in front of legions of reporters, I will release the information to the press about what you required of these boys."

"They would never confirm it."

"False hopes will not serve," Turner said. "As you said, these are not the first band members you required sexual favors from. Once it becomes public knowledge, it will snowball. Certainly, some of the former victims will talk. People who your victims have confided in will come forward. Others will want their fifteen minutes of fame connected to this band."

"I resign and you say nothing?"

"Yes."

"I'll think it over."

"No, you won't," Turner said. "You will do it, or I release the news. And the rest of the band members will be allowed to renegotiate their contracts and be free to choose other companies."

Zawicki's angry glare didn't indicate to Turner that he was in any way prepared to be cooperative.

Turner said, "I almost hope you try to bluff us. One boy is dead. One has had a breakdown. One is missing. We're going to talk to the last two again. My guess is there's more ugly stuff that is going to come out."

Zawicki said, "You do what you have to do. I will do what I have to do."

Turner asked, "Where are the rest of the boys right now?"

"In their rooms. We doubled security."

"Send for them please."

Zawicki picked up the phone, tapped several numbers, and gave the requisite orders.

"What happened with Jason Devane?" Turner asked.

"We don't know. The other guys don't know. He wasn't in his room. Contrary to what you might think, I am worried. They know better than to just walk off. Pastern is an idiot. It would look bad to get rid of him now, and it would cause chaos. He'll be gone days after we all get back home."

"You told us last night that everyone in the band got along fine. Dexter told us that there was dissension in the band. That Roger was planning to leave. Was that true?"

"His contract was ironclad."

Turner put pauses between the next words long enough to encompass an ice age. "Cut. The. Crap."

"Yes, Roger was unhappy. They could all be unhappy. They could all be incredibly happy. They danced and sang. I did not cause anyone's death."

"Maybe not directly," Turner said. "Maybe you're completely innocent, but as of tomorrow, you are out of the picture."

Defiant silence.

Fenwick asked, "What did you and Blundlefitz discuss this afternoon? Why'd you pick him as the shill for your little charade and why bother to berate us? Last night Blundlefitz accused us of being in league with you in some kind of cover-up. Now, you guys are buddies against the bungling detectives. Why the change?"

Zawicki said, "Have you found the killer? I don't see anything getting done. Even now, you threaten me, but how does that get you closer to the murderer? As for Blundlefitz, he's a fat fool. He was pissed at you. I wanted to use him as much as he wanted to use me. He will lead the publicity barrage against you. He thinks he's some kind of goddamn Miss Marple who's going to find out who killed Roger. Ha!"

Fenwick said, "That moronic twit will be sorrier than you are."

"I'm not sure how sorry I need to feel." Zawicki stood up. "Feel free to use the suite as long as you wish." He left.

Fenwick turned to his partner. "Who do we believe about the security guy being fired—Pastern or Zawicki?"

Turner said, "I feel neutral about Pastern and don't like Zawicki, but I'm not ready to make that decision yet. I can picture Zawicki and his minions making that kind of thing up. Look how he's trying to smear us."

Fenwick said, "And why frame Pastern? Is he trying to shift suspicion away from himself or do his own cover-up?"

"Don't know," Turner said. While pulling out his cell phone, he added, "We're getting the local beat cops involved with finding this kid." He talked to a dispatcher for several moments then the commander of the local district and Molton from Area Ten. He hung up and said, "The local district cops will get on it. I'm calling Ian. I don't want to get out of my depth here. The department might help us out, but I think I should get Ian on board. He'll know more about releasing information about this guy to the press."

"Zawicki's going to fight," Fenwick stated.

"If he is, I'm going to be as ready as I can." He punched in the pager number of his friend Ian Hume, the reporter. Turner knew he would be at the office late on a Sunday, deadline day for the weekly paper. Ian worked late nearly every day. In moments Turner's phone rang. Turner said, "I need some help with a press problem, and do you guys have a music critic at the paper?"

"Yep."

"Could you meet me around eleven and get the music critic there about twelve? I know it's a Sunday night and you're on deadline."

"I'm always on deadline. I always wonder about reporters who are so frantic when a deadline looms. Is it a surprise to them that they have a deadline? You always know your deadline so get off your ass. As for the critic, he's a part-time bartender up at a place on Halsted. We can meet there and talk to him after his shift is over."

"Thanks."

"What's going on?"

"The Stendar murder." He gave Ian a sketch of the important details. Turner didn't have to tell his friend that what he was saying was confidential. The reporter would reveal nothing without permission. Besides being an old friend, Ian had also been a cop before turning to journalism. Turner trusted him implicitly. He said, "We've got people to talk to. If we get delayed, I'll call you." He hung up.

There was a knock on the door. Pastern brought in Danny Galyak and Ivan Pappas.

.12.

Turner led the two boys to a dining area. They sat around a glass-topped table. Both boys wore running shoes, faded jeans, and sweatshirts, Danny's with BOYS4U stenciled across the front, above which was the bright, swirling logo. Ivan's had a picture of the Eiffel Tower on it.

"What's happening?" Pappas asked. "Have they found Jason?"

Turner said, "The local police are on it. Did Jason ever do anything like this before?"

"No," Galyak said. "If anybody was going to stick around the hotel, it was Jason. Him, and Dexter, too, would stay in the bus instead of going out. I guess they felt safe there. Jason didn't like going out. He would party with us only once in a great while. Do you think he's dead?" All trace of bravado was gone from his voice.

"We don't know," Turner said. "What happened after we talked to you last night?"

Galyak said, "We all got on the bus to come back here. We had to wait until everybody was done. They've got that underground entrance, big enough for buses so bands like us don't get mobbed. Most places don't have that. Waiting got kind of boring. We were all nervous. As each of us got back to the bus, we grilled the others on what they'd been asked. Nobody remembered anything special and we didn't know what was happening. It was like none of us could believe it. I still don't. For a while after we talked I listened to music. Dexter looked kind of out of it. He kept walking up and down the center aisle. Kept pestering us. He always needed somebody to pay attention to him. He always bugged Roger. Mostly Roger put up with it, but he could drive you nuts. He was younger than the rest of us, and he never shut up."

Turner said, "He's had a nervous breakdown. Maybe he was looking for someone to talk to."

Galyak said, "He was always trying to talk to somebody. It was boring. Even Roger got fed up once in a while. Dexter was a wuss. We didn't make him needy. He came to us that way. We all figured Dex was a fag."

"Gay," Turner said. "The word is gay."

"I didn't mean anything by it," Galyak said.

"Good."

"I know I saw Dexter writing for a while in that stupid journal he keeps," Galyak said.

"He kept a journal?" Turner asked.

"Yeah."

"Where is it?"

"I don't know."

A journal? The detectives knew a possible gold mine when they heard one.

"I was reading a book," Pappas said. "An Agatha Christie mystery. I like them. They relax me. No matter how tense I get, they put me to sleep."

"What did Jason do?"

"He played video games on a Game Boy. He turns the sound way down. He knows it drives us nuts. He plays that thing for hours on end."

"Do you remember anything at all Jason might have said to you?" Turner asked.

"He talked on the phone for a while," Galyak said.

"To whom?" Turner asked.

"I don't know. He calls his parents a lot. Maybe them. He talked for about twenty minutes."

They'd have to get his phone records. Turner asked, "What happened after you all got to the hotel?"

"Jordan told us we had a meeting. It was late. We were all dazed by what had happened. It was odd. Roger not being in the bus. The five of us had done a million concerts together, coming and going on that tour bus. He was always happy and dancing and moving and the life of the party after a concert. We had planned to go out to Naked Surfers, a new after-hours club. That was cancelled. After we got back, we met with Pastern, Eudace, Hinkmeyer, Zawicki, and Davis. It was boring. They kept asking us if we were all right. Dex just bawled. Jason was crying, too."

"We all were," Pappas said. "Then Hinkmeyer gave us our new room numbers. She said we'd have to put up with less than first class for a night or two. I didn't care. By that time everybody just wanted to go to bed."

"Did you see Jason?"

"Yeah," Galyak said. "I was on the eleventh floor and he was on the tenth. We rode the elevator down together."

"Did he say anything?"

"Just good night."

"And you didn't see him today?"

"No."

"Where would he go?"

"We've thought about it," Pappas said. "He didn't go places a lot. None of us did. Girls camp outside our hotel. They watch every entrance and exit."

Fenwick said, "A hat pulled low, some dark glasses, how much more do you need?"

"Fans stake out the hotels. They trail after anyone that looks likely. It can be a hassle for guys with similar builds who are staying in our hotel. We've deliberately sent body doubles out, but that doesn't always work, either. We could leave, but only with security or limousines with tinted glass. It wasn't like we were prisoners."

"It felt like it sometimes," Galyak said.

Pappas added, "But Jason didn't go a lot of places. He'd order room service and just play video games in his room."

"Would he go to a video parlor?"

"No way. With all the kids, he'd be recognized in a second. He'd be mobbed. That's why it's so hard to think that he disappeared. He can't go far without being recognized."

Galyak said, "Maybe he just fell asleep in some other hotel room by himself."

"There are records of who's in what room," Pappas said. "He'd have used a credit card. They'd know."

"Has he ever walked out before?" Turner asked. "Gone off by himself?"

"No," Galyak said. "Roger sometimes did. He was a thinker, used to read books on philosophy. He finished his first year of college. None of the rest of us ever went. Roger would want to be by himself. Even Dex knew to leave him alone at those times."

"Was Roger depressed at those times, angry?"

"No, he was just private."

"Did Jason have any friends in town?" Turner asked.

Neither one knew of any.

Turner said, "Dexter told us about the dissension in the

band. Ms. Haupmin claimed there were problems. That you guys hated Roger. Last night you both said everything was good."

Galyak said, "Sherri Haupmin is a vicious jerk. You can't believe a thing that bitch tells you. She tried to break this band up. We're the ones who helped her out. She was singing at junior-high dances when we gave her a big break."

Fenwick said, "Did it bother you that you were forced to have sex with Mr. Zawicki?"

Galyak stood up. "Hey, what?"

Turner and Fenwick waited.

"Who told you that?" Galyak asked.

Fenwick said, "Zawicki confirmed it a little while ago."

"Oh," Galyak said. He sat back down. His eyes didn't meet theirs. "I, well . . ." He fumbled. They waited. Galyak said, "How come you guys don't say anything?"

Pappas said, "You're not going to tell anyone about it, are you? I never told anybody about doing it with Zawicki. It was only once and over pretty quick. Lots of guys think we're gay because we're in the band, but if that got out, it would be bad. It wasn't a big deal for me. It's just kind of embarrassing."

"You never told anyone?" Turner asked.

"No, they'd think I was gay," Pappas said.

"Was it embarrassing for Roger or Jason?"

"Nobody ever talked about it. I think we must have guessed the others were being made to do it, but nobody ever said."

Turner asked Galyak, "Did you ever tell anyone?"

"No. Look, it happened. I got used. It was just once. I think we were each like little trophies to Zawicki. So what? You wanna be famous, you gotta make sacrifices."

Pappas nodded. "All the time."

Galyak continued, "It's not like we're innocent. We're

always getting offers. Real rich guys offer us all kinds of things. Women, too. Couple years ago one fourteen-year-old kid sent her butler to proposition us for her. We turned her down. Fourteen, that's sick. But, like one guy offered to put all of us up in his house in Paris for a weekend. Offered us a million bucks. He wanted us to perform just for him. We figured he wanted sex, too. We said no."

"Neither of you guys resented Zawicki for screwing you?" Fenwick asked.

"This thing isn't about sex," Galyak said. "Everybody's obsessed with sex about us. The most frequently asked questions we get are about our underwear. I'm sick of the fucking underwear bullshit. People need to get a life. I'm telling you, the band and our lives don't revolve around sex. This is all about the music."

"They didn't hire the five ugliest guys to do the singing," Fenwick said.

"You a critic?" Galyak asked.

"Just making an observation," Fenwick said.

Pappas said, "I wanted to be in the band. I would have done anything anybody said. We did a lot of stuff that you wouldn't normally do."

"Like what?" Turner asked.

"You don't see your families much. You live out of a suitcase for months on end. You practice from ten to twelve hours a day. You're too exhausted to do anything after that. You don't have much of a place to call home. Each of us dumped a girlfriend. Riveting Records didn't care as long as we made them money. Lots of times they wouldn't let us bring girlfriends along, or at least they wouldn't pay for them to stay in the hotels with us."

"You were rich," Turner said. "Why wouldn't you guys just pay for them yourselves?"

"Sometimes we did, but even the most desperate gold

digger gets bored. When we were overseas, most of the time it was just the five of us with Jordan. You'd get girls sometimes, but it just never worked out. It's not required, but it's nice to speak the language of the person you're with. Sex might be fun for a while—and it was—but we were there for months. I'd rather have a relationship, not just the sex."

"You could have almost any girl in the audience for the asking," Fenwick said.

"Got that right," Galyak replied. "Any of us could. Roger always got the most."

"Was he cheating on Sherri Haupmin?" Fenwick asked.

"I sure thought so," Galyak said, "but I got no proof."

"Was Jason forced to have sex with Zawicki?" Turner asked.

"He must have been," Pappas said. "He never talked about it if he did."

Fenwick said, "We were told you had to make it with other executives in the company."

"I never did," Pappas said.

"Me neither," Galyak said.

"Did you force other people to make sacrifices for you?"

"Hey, I'm not like that," Galyak said.

"Me neither," Pappas said.

"Was Roger, Jason, or Dexter?"

Galyak said, "Dex? Ha! He was scared of his own shadow. I got free stuff and lots of sex. I didn't have to hire anybody or force anybody. I was hot. The girls wanted me."

"Roger used people," Pappas said. "I never thought much about the people and groups in our production company. That was a big deal to him. Maybe he did." He shrugged. "I don't know."

Galyak said, "He never told me he did anything like that."

"Was Roger going to leave the group?" Turner asked.

Pappas answered. "He would have discussed it with us. He would never have left us."

Turner said, "Tomorrow morning Mr. Zawicki is going to announce his resignation as the head of the company."

Both boys looked startled. "What's going on?" Galyak asked.

"He's not going to use his position to hurt people again," Turner said.

"He was always creepy," Galyak said. "Who would want such a weird thing from straight guys? That was sick."

Pappas said, "That press conference was weird. We've had it drilled into us. Whenever anybody asks questions, everything was supposed to be perfect. Really it was. Mostly. Roger did always have big ideas and dreams. Things always had to be Roger's way. Always. Then that bitch Haupmin showed up."

"Why not tell us this last night?"

"Jesus, the guy was dead. How can you say bad stuff about him when he's dead?"

"What's the difference now?" Fenwick asked.

"Maybe we'll say something that will help save Jason," Pappas said.

"You think he needs saving?" Fenwick asked.

"I hope not."

Turner asked, "Why did you say Ms. Haupmin is a bitch?"

"She is," Pappas said. "She is a cross between a den mother on speed and the Wicked Witch of the West. When she was around, she didn't want us messing with different girls. We were supposed to date them. We were supposed to be in at a certain time. We could laugh off that crap. We're over twenty-one, but it was Roger who she changed. After he started with her, he'd never see any other girls on the road."

Galyak said, "That was okay, but then he'd get on our cases. That wasn't bad really. He just kind of teased. It was band stuff that got tougher. We've had the same choreographer for our first three albums. All of a sudden, Roger had big questions. Our choreographer is really good. She has great ideas. She takes her time with us. She drives us hard, but we look great. She has a knack, but Roger would tell her we needed to do things differently."

"Did they fight?" Turner asked.

"Not really," Galyak said.

Pappas said, "But they went after each other sometimes. It was like Roger would get stubborn. We knew it was Haupmin who was putting him up to this. Roger was a good dancer. He took lessons for years when he was little. We'd all make suggestions sometimes. Some stuff got pretty funny, especially when we'd first be learning something."

"It was so cool," Galyak said. "The first time you did a routine to music and it worked. It was magical. It was like we were all brothers. It was neat."

"But Haupmin." Pappas shook his head. "She wanted Roger to be more prominent in the routines, out front more often. Like the rest of us were backup singers. She wanted him to have more lines to sing. She wanted more for him. At least she claimed it was for him, but I think it was for herself mostly. She wanted to be the next Britney Spears. I think she was using Roger."

"Did you tell him this?" Turner asked.

"Once," Pappas said. "It did no good. He just kind of laughed and said I shouldn't worry."

"Did you believe him?"

Both boys shrugged. Galyak said, "In this business nothing is for sure. We made lots of money. We'd hate to see that come to an end. Somebody should do something to Sherri Haupmin. It would save everybody she comes into contact with for the next fifty or sixty years a lot of grief."

Pappas said, "We weren't going to break up, though. That

was not true. And killing Roger would for sure break us up. What would be the point?"

What indeed, Turner thought. *Who benefits from the kid dying?* He asked, "Did you know Jordan Pastern was going to be fired before this happened?"

"No way."

They both averred this was the first they had heard about it. The boys knew nothing more that was helpful and they left.

Fenwick said, "I know I feel better that the boys in the band had some disagreements. If we could get them fighting constantly, I'd buy all their CDs."

"Seems like a pretty mild form of dissension. A lot of it centers on Haupmin, but she's not dead. Roger is."

Turner and Fenwick talked to Devane's and Stendar's personal assistants. They could shed no light on what had happened.

Before they left, they hunted for the diary. Clendenen's hotel room yielded nothing. They tried the tour bus, which was a huge metro coach liner and a bus only in terms of its shape. Inside it was the epitome of luxury. All the sounds were muffled. Even the insulation and soundproofing must have been state of the art. The few seats in back of the driver were covered in soft, buttery leather. Through a doorway were deep plush couches, a fully stocked refrigerator and bar, an electronics area dominated by a sixteen-by-thirty-six-inch flat-screen television, individual sleeping quarters for five, phones covered in gold leaf, and much more. Turner thought the bus and its contents might be worth more than his entire home.

The two detectives searched for nearly an hour. Nothing. They called the hospital and asked the nurse to check in Dexter's room for the backpack. She found nothing.

13

Joan and Judy's bar was on Halsted just north of Belmont. Everybody assumed it was named after Joan Crawford and Judy Garland. The owner was an old folk-music fan. He'd named it in honor of Joan Baez and Judy Collins, the greatest women folk singers who came out of the sixties. The interior was shabby linens and crushed velvet, lots of deep reds and brown leather. Photos on the wall above the bar were of folk concerts from the early sixties. As you walked in, the bar ran along the left-hand side and stretched all the way to the back. The floor had elegant seating arrangements of comfy chairs and love seats with little cocktail tables in front of them. This establishment catered to an older crowd. A few twinkies would sometimes show up. Most were either trophies on a sugar daddy's arm or hoping to be a twinky on a sugar daddy's arm or paid-for twinkies on a sugar daddy's arm. And as Paul's friend Ian often said, if it's a twinky on a sugar daddy's arm, there is always a price to be paid. There were three pinball machines in back. The few times he had been here, Paul had never seen anyone playing them. Mostly men chatted amiably in the usually crowded living room area. The music ranged from blues, to mellow jazz, to big band, to fifties and early sixties rock, and, of course, any folk music from any era.

Ian had his lanky frame sprawled on an overstuffed couch in a quiet alcove. His ever-present slouch fedora was pulled low over his eyes. The youngest-looking man in the bar sat chatting with him cheerfully. When Ian saw Turner and Fenwick and waved them over, the young man looked disappointed. He stood up and left. Turner and Fenwick sat on soft leather chairs opposite Ian.

"You make a new friend?" Turner asked.

"I'm the one in the place closest to his age. I think he was hoping I might be willing to afford him. 'No' didn't seem to be in his vocabulary. I was attempting other one-syllable words to communicate 'no.' I wasn't having a lot of luck."

A bartender in a tux took their drink order: soda for the detectives, lite beer for Ian.

"So, what's the deal on Stendar?" Ian asked. "Was he gay?"

"Why does everybody thinks these guys are gay?" Fenwick asked.

"They're young, cute, and rich. For this community, I think it comes down to, if they're gay, I can feel better about myself being gay."

"They all claim they're not," Turner said.

Ian said, "They need to sit down with their wise, old, friendly, local gay reporter, and they would realize the error of their ways."

"They may not be gay," Turner said, "but they were having sex with Jonathan Zawicki."

"All of them?"

"All."

"Son of a bitch. Every queen's wet dream. The slimy shit was living out the fantasy of half the gay teens in America

138

and probably most of the girls. Zawicki's got as much fame as anybody. He quietly gives to lots of gay causes, and supports gay politicians, but he's never officially come out, which pisses off a lot of activists. The music industry seems to be gay-friendly, but only up to a point. The band members still need to be fairly discreet. Some second echelon band members have come out, but with the exception of Elton John, whose sales have plummeted since that Grammy fiasco with the Nazi, nobody really has. How did he convince them to have sex with him?"

"To get in the band they had to let him fuck them," Turner said.

"Nobody told?" Ian asked.

"Apparently not," Turner said.

Fenwick added, "They felt it necessary to make sacrifices for their art."

Ian said, "Art? Bullshit. They wanted to sacrifice for their ambition and to make tons of money. Not the first time in the history of the human race that's happened. Are you saying somebody wants to tell now?"

"Yeah. Me," Turner said.

"Ah, and you have come to enlist the support of your wise, old, friendly, local reporter from the gay press."

"Yes, but you'll do," Fenwick said.

"That is a very old and not very funny joke," Ian said.

Fenwick leaned over closer to Ian and whispered. "Is that guy you were talking to when we came in making eyes at me?"

Ian stared blatantly at the young man. "I do believe he is. Madge would be jealous."

Madge was Fenwick's wife. She was one of Turner's favorite people. Their families spent a great deal of time together.

Fenwick said, "Madge would laugh her ass off at the very notion."

"Try not to break his heart," Turner said.

"I break their hearts whether they're gay or straight," Fenwick said. "Let's get on with this."

Turner said, "I threatened to expose Zawicki if he didn't quit as the CEO of Riveting Records. I'm afraid he's going to call my bluff."

"Were you bluffing?" Ian asked.

"That's why I'm here. I can't have the department doing this. Nobody would, even if I asked them, and I wouldn't ask them."

"What exactly did you say?"

Turner told him.

Ian said, "What you really need is somebody to leak all of it to the press, a well-orchestrated smear campaign."

"After the press conference," Turner added. "And only if it's necessary."

"Not a lot of time to work with. Let me think. We can talk to Mickey, our music critic, while I mull it over."

"Can we trust this guy?" Turner asked.

"I do."

"He's not going to blab anything we might tell him about the band?" Fenwick asked.

"He won't even be tempted. He is discreet. I know. He's worked for the paper nearly as long as I have. We share secrets. He is very good at keeping his mouth shut."

Turner accepted Ian's word. His friend was an excellent judge of character.

Mickey Pendyce was in his mid-thirties. He had the slender, muscular build of a tennis player. He wore a tight-fitting, pink thunder-and-lightning cowboy shirt and black jeans. He smiled as he swung a chair around to join them. Ian performed the introductions.

Turner said, "First, I need some background on these

people. I've only been part of their world for a little over twenty-four hours, and I don't get it."

"Big egos? Lots of attitude?" Pendyce asked.

Turner nodded.

Pendyce smiled. "I've been in a couple of not very famous bands, and I've worked behind the scenes for others. Ninety-nine-point-nine percent of the people in the music industry take themselves very, very seriously. Normally the band members who make it to the top actually have talent. The same percentage certainly have a high opinion of their ability to influence the world, especially, but certainly not limited to, the world of music. I can't tell you how many press releases I've read where a publicist claims that some new CD will cause a rock or a pop or a hip-hop or a rap or a whatever revolution. Every band is on the cutting edge. Every band is the next incarnation of the Beatles. Every solo artist will sweep the world. So many of them think what they've got is on a par with the Second Coming. Their world is filled with reams of adjectives and mountains of adverbs that don't add up to much of anything. To be fair it's the same kind of hyperbole you see in a lot of the entertainment industry. After a while I suppose it's hard not to believe your own press."

Fenwick said, "What I've seen mostly on television is the ability of the guys in all that makeup to stick their tongues out at cameras."

Pendyce laughed. "Think about it. These aren't college professors. Most guys in bands didn't attend college, many barely finished high school. A lot of them were involved in music from an early age. Most likely they spent a lot more time on music than they did on their studies. If you're going to be at the top in any profession, you have to make sacrifices. Academics is often among the first to go, self-awareness the second. As for the tongue-sticking-out shtick . . ." He chuckled. "That's mostly heavy metal silly nonsense. They like to emphasize their bad boy image. They like the world to think they're tough. How being tough or rebellious or being your own boss became synonymous with sticking out your tongue, I don't know. See, those guys claim they are doing what they want when they want. A continuous party with no one telling them what to do. Defiance as lifestyle. Defiance as myth. All bullshit. My opinion, I think they stick their tongues out because they're inarticulate morons who have no other way of communicating their feelings of anger."

"But I don't get it," Fenwick said. "What are they angry about?"

"Whatever they want to be angry about: growing up, being told what to do, having to get a job, breathing. Who knows? Some people say it's sensuous, a sexual invitation."

"To who?" Fenwick asked. "Deranged morons?"

"To anybody who thinks it is."

Fenwick said, "Didn't I see on the Discovery Channel some kind of monkeys in Africa use tongue-sticking-out as a sign of sexual interest?"

"You watch the Discovery Channel?" Ian asked.

"In my secret life, I do. Or maybe I just think these guys are fucking morons."

Pendyce said, "I doubt if any of those activities apply to what you want to know. This is a boy band not normally associated with inarticulate anger. I was at their first concert this week. They were great. I enjoyed them. In a lot of ways they did fit the cliché of self-important jerks, but I got to talk to them a few years ago before they hit it big. They seemed to be regular guys who worked very, very hard to perfect what they were doing. Long hours of grueling practice for days on end is the rule, not the exception, if you want to get to the top. It is not easy to sing and dance at the same time.

They weren't just sashaying around that stage. They were moving, and they knew their moves. It wasn't traditional ballet, but a lot of the time it was as good as any modern dance company. It was well choreographed and well scripted. It has to be. It's a show. These guys were very, very good. They had talent, enough to spare. They could be at the top for as long as they wanted. Lots of critics put down these guys for being superficial and pandering to the masses. Blundlefitz, the critic for *Hot Trends*, is one of the most negative."

"What's his story?" Turner asked.

"A poster boy for Arrogant Shits Anonymous. You look up *arrogant* in a dictionary, you'll see a picture of him. A bully, so, of course, a coward, but more dangerous than a frightened rat when cornered. I'll give you one example of the kind of shit he is. He refuses to go to any concert by any local group."

"He can be a critic for a major Chicago magazine and get away with that?" Fenwick asked.

"Some of the people in the music industry are very provincial. Unless you've played Carnegie Hall, so to speak, you aren't worthy of their notice. And whatever you do, don't ever dare try to criticize Blundlefitz, or any other critic for that matter. Most of us critics have egos as big as those of band members. If you try to criticize us, then we beat the drums of you're-a-petty-musician-who-doesn't-understand-the-freedom-of-the-press. As if there isn't a difference between good criticism and bad criticism. One time I heard Blundlefitz explain the reason he gave so many negative reviews. He said, and I quote, 'People are so busy, I have to be negative.'"

"That doesn't make sense," Fenwick said.

"Of course not. A concert or a CD review should be based on the merit of the work involved, not how busy the people are who might go to the concert or listen to the

143

music. He was born vicious. He doesn't use words just to communicate. Like William F. Buckley, Jr., he uses them as a bludgeon to intimidate and overwhelm, especially when his logic is lacking. He could take apart a group's performance in fewer words and nastier ones than almost anybody I know. He hated all the boy bands. Hated."

"Maybe he couldn't sing and dance," Fenwick suggested.

"He hasn't exercised since the Carter administration. A lot of people in this town would love to see him taken down a peg. I saw bits of that performance he and Zawicki put on at the press conference before I came to work. He will run with whomever is likely to give him the biggest story. Attacking you is big now. He can be nasty and underhanded. I'd watch myself."

"I think we might be able to do a little in the peg-taking-down business," Turner said. He told them about the stolen underwear.

Ian laughed. Mickey looked thoughtful.

Ian said, "You know something that millions of teenage girls and gay boys have been dying to know."

"What's that?" Fenwick asked.

"Whether they wear boxers or briefs," Ian said. "You could sell your story to every teen magazine on the planet. If you put them up for auction on the Internet, I bet you could retire on the profits."

"Not today," Fenwick said.

"He's got nasty lawyers adding pressure," Turner said.

"The lawyers are going to be like King Canute trying to keep back the tide," Pendyce said. "Once this gets out, he's toast. Stealing a dead kid's underwear? That goes beyond those photographers who sneak in to celebrity funerals to try and take pictures of the corpse. Sick, but if it's a celebrity, the tabloids pay a fortune for it."

"We need to make sure no one knows this is coming from us," Turner said.

"That's not a problem," Pendyce said. "I can get this story out. The music world is not a very big one. Everyone knows everyone else. This is almost too good."

"Thanks," Turner said, "We appreciate the help."

"Ian's a friend. When this can be public, do I get a scoop?"

"Of course," Turner said.

"Excellent."

"What can you tell us about Sherri Haupmin?"

"A no-talent, wanna-be hack. She seemed to have Roger Stendar tied around her twat."

"How do you know these inside gossip things?" Fenwick asked.

"There are often gay crew members. I know one on this tour with Boys4u. I make it a point to seek them out. I'm kind of known in my own small way. The one on the current tour is a good friend." He sipped from a bottle of imported water.

"Can we talk to him?" Turner asked.

"I'll give him a call and make sure he's comfortable with that."

Neither detective interjected that they didn't care if the guy was comfortable or not with them talking to him. They were getting help and it was no time to be surly.

Ian said, "You'll help them with Blundlefitz?"

"Absolutely. I'd be delighted."

"Can you really do something?" Fenwick asked.

"It's not more than a call or two away."

"You can never reveal your sources," Turner said.

"I never would anyway." Pendyce leaned over to Fenwick, "Why is that guy at the bar constantly staring at you?"

The detective looked. "He is smitten."

"No accounting for taste," Turner said.

"Hey," Fenwick said. "Just because I'm fat and straight, doesn't mean I'm not hot looking. Look at all the women who are married to fat, straight men."

"You are in the majority," Ian observed.

Turner said, "If we could take our mind off Fenwick's latest conquest. What was the deal with Haupmin? Was she trying to break up the band?" Turner asked.

Pendyce said, "I heard Roger was screwing her. I was told they did it up on that high platform after the second concert here. One of the guys in the crew tried to take pictures, but he almost fell from one of the rafters in the ceiling. Haupmin showed up with Roger about a year ago. She sings her little heart out. She's awful. I felt so bad for her I almost didn't include her in the article I wrote for the paper. Then I decided people were so busy, I'd better mention it." He shook his head. "I don't get Blundlefitz's logic." He shook his head again. "You want gossip? She was the classic leech, a gold digger of the first order. A nobody who got her claws into someone famous and wouldn't let go. She figured she got the prize. She was screwing the guy millions of teenage girls had the hots for. That's got to be a hell of a rush. She went about exploiting that relationship for her own gain. She got the recording contract from the band's production company because Roger insisted on it. She wanted him for herself. She always put it that she was acting in his best interests, as if he were too dumb to know what those were."

"Was he too dumb?" Turner asked.

"Not from what I could tell. He seemed like a reasonably intelligent young man when I interviewed him. He was certainly pleasant enough to any interviewer. He had a positive reputation. Haupmin wanted him to do fewer interviews with the press. If there was a decision to be made, she campaigned for the dumb choice."

"Was he cheating on her?" Turner asked.

"I don't know if he was monogamous. He could get almost any woman he wanted. These guys weren't just tempted. They were given the whole candy store and invited to dive in."

Turner asked, "Can we trust what she says about dissension among the band, and Stendar planning to leave?"

"My opinion? Maybe. Sorry I don't have a better answer. I know some gossip. I don't know all."

"What about Jonathan Zawicki?" Turner asked. "What's his story?"

"A very tough, smart businessman. He's made decisions for that company that have caused record profits for seven straight years. And he's ruthless. If you don't make the bottom line, you don't stay hired. He's dumped more than one popular old act from his label because they were no longer the draw they once were."

"We've got information about his requirements for a guy being in one of his bands," Turner explained.

Pendyce said, "Everybody thinks all the guys in boy bands are gay. The poor guys parade around with a host of gorgeous women. Even if you released a video of each one of them screwing a woman, I'm not sure it would make a difference. They sing. They dance. They're thin. They're cute. They're clean. They have a sense of fashion, even if that sense comes from being able to hire expensive fashion designers. One, some, or all of those could be considered acting gender inappropriately. You don't have to be as blatant as a drag queen for someone to think you're gay."

Turner asked, "How did they feel about what the public thought about them?"

"As for their public image, they had teams of people pumping out reams of positive press. They didn't have to worry about that. Privately, I'm not sure. You walk into an exclusive restaurant where you don't want to be bothered and you hear somebody yell out, 'you're gay,' that can't be a good feeling. With as much money as they make, I'm not sure how much they cared. I know if I made that much money, I wouldn't care if they accused me of much of anything."

"Why don't the groups he's dumped sue him?"

"He's smart. He's dumped old groups from before he took over the label. He knows how to manipulate people and contracts. And he's careful."

"He's taking an awful big risk," Turner said.

"Worked so far," Pendyce said.

Turner asked, "Anybody else you can think of who might be able to give us inside information on these guys?"

"You might want to talk to Jeremiah Boissec. He's got a small record company in Chicago. He used to work for Riveting Records. He can tell you more about Zawicki."

"Thanks," Turner said.

A shadow loomed over their group. It was the young man who'd been staring at Fenwick. He put a hand on the detective's brawny shoulder and in a baritone voice mixed with a Southern twang, he said, "Can I buy you a drink?"

"I'm old enough to be your dad."

"I know."

"I'm not gay, but these guys are. Why don't you ask one of them?"

"You don't have to be gay," the young man said. "You just have to hold still."

Fenwick said, "I'm flattered, but the answer is no. And if you don't go away, I will take out my cop identification and make your night unnecessarily unpleasant."

The kid looked crestfallen. He turned and walked out of the bar.

"Score one for you," Ian said.

"I lost count years ago," Fenwick said.

"Where would one of these musicians go if they wanted to disappear?" Turner asked.

"One of them is missing?" Ian asked.

Turner nodded. "Jason Devane."

"A nice guy," Pendyce said. "I spent some time with him after I did that interview with Stendar I mentioned earlier. He was down-to-earth, reasonable, and gave me sensible answers. Some of them give dumb answers because they're dumb. Galyak gave stupid answers because he thought it was funny, or maybe he thought he was putting one over on the press or the fans. Devane didn't do any of that. He had a good head on his shoulders. Of course, that was when they were desperate for media attention. They'd give interviews to anybody who would stand still for five seconds. Where would he go? I don't know. The big question is why? Staying behind security is important for these guys. They could literally get trampled. You can disguise yourself. Once you escape from the hotel, it's not so bad, but you've still got to be careful. If you're recognized, look out."

"We don't think he left town," Turner said.

"Do you think he's dead?" Ian asked.

"I'm not optimistic," Turner said.

"If he had a friend in town," Pendyce said, "he would try to go there. I don't remember any of them having relatives in Chicago. Although there's always a cousin or two emerging from the woodwork the more famous these bands get."

Turner said, "Nobody from the company mentioned friends or relatives."

Ian said, "I watched that press conference down at the office. They blistered you guys. Did they know at the time that Devane was missing?"

"Yes."

"What kind of crap is that?" Ian asked.

"The nasty, vicious, unpleasant kind," Fenwick said.

They asked about Hinkmeyer, Pastern, and Eudace.

Pendyce said, "Ethel is a hard-working woman who would do anything to help anybody out. A genuinely kind person who has a lot of ambition but won't go anywhere in the industry until she toughens up. I don't know if she can. Pastern is a mix. The guys like him. The bosses don't. I can believe they were planning to fire him. He could be rough if things weren't going his way, especially if he thought the guys were in jeopardy. I think he pictured himself as a superhero. Eudace has the reputation as the grasping, evil, Hollywood agent, although in the few dealings I had with him, he was actually very nice. I'm not sure which is true about him."

They talked strategy with Pendyce about Blundlefitz then Pendyce went home after promising to set up the contact with the gay crew member. After he left, Turner, Fenwick, and Ian discussed plans for handling Zawicki.

14

The call came over the police radio as they turned east on Belmont. The dispatcher said, "You need to get to Lake Shore Drive opposite Buckingham Fountain. We've got a body in the lake, and I was told you were the ones to notify."

Turner acknowledged the call and switched off. He said, "Gotta be connected to the Stendar killing. They probably don't want to put that over the radio. Too many reporters listen to scanners."

Fenwick said, "I don't like Jason Devane's chances for ever singing or dancing again."

Fenwick put the blue mars light on the roof of the car. It made no difference in the speed with which they traveled, but this way the cars and pedestrians had a fighting chance of getting out of the way.

As Turner shivered in the car's almost warmth, he realized that in fact in all these years, Fenwick had not actually hit anyone. That his madcap driving was well orchestrated. Perhaps a macho image thing. Turner decided to keep this insight to himself.

As they crossed the Chicago River on their way south, Turner said, "Maybe the killer just wanted to wreck the band."

"What for?" Fenwick asked.

"There are people who just like to wreck something good somebody else has going, although we've got plenty of people with lots of motives."

They drove up onto the wide sidewalk on the west side of Lake Shore Drive. Buckingham Fountain sat in splendid isolation. No water spewed from it. The fountain operated only in the summer. They hustled across the Drive to where three blue-and-white squad cars had their spotlights and headlights trained on the edge of the lake. Two fire engines rested along the periphery. The crime-scene van pulled up as they neared the other vehicles. A couple of techs were setting up some outdoor lights. An ambulance rested feet from the water's edge. The wind gusted off the lake adding even more chill to the below-zero misery. Fenwick stubbornly refused to wear a hat no matter what the weather. Turner had donned his heaviest sweater and warmest synthetic-fiber winter coat as well as a thick scarf and a knit hat. He wasn't warm, but his clothing kept out the worst of the cold, especially the wind.

There was a rim of about ten feet of ice around this part of the harbor. Some years the shore near the lake froze in winter, some years it didn't. Depended on the weather and the direction of the wind. Mists of condensation rose from the ice-free portions of the lake. A body was floating in the water at the edge of the ice.

Mike Sanchez, a beat cop they knew and respected, found them. "What's up?" Turner asked.

"Thought the body might have something to do with your case."

"Don't recognize him from here," Fenwick said.

Sanchez pointed, "See that gold shiny thread on his jacket? You can see it every time the body bobs slightly this way. Guy who found him says that's a Boys4u logo. Kind of like their trademark."

Turner and Fenwick looked. Both recognized the miniature version of the immense banner they had seen hanging in the All-Chicago Sports Arena.

They watched the firemen preparing for the rescue, although Turner thought that was too strong a word. Anybody in the lake with the water this cold would either be jumping madly and trying to get out, or he was dead. The firemen put a lifeline around one of their own. They inflated a little blow-up boat. A rescue worker carefully walked a step out onto the ice. He bobbed on it gently.

"It's not gonna hold," he said. They all heard a crack. He shoved the little boat farther toward the water and got in from the landward side. Another little boat was inflated and passed to him. He placed this one beyond the other and stepped from the one to the next. The ice cracked. A five-foot-wide swath of water appeared. The boat began to float among chucks and bits of ice. He reached the body. With a gloved hand he dragged it to the boat. He tied a rope around it. Some of the others grabbed the line to the boat, others the one to the fireman, and two more grabbed the one to the body. Coordinating their efforts they pulled boat, man, and body to the shore.

The corpse's clothes were wet but not frozen. In the stiff wind and bitter cold a crust of ice could be seen forming on the edges of the pants and jacket even in these few moments it had been out of the water. Still, the paramedics obeyed procedure and attempted CPR. They took out an AMBU bag, which looked like a big syringe with a facepiece and a valve over it. After adjusting the AMBU bag, they pumped it a few times. They got absolutely no response from the corpse. One of the paramedics pounded on the lifeless chest for a minute.

Now that the corpse was on the shore, Turner and Fenwick could see that it was definitely Jason Devane. He wore a hat, gloves, and warm outer clothes. Turner knew that once he was in the water, the heavy winter clothes were more likely to pull him down than they were to keep him warm. If he'd even been alive when he went in. Turner knew the frigid water could kill in minutes. Devane had a Game Boy clutched in his left hand.

Fenwick said to Sanchez, "Better set up a huge perimeter. Don't let anybody onto this side of the Drive between Balbo and Monroe. Especially make sure nobody from the press gets through."

"I'm not sure we've got enough tape to cover that much space," Sanchez said.

"There's more in the trunk of our car."

Sanchez hurried away.

"Frozen," the ME said.

"A bandsicle," one of the evidence techs said.

"A boysicle," Fenwick said.

Turner growled. "This is going to stop or there's going to be a copsicle around here."

While the ME and crime-scene crews worked, Turner and Fenwick took their flashlights and examined the shoreline. Turner went as far as the fences of the Adler Planetarium to the south. Fenwick got as close to Navy Pier as he could along the shore. Neither one saw any evidence of a body being dragged along the ground to the lake and no evidence of broken ice, which they would hope to see if someone had tried to toss or roll the body into the lake. The ground was so firm it would be unlikely to show anything less than a major disruption. A late January thaw had melted the early winter snows. Since then it had been dry and very cold. Where the body had floated from would be difficult to determine. The wind direction would be the most telling thing in the harbor. The direction the boy had taken could also have been influenced by the wakes of the larger pleasure boats that still cruised from Navy Pier during the winter. Since the wind was from the northeast it would be toward the pier that they would need to concentrate asking questions.

When they got back to the area around the body, Fenwick asked Sanchez, "Who found him?"

Sanchez nodded toward a man sitting in the back of the crime-lab van. "Guy's name is Alfred Hazelow. Says he was getting in his nightly run."

Fenwick and Turner hurried through the cold. Warmth emanated from the van. At least they'd be out of the wind. They squeezed inside with Hazelow. He was dressed in a yellow Gore-Tex bodysuit, thick boots, heavy gloves, a knit cap under the hood. A heavy scarf and skier's face mask sat on his lap. He'd look like a bloated blow-up doll if he came trotting down the street toward someone. He was drinking coffee. Hazelow looked to be in his mid-to-late teens.

Turner and Fenwick introduced themselves.

"Was it really one of the guys from Boys4u?" Hazelow asked.

"Yeah," Fenwick said.

"I've never seen a dead body before. I've never even been to a funeral. I didn't get close or touch it or anything, but it was still creepy. I thought at first I should try and rescue him, you know, crawl out on the ice, but he wasn't moving or anything."

"You might have fallen through the ice," Turner said. "You could easily have drowned yourself."

"Wow." He sipped some coffee and repeated, "Wow. Poor guy. What a terrible way to die. Freezing to death. Like the people in the water at the end of the movie *Titanic*."

"You knew who it was?" Turner asked.

"I wasn't sure about that, but I recognized the logo. I tried to get one of their sweatshirts. For my girlfriend," he said a bit too quickly. "The girls love anything that's connected to these guys."

"The water's edge is pretty far from the sidewalk," Fenwick said. "How'd you happen to see him?"

"You've got to be alert out here. I run every night about this time. Gives me a chance to think and get out of the house. I live with my mom in a condo up at Buckingham Place. I like to exercise at night. It's quieter. That's why I wear yellow. So drivers can see me. I watch everything. Always have been observant. I'm going to be a NASA scientist if I can. If you're going to do science, you've got to observe."

Both Turner and Fenwick wished there was a "just the facts" pill they could give to peripheral witnesses. The detectives hesitated to stop anyone. The majority of killers know their victims and can't hold back from talking about the horror they've perpetrated. Eventually, Hazelow got to the point. "The light from the stars and the rising moon shone off the water. There was a blank spot a foot past the ice that wasn't shining. That struck me as odd. There are no boats in the harbor. Haven't been for months. Then I saw a glint that looked out of place. Later I realized it was the gold of his wristwatch or maybe a ring with a bright stone catching a beam of streetlight. I trotted over. I couldn't believe it was a dead body."

"What did you do?"

"I went back to the Drive. I flagged a cab down. He called it in."

"Did you see or hear anything suspicious?"

"Nope. Sorry. I was just running. Can I begin heading back now? My mom might start to worry."

They made sure they had his name and address, and he left.

Back at the body Fenwick asked, "Any notion of how long he's been in the water?"

The ME said, "Won't know until I look inside. Cause of death probably won't have anything to do with how long he was in the water." He turned the body over. There was a black hole in the back of the young man's head. "I don't think he drowned or froze to death."

"Execution style," Turner said. "Just like Stendar."

Fenwick said, "Who the hell starts executing the members of a boy band?"

"Anyone with a taste in music?" an evidence tech opined.

The ME said, "I can't tell from this if he was shot and fell into the water immediately, or if he was shot much earlier and then dumped into the water. I can give you that later. Most likely the water washed away any blood."

"What time did his watch stop?" Turner asked. He bent down to the frozen corpse. The smashed watch face could tell him nothing.

"Did the killer do that or did he break it when he got pushed or fell or dumped into the water?" Turner asked. "Or why didn't the killer just take it?"

"Might have forgotten about it," Fenwick said. "The gunshot was it for sure?"

"Most likely. Unless he fell in the water immediately after being shot and his body functions didn't shut down until he swallowed too much water. Or he got pushed into the water and somebody used him for target practice, or he was taking a refreshing dip in the lake and got shot by a random killer out for a casual stroll who happened to . . ."

"I get the drift," Fenwick said.

The ME said, "I'll be able to give you an approximation on the time when he was attacked."

The wind whistled around their heads as Turner and Fenwick hustled back to their car. They crossed at the light between Balbo and Jackson. Turner thought it was the most annoying traffic light in the city. It did little more than help cause major traffic headaches. The light had been placed there for the convenience of pedestrians who couldn't take the exhausting walk of a half block to the major intersections to the north and south.

15

In the lobby of the Hotel Chicago they found Jonathan Zawicki and Sherri Haupmin. The young woman's screeching echoed through the elegant lobby. Factotums surrounded Zawicki. As the detectives approached, Haupmin's megadecibel shrieking headed off the high end of the human hearing spectrum. "You never cared for these guys! You just wanted to screw them!"

"Do make as many wild accusations as you like, young lady," Zawicki said. "You will be sued for slander for the words you just uttered."

"Utter your ass," Haupmin said. "Roger Stendar told me all about you. It's your fault that he's dead. If you didn't actually pull the trigger, you were an indirect cause."

"Kindly take notes," Zawicki said to one of the men in the crowd around him.

One of the hotel employees from behind the registration desk arrived. He said, "Could we take this to a private room?"

Zawicki snapped, "I'm not going anywhere with this creature."

"Please, sir."

Zawicki glared.

Haupmin was not out of rage yet. "You don't have to go anywhere with me. I'm going to stick to your butt closer than a thong until you tell me all that I want to know. I'm going to get what's coming to me."

"I certainly hope so," Zawicki said.

Haupmin narrowed her eyes at him. She seemed to have caught the more universal implications of what he'd said.

Turner and Fenwick stepped forward.

Zawicki said, "Arrest this woman. She's making a public nuisance of herself. She's not allowing me to quietly go to my room."

"So go," Fenwick said. "If she commits a crime, we'll arrest her."

"The Chicago police are going to be so sorry you hassled me," Zawicki said.

Fenwick said, "I get that from gang-bangers at least once a week, but here I still am, able to parade my Chicago cop, donut-filled ass in front of the public."

Zawicki said, "I want nothing to do with any of you." He began to turn away. Haupmin jumped in front of him and drew in a deep breath. Turner presumed this was for another oration. Two of the guards around Zawicki moved to block Haupmin.

Turner said, "I have news."

The little assemblage turned to him.

"What?" Zawicki asked.

"Jason Devane is dead."

Haupmin's inarticulate moan rapidly rose to incoherent keening, then spilled to bellowed, barely recognizable words. "Someone's trying to kill the whole band! What a loss to the world! They were . . ."

160

"Oh, shut up," Zawicki said.

For once Turner agreed with the evil villain of the piece.

"What do you intend to do about it?" Zawicki demanded.

"I was thinking about investigating," Fenwick said. He turned to Turner. "What about you, Paul? You think we should investigate this one?"

Zawicki snarled, "How dare you treat this frivolously?"

"I may or may not be frivolous," Fenwick said, "but you, sir, are reacting strangely to another one of your band members being dead. No curiosity about what happened. No concern for the boy. No thought for the parents. The lack of one of those is odd. The absence of all of them is suspicious."

"I did not kill these boys. They were making me rich."

Through a cascade of tears, Haupmin piped up. "You cheap fuck. You'd do anything to harm these boys."

Zawicki turned on her. "Since you first put syllables together not that long ago, have any two consecutive ones of them made sense? And has any one of them been produced at less than the decibel level which you are using now?"

Turner hated the guy, but as put-down comments went, he appreciated its thoroughness and depth. Two beat cops walked into the lobby, spotted their group, and came over.

The younger one said, "We got a complaint."

Fenwick said, "We are the complaint, you twit. We're from Area Ten."

"Oh."

Fenwick nodded at Haupmin. "Take that young woman and escort her to the opposite end of the lobby and keep her there." They ushered the squawking woman away.

"We need to talk to everyone again," Turner said.

"They're asleep," Zawicki snapped.

"Not for long," Fenwick said. "And we'll need to know your movements for the past twenty-four hours."

"You'll need to speak to my lawyers. I have nothing to say to you." And he walked away. The speed with which Fenwick inserted himself between Zawicki and the elevators, belied the detective's huge bulk.

Fenwick said, "This is a murder investigation in the city of Chicago. We are not underlings."

"You're going to be out of a job."

"Until then, we're going to talk to your people."

"You may try anything you wish with them. They've been warned. I know better. I am not under arrest, so go away." He took out a card. "Here's my lawyer's name and address."

"You have a local lawyer?" Fenwick asked. "You knew you'd need someone so you checked ahead?"

Zawicki stepped around Fenwick and proceeded to the elevator.

They woke up Ethel Hinkmeyer who promised to assemble everyone as quickly as she could. Pastern and Hinkmeyer were the first ones down. Neither looked like they'd had much sleep.

Hinkmeyer said, "We've been ordered not to talk to you by Mr. Zawicki."

"Did his lawyers tell you that?" Turner asked.

"No," Hinkmeyer said. "He did. He said I'd lose my job. I'm sorry. That makes no sense. One of these boys is dead. We've got to find the killer. I'm willing to help any way I can."

"Me, too," Pastern said. "What's going on?"

Turner gave them the news about Jason Devane.

Hinkmeyer put her fist to her chin and started to cry. Pastern swore. "What the hell is going on?"

Danny Galyak, Ivan Pappas, their personal assistants, and several other members of the band's entourage joined them.

Turner gave them the news. They all looked stricken. "We need to talk to all of you again."

"How can we talk at a moment like this?" asked one of the assistants.

"It's the second murder," Turner said. "All of these boys could be in danger."

Galyak said, "Zawicki told us not to talk to you anymore. That's stupid. Now two of us are dead." Any remaining trace of his youthful bravado from the first time they'd met was gone. "I think something is wrong. Really, really wrong."

The hotel let the detectives use a conference room just off the lobby. They interviewed Galyak and Pappas first.

"What is it that you think is really, really wrong?" Turner asked.

Galyak licked his thin lips. "I'm really scared. That's two people. Roger getting killed was bad, terrible. It was so hard to believe at first. Now, it's starting to sink in. But Jason. Everybody liked Jason. He was so quiet. He never hurt anybody." Galyak started to cry. Ivan put his hand on his friend's shoulder. Tears were running down his cheeks as well. The detectives waited for them to compose themselves.

"Are we really in danger?" Pappas asked.

"We have to assume so," Turner said.

"But who? Why? What did we do?" Pappas asked.

"It's hard to tell what sets people off," Turner said.

Galyak said, "We're rich and famous. Bad things aren't supposed to happen to us."

Turner forbore pointing out that everybody has problems.

Pappas said, "There's gotta be something we can do to stop it."

Turner said, "Until we find the killer, we want you to stay in the same hotel room. We'll have one of our officers on duty. If you want some of your security inside or outside the room with you, that'll be fine, but we want our people there."

"Okay."

Turner said, "Danny, you mentioned that everybody liked Jason. Did that mean there were some who didn't like Roger?"

"No. I guess not. It's just Roger pushed us all hard. We needed it a lot of times. I guess I meant that Jason was a good guy, easy to talk to. If you wanted a buddy, he was the one we all went to."

They both claimed to have been in their rooms catching up on sleep. They knew nothing else. The two young men left.

Turner and Fenwick talked to all the people in the immediate entourage. Some were forthcoming. Some had obviously been convinced to keep silent by Zawicki's warning. None of them clammed up completely. None of them revealed anything helpful.

When the detectives were finally alone in the room after all the interviews, Turner said, "Donut-filled ass? What did that mean?"

"I'm not sure. I just liked the sound of it."

"I gotta get that down in my 'Sayings of Chairman Fenwick' collection before I forget it. Zawicki didn't look impressed."

"Somebody mentioned the Second Coming early tonight. I don't think anything short of that would impress Mr. Zawicki and even then, he'd have to have been specially invited and know how it was going to make him some money. Why the hell doesn't that guy ever look sad that these guys are dead? He's cold. He's hard. He makes a great evil presence, but I don't get it. Nearly half of this hugely successful moneymaking band is dead, and he's not bothered?"

"I think he's bothered," Turner said, "just not the way we think he should be."

Fenwick said, "We haven't had a great villain in a while.

All we need is some gritty streets to add to the mix, and we could become a classic act."

"Don't forget ethnic diversity," Turner said. "Grit and diversity get your picture in the paper and positive reviews."

"Why don't the killers we know provide that?" Fenwick asked. "It's their fault we're not richer and more famous."

"Doesn't 'more famous' imply that we were at least a little bit famous to begin with?" Turner asked. "I think I missed the 'little bit famous' phase of this relationship."

"That's so like you," Fenwick said.

"Leaving fame and fortune behind for the moment," Turner said, "it is very possible that Zawicki is frightened as well. He's used to power and having people respond the way he wishes. That's not happening here. People are dying outside of his control."

"Unless he's the killer," Fenwick said.

"We'll have to talk to him with his lawyers. Why the big hang-up about telling us where he was, unless he is the killer?"

"He'd make a great suspect," Fenwick said. "The villain being the killer. What could be better? What could be more dramatic? Truly evil villains whet my appetite."

"You ever know of one of our cases working out that neatly?" Turner asked.

"No."

"And is there something on this planet that doesn't whet your appetite?"

"If there is, I haven't discovered it yet."

Turner picked up his cell phone. "I should call the hospital where Dexter Clendenen is. He should have protection as well."

He found the hospital's number in his notes and called. When he identified himself, the purpose of his call, and asked to speak with the nurse on the floor, the operator said, "But Mr. Clendenen is no longer in this hospital."

"What hospital is he in?"

"I'll have to transfer you to the nursing supervisor."

After identifying himself sufficiently so that she would not think he was a crazed fan who got lucky in locating a member of the band, he said, "Dexter Clendenen is gone?"

"Yes. He left with Mr. Jonathan Zawicki late this evening."

"Did Clendenen's parents arrive?"

"They hadn't by the time he left. Mr. Clendenen is over twenty-one. We were not required to wait for his parents to arrive."

"I understand," Turner said. He hung up and told Fenwick, who said, "Son of a bitch. I'm going to that asshole's room now, and it's not going to be pretty."

Turner and Fenwick marched to the front desk. The head of hotel security accompanied them to Zawicki's room. Fenwick insisted on doing the honors of being the one to bang on the door until someone answered.

A heavily built man in a sport coat and dress pants answered almost immediately. "Mr. Zawicki doesn't want to see you."

Fenwick said, "Another one of his band boys is missing."

"What?"

The door swung open. Zawicki, still fully dressed, appeared in the entrance. "Who's missing?"

"Dexter Clendenen."

"He's not missing, you fool. He's here in this suite with me."

"In your bed?" Fenwick asked.

Zawicki banged the door shut. They arranged for a guard outside the suite and left.

16

"You are not making any friends in this case," Turner said as they drove back to headquarters.

Fenwick said, "My goal in life is to be best friends with all our suspects."

"I must have been absent the day they taught that at the academy." Turner sighed. "Why'd he go get the kid? Is he covering something up? Does he really care? What is it with these people?"

"Terminal egotistical bullshit."

At headquarters they talked with Fred Falcoli, the night-shift lieutenant. His response to all their information was, "Be sure to get started on the paperwork."

On the way to their desks on the third floor Fenwick said, "I hope a tree falls on Falcoli some day. I think that would be great revenge for all the forests he's destroyed with his insistence on paperwork."

"An environmentally sensitive Fenwick is a new concept," Turner said.

"And still not true. I don't care so much about the tree as

I do about poetic justice. Him dying under a falling tree fits my sense of what is right in the world."

"Which is getting a little macabre."

Arnie Krempe was at his desk writing. He looked up at the detectives, gave a brief wave, and walked over. Turner kind of liked Krempe. He thought they needed fresh faces on the squad. The new guy was young and enthusiastic.

Krempe said, "You guys having any luck?"

"Not much," Fenwick said.

"That Carruthers guy was here," Krempe said. "He just came back from vacation. I hadn't met him before. Is he nuts?"

"Pretty much," Fenwick said.

"He wanted to talk about your case. I told him I didn't know anything. He talked on and on. Can anybody stand the poor guy?"

"You've learned one of the most important lessons of the Area Ten detective squad," Fenwick said. "Avoid Carruthers at all costs."

Krempe smiled. "I'll remember." He returned to his desk.

Carruthers was the one on the squad who organized all the social events. He'd turned being inept into a lifestyle. It's not that some of the detectives didn't socialize or honor important events in each other's lives such as promotions and retirements. Carruthers wanted to turn them into intimate events on an incessant basis. No one cared as much as Carruthers, and their failure to be at his level of caring irritated him. He irritated all of them all the time.

Turner and Fenwick went over the records of the people the beat cops had interviewed to check if any of them had seen anything out of the ordinary or heard gunshots. They found nothing.

They pored over their notes from the recently completed

interviews. Then they spent a half hour making a chart of the whereabouts of everyone in the immediate entourage since early Sunday morning after the meeting Zawicki had with all of them. When they finished, they examined their handiwork.

Fenwick said, "It's a perfectly done chart. A thing of beauty, wondrous to behold. I don't see a thing here that's going to help."

Turner agreed.

They read over the band's schedule during the performance, particularly the timing of the special effects with the chart they had of people's movements during the concert. Nobody appeared to be out of place. Even though many people had very specific functions and could report where they were, few of the schedules were perfectly exact. While the special-effects people had to perform their assigned tasks with split-second precision at the same place and time, others were less rigidly structured. The venues might change, but the tasks remained the same. Also, people busy performing essential tasks were not likely to be consciously looking for strangers.

One of the beat cops from downstairs entered with a phone message from Mickey Pendyce. All it had was a name. Jose Oxaka. Turner called the Plaza Mart and found Jose Oxaka was registered there. He showed it to Fenwick who said, "We should go see this guy now. We've got to move before this entire band is dead."

Fenwick agreed. They arranged with the lieutenant for beat cops to help with interviewing the rest of the crew. They had to find out where all these people had been at the time of this new death. Someone might criticize the detectives for making a lot of useless charts and doing extra work. More of their dogged police work than Turner cared to admit was useless but until criminals came equipped with an instant confession button, the detectives had no choice. They didn't know which bit of apparently useless information would turn out to be the golden nugget that led to a killer.

They hurried through the bitter cold. The wind blew harder than it had when they were at the lakeshore. Record cold was predicted to continue for the next three days.

They found an agitated crowd babbling away in the Plaza Mart lobby. The news of the second death had spread like wildfire. They arranged for beat cops to begin interviews. Turner and Fenwick started with Jose Oxaka. He was in his mid-twenties. He wore a gray sweatshirt with the band's logo on it, black jeans, and running shoes. He was five foot six and might have weighed one twenty. They talked in the office of the head of security of the Plaza Mart.

Turner said, "We talked to Mickey Pendyce early tonight."

"He called me. I said he could give you my name."

"We need the real story behind these guys," Turner said. "What can you tell us?"

"A lot. Sometimes the guys in the crew see things. We hear stuff. Some of us become friends with the guys. I went with them for those early tours to South America and Asia. You learn a lot about each other when you're stuck together, and you don't speak the language, and you aren't very famous, and you don't have a lot of money."

Turner said, "How was Roger Stendar's relationship with the rest of the band?"

"Roger was basically a good guy, but he was driven. They all are, but he was more than most. The other guys resented it sometimes, but most times not. Roger insisted on practice and perfection. He'd stay longer than anybody else most days. He'd work with the choreographer for hours. And he'd help the other guys."

Turner said, "Dexter told us he helped him a lot."

"Definitely. And Dexter needed a lot of help at the beginning. He wasn't real coordinated. When he started, he was just out of high school. He was a little young, but hell, they all were. Dexter had sung in school choirs since the fifth grade, but he'd never had any formal training."

"Which guys were friends outside of the band?" Turner asked.

"There wasn't really any 'outside the band.' They didn't go over to each other's houses, because they all lived in the same house when they were practicing. When they were touring, they all lived in the same hotel. There hasn't been a lot of time in the last few years when they weren't touring or practicing. They got along. I'd say Danny and Ivan were closest. Danny could be kind of a pain. I haven't laughed at one of his jokes in three or four years. Pappas was the most like a real adult, very responsible. Jason was buddies with everyone. Dexter kind of clung to everyone. He clung to Roger the most, and Roger put up with him the most."

"How'd they get along with Mr. Zawicki?" Turner asked.

"You mean the sex?"

"The crew knew about that?"

"Everybody knew about that."

"They said they never told anybody about it."

"You hang around long enough, you begin to see a pattern. Us guys on the crew never said much. Zawicki used to enjoy making Roger have sex."

"He made him service him often?" Fenwick asked.

"Roger was very independent. He wanted things his way. Zawicki liked forcing Roger to do his bidding. That's how Sherri Haupmin got to be an opening act. Technically, she might be under contract to the band's production company, but Zawicki gets his way when he wants to get his way. If Roger wanted her to sing, then he had to let himself get screwed. Zawicki worked that way a lot. He'd play the guys off against each other. He'd play different bands in the company off against each other."

"What for?" Fenwick asked.

"To make more money. To push guys to the edge. To get them to perform better."

"What's the point?" Fenwick asked. "These guys were at the top."

"There's always more money to be made, and Zawicki was about making money," Oxaka said. "You sell three million CDs in a week, your next one needs to sell more. Who cares if three million makes a huge profit? It's a style of leadership more suited to the army than a band. The atmosphere around the band might be different from a marine boot camp, but the discipline isn't. Zawicki spoke and the boys bent over."

"But none of these guys were gay?"

"They hung around with women, if that's what you mean. I never saw them with any kind of boyfriend. If I had to pick one as gay, I'd say Dexter, but I've got no actual evidence of that. You guys think the pressure of having to give in to Zawicki could have driven Stendar over the edge?"

While Turner conceded to himself that that was a possibility, it didn't make much sense as a motive for this murder. If Stendar had been driven over the edge, most likely Zawicki would be dead. "We're not sure," he said. "Who were their enemies? Who'd they have fights with?"

"Some of it was simple stuff. The personal assistants were at each other's throats half the time, but for most of them it's an entry-level position. If the boys wanted bagels on the buffet in Buffalo and there were no bagels on the buffet, you could lose your job."

172

"Their positions are that insecure?"

"The guys in the band might be rich, and a few people in the permanent crew are well paid, but people who do the bidding and fetching are on the lowest rungs of the music-business ladder. They do it to be close to fame. They aren't getting rich. Lots of intense competition among some of them and jockeying for position to be noticed by Zawicki and other executives.

"Haupmin was a cause of dissension. She had all kinds of plans for herself and none of those included Roger being in this band. I think she was jealous of the time he spent with the guys. Being on the road is hell on relationships."

"What's the story on Eudace?" Fenwick asked.

"Their agent? He and Zawicki are close buddies."

"Would Eudace be using them for sex?"

"I never heard anything like that. He'd be using them to make himself rich, and he would get rid of anything that stood in the way of him becoming rich."

"Even one of the members of his own band?" Turner asked.

"If he thought they were going to break up, maybe. The CDs are going to sell through the roof for the next few months. He'll get his percentage of that. He'd make a lot more from years and years of CDs."

"If they weren't breaking up," Turner said.

"Nobody in the crew knew anything about a band breakup."

"What about Jordan Pastern?"

"He's a funny guy. The crew doesn't like him. He considers us beneath him. To him, we were nothing more than the hired help and needed to stay away from the band and security. He'd find minor rules for us to comply with. Keep us away from the band when there was no point in us being away from them. I don't think he'd harm them. He really liked them."

"We heard he was going to be fired."

"That rumor flew every time he had a dust-up with some executive from Riveting Records. I never believed it." He shook his head. "I still think this was all done by a sicko fan. These guys live under constant pressure. If these fans were given the slightest chance, they'd trample these guys like blades of grass before herds of stampeding buffaloes."

"Dexter seems to have had some kind of breakdown," Turner said.

"Yeah. We all kind of liked Dexter. He was sort of the crew's pet. He never hassled us. As the other guys got more famous, they got more demanding about little things, special attentions. They weren't as bad as some bands. Heavy metal guys are usually the worst. Dexter said he always trusted us. He was really sweet. I think Zawicki took advantage of him most of all, screwed him the most, but Dex was messed up before he got to us. Dexter didn't get along real well with his parents. This band was a great thing for him."

"Any special connection you know of between Stendar and Devane?"

"They sang together before joining the band is all I know."

After another fruitless round of interviews and talking to the beat cops about the people they had spoken with, Turner and Fenwick returned to headquarters.

Turner said, "I think we need to find out if there's some unique connection between Stendar and Devane."

"Nobody said so. We've got charts and movements, but we've got too many people with too few or too many alibis. They were either standing around in a lobby and talking to a herd of people, or they were fast asleep. I'm not sure which I prefer."

They spent an hour wading through a depressing amount of paperwork.

⸜17⸝

Breakfast was its Monday self. It was Brian's turn to cook for the week. He'd chosen to do baked eggs with broccoli, zucchini, and onions. Paul hated zucchini. He ate every bit. He wasn't about to be anti-vegetable with a teenage boy who was willing to eat them. Jeff picked all the zucchini and broccoli out of his. Then he slathered the entire concoction with mustard. Paul had no notion where his younger son picked up the mustard habit. Five months ago he'd been burying everything he ate, except oatmeal, under heaps of salsa. He figured maybe Jeff was trying to establish his own niche by matching his older brother in having odd food habits. Jeff's requests were never the same as Brian's, but lately, every time Brian came up with one oddity, Jeff came up with another. Sibling competition. So far this wasn't causing squabbles, so Paul was willing to let it be.

Ben said to Paul, "You going to be able to get some rest?"

"I hope so."

After making sure all three of them were sufficiently bundled against the bitter cold, Paul decided to finish a couple of calls before getting some sleep. He stacked the dish-washer then called his friend Grannett. The psychologist hadn't left for his office. Grannett said, "At the hospital Zaw-icki showed up with an entourage which included a very insistent lawyer. They demanded to see the kid. I advised against it, but Dexter was awake. He said it was okay. I was explicitly told I was unwanted. That I couldn't possibly understand the rich and famous. If I hadn't walked out of his room, I'd of been thrown out."

"Who told you all this?"

"Guy named Eudace and a woman named Hinkmeyer plus the lawyer. Eudace talked the most, with the other two as a kind of chorus. The lawyer reminded me that I wasn't a relative. I pointed out that they weren't, either. There was nothing I could do. I had no standing. Next I knew, they were all marching toward the exit."

"You did your best," Paul said. "I appreciate it."

"Kid's going to need more help and soon, if I'm any judge of these things."

Turner agreed. He called the office. Nothing new had been reported. He switched on CNN. They announced there was going to be a press conference with a statement concerning major developments in the case. The announcer said, "Since early this morning unconfirmed rumors of Jonathan Zawicki's resignation from Riveting Records are all over the Internet, many contradictory. After such a devastating loss of two of the members of the most popular band in the world . . ." The background for the CNN telecast was the ballroom of the Hotel Chicago. A mass of reporters surged between the walls. As he surfed through the channels, he saw that all the major cable networks were doing all-dead-Boys4u all the time. Fox had a right-wing religious nut masquerading as a normal human being claiming, "It is safe to assume that these boys led a lifestyle that is all too familiar to the rock musicians of today." MSNBC had a therapist who was saying, "It is safe to assume that the lifestyle of these boys—and we can't really call them men, can we?—is incredibly stressful. It's more stress than they can handle. In my book . . ." The CNN reporter was saying, "Again, this is an unconfirmed report. The head of Riveting Records is expected to resign today. A scandal of major proportions that is expected to rock the music world is in the making. This follows on the heels of the murder of two members of the most famous band in the world. The streets of Chicago are dangerous this morning."

Turner loved this last exaggeration as if the millions of people in the city had all suddenly woken up and gone to work looking over their shoulders.

Turner called Ian. He knew calling before ten in the morning was unlikely to get a response, but he wanted to see what his friend knew. He was surprised when the phone was picked up on the first ring. "Haven't been to bed," Ian told him.

"You need to look at the news reports." Turner waited for Ian to switch to CNN.

A new reporter spoke into the camera. "The police are saying nothing. Some are suggesting that perhaps the police themselves are hiding something. Conspiracy theorists are flooding the Web with . . ."

Ian snorted. "Because I have a computer, I have wisdom and credibility? The story is not serious enough or complicated enough that they have to quote from the World Wide fucking Web?"

Turner said, "I'd go with an alien pod-people theory."

"You've heard those theories?" Ian asked.

"Don't need to. If there isn't an alien pod-people theory about who killed these guys, there should be, or there will be. On the Web and on call-in right-wing radio and television shows."

The CNN reporter droned on. "The death of these two young men has caused an upheaval in the music world the likes of which has not been seen since the deaths of Elvis, John Lennon, and George Harrison. And here we have two dead young men. The president issued a statement . . ."

Turner said into the phone, "Do you know if that reporter knows what's going on?"

"Yes. They can't go with the full story until they've had a chance to talk to Zawicki, or get it confirmed from another source. I'm working on getting another source. It's still too early on the West Coast. Zawicki dropped a band last year at the last minute. All cute young guys. The market was starting to be flooded with boy bands. They got some tryouts but went nowhere. Was it business or lack of pleasure that got them dropped? Either way, I bet there's some connection with them getting screwed literally and figuratively. I'll be getting some confirmation before long."

"He may use counter-propaganda hard," Turner said.

"He's not my boss."

"This can't be traced back to me or the department?"

"It can't even be traced back to me," Ian said.

"How can you do that?" Turner asked.

"An anonymous call here, an anonymous call there, a few suggestions to friends of friends. Pop in a few Internet rumors which are the lifeblood of senselessness and silliness in the new millennium. The Internet has the best, most vicious, most unconfirmed bits of news. God bless the Internet. A number of people were prepared to believe anything about Zawicki. You don't get to the top without making enemies, and he's got more than most."

"They must be legion," Turner said. "Maybe one of them killed these guys to try to ruin him financially."

"I suppose these deaths would be a setback, but the guy

is rich in his own right. He does own fifty-one percent of the stock in Riveting Records, which might suffer in the long run from these two deaths. In the short run, my guess is people will flock to buy the band's CDs. My sources say that Zawicki has huge investments outside the company. He's probably made enemies, but I don't know if I'd believe old men in corporate boardrooms would just order the elimination of a rival's band."

"Think *The Godfather*," Turner said.

"I have no feel for any kind of connection like that here," Ian said, "but I've only been at this a few hours."

"Don't you ever sleep?" Turner asked.

"You never used to ask me that when we were lovers."

"We were young then."

Turner watched the news coverage for several more minutes. A reporter was saying, "We have further unconfirmed rumors of sabotage. That the whole band may have been a target of one or more assassins."

Turner said good-bye to Ian. Against the background of the hotel ballroom, he saw Blundlefitz being fitted with a mike on the Fox morning news. Seeing no useful gain from the news shows for the moment, he reached for the remote. He was exhausted. He hated working nights.

Just before he pressed the off button, there was a flurry of activity near the door in the background. Turner saw television lights follow Jonathan Zawicki into the ballroom. He led Dexter Clendenen, Danny Galyak, Ivan Pappas, and several other members of the band's entourage to the podium.

Zawicki held up his hand for silence. Dexter looked lost and disoriented. An older man and woman stood ramrod straight next to him. Paul guessed they were Dexter's parents.

Galyak and Pappas barely looked at the cameras or the

crowds. "I have an announcement," Zawicki said. He looked totally serene and in control. He wore a dark gray suit, white shirt, and conservative tie. The room quieted down.

"Ladies and gentlemen," Zawicki said. "You've heard rumors about a possible scandal. I'm here to put those rumors to rest. I believe we need to spend this time mourning the deaths of two fine young men. I haven't slept. None of us has. This is a terrible tragedy. Yet, ugly rumors have surfaced. At the time of such horrific events, I am loath to waste even an instant on these lies, but I feel I am forced to. I will start with the simplest. You heard about my possible resignation from this company. That is not true. I am the majority stockholder. I will not resign."

Zawicki motioned to Clendenen who stepped to the microphone. Zawicki said, "Rumors have circulated about sexual activity connected with the band. Dexter has a statement."

Paul thought Clendenen might start the rocking and banging again any second. If this was his child, the last place he'd want to have him right now was in front of a horde of reporters. When Clendenen spoke, his voice was soft but clear. "Mr. Zawicki has been nothing but a friend to us. Whoever would spread vicious rumors at a time like this doesn't deserve to be considered human. Two of us are dead. Please help us find who killed them." When he finished, Dexter faded into the background, and Zawicki returned to the microphone.

Interspersed with the coverage of the press conference were shots of sobbing teens and the sea of candles outside the All-Chicago Sports Arena. The mound of teddy bears was now at least ten feet high.

Turner thought Zawicki had abused his position. The guys had confirmed it. How could Zawicki be sure the remaining members of the band wouldn't turn on him? The man could be reasonably sure the police wouldn't make an announcement. The police had no choice but to respect the rights of suspects and witnesses. Still, people blabbed.

Blundlefitz was recognized from among the mass of reporters. "Is it true they found someone who saw Jason Devane last night after he left the hotel?"

"Yes," Zawicki said. "We found this person only a few minutes after an appeal this morning on the networks for anyone with information to come forth. Why the police hadn't found her is a mystery to me."

Turner called the police station and got the commander. "You watching this?"

"Yeah."

"Who is this witness?"

"I know about the appeal because I heard it on the radio while driving in. This is the first I heard that someone saw something. You and Fenwick better get back down here."

Tired as he was, Turner knew he didn't have much choice. He hung up but watched for a few more minutes.

Numerous reporters jumped up to be recognized. The first one was a woman in a pink woolen skirt and navy blue top. "Where is this person?"

"Safe from the police."

Blundlefitz was recognized again. Several of the reporters around him did little to disguise looks of disdain. Blundlefitz asked, "Do you know the source of these rumors about yourself?"

"We're doing everything we can to track them down. We will not rest until we find out where they came from."

"What are the police doing?" Blundlefitz being allowed to do a follow-up seemed to irk those around him, but they kept writing. "Are the police doing enough?" he asked.

"Obviously not. Two of these boys are dead. The way to honor their deaths is to find their killers."

Turner's phone rang. It was Fenwick.

"Are you watching this shit?" Fenwick asked.

"Yes."

"Your blood boiling yet?"

"Almost as much as yours on a bad day."

"And this is one of the worst. See you in half an hour."

Paul took a shower that seemed to rearrange his tiredness rather than revive him. He headed back to work.

The press conference was over. Reporters swarmed in and outside the station. The ones outside were desperate to be one of the lucky ones inside and out of the cold. Turner used a side entrance.

In the commander's office, Turner and Fenwick found Zawicki, two of his lawyers, representatives from the offices of the superintendent of police, and the mayor.

The detectives stayed near the door. The lawyers flanked Zawicki in chairs near the superintendent's desk. The official representatives sat off to one side. Zawicki barely deigned to look at the detectives. "I want these two off the case."

Molton said, "No."

"There are people here from high-up offices that you have to listen to."

"I will listen when they have something to say. Right now I'm listening to you."

Fenwick said, "We have your own confession that you required sex from these boys for them to get into the band."

"I said no such thing."

Fenwick, Turner, and the commander exchanged glances.

"What?" Fenwick said.

"I don't know why you would repeat such a thing. I assume you are the source of these ugly rumors?"

"We have statements from the members of the band," Turner said.

"I invite you to talk to them with my lawyers present. And you will be talking to them only with lawyers present from now on."

"What kind of hold do you have on these guys?" Fenwick asked.

"I don't have a hold on them. I want them to tell the truth. Sex has nothing to do with this case."

"Do you really think that kind of activity can be kept quiet?" Turner asked. "Aren't you risking a lot on the hope of silence? You cannot control these people."

Zawicki spoke directly to the commander, "If the police have been concentrating on sex, no wonder they haven't gotten anywhere with the inquiry. I'll have an army of private investigators looking into the murders and the actions of the police."

"Where were you yesterday afternoon and evening?" Fenwick asked.

"I had nothing to do with the murder of either of these boys."

"Answer the question, please," Molton said.

"My lawyers will provide you with a detailed account of my activities."

"Where is this witness?" Molton asked.

One of the lawyers spoke. "She's waiting in a limousine outside."

"If she can help with the case, why didn't you bring her to us immediately?" Molton asked.

"We're not sure we can trust the police in this matter," Zawicki said.

Molton picked up his phone and punched two numbers. "There's a limo outside with a witness in it. Bring her in here." He hung up. He turned to the lawyers and Zawicki and said, "I'm not sure you have a choice about trusting or not trusting the police. We're in charge of the investigation.

We're the only ones who are going to be in charge of the investigation. You need to work with us, not against us."

Zawicki said, "I will work for what I think is in the best interest of the remaining band members."

"Dexter Clendenen is in bad shape," Turner said. "He needs help."

For the first time Zawicki favored him with a glance. "What is your role in helping to bring him to the state he is in?"

"He's twenty-three years old," Turner said. "He's had twenty-three years of life before I met him Saturday night. He's had six years of intense work, the last few with the spotlight of fame and fortune. Whatever condition he is in is not the result of a few moments of kindness in the past thirty-six hours."

"Did you hold him captive in your home? What's the press going to say when they learn the police compromised their investigation by having one of the members of the band in their home? They will have lots of questions. There don't have to be reasons or answers. Suspicion of impropriety is enough."

Turner knew the press in today's feeding-frenzy mode didn't need facts. Rampant speculation was enough. Then they would have people on their shows discussing as factual the speculations and then debating the speculations rather than dealing with the facts. The right-wing media especially hated facts and not having enough didn't stop them. If they didn't have a bloody piece of evidence to wave, they speculated about whether there should be a bloody piece of evidence to wave, and why there wasn't a bloody piece of evidence, or who might have a bloody piece of evidence, or who might be covering up a bloody piece of evidence. Never mind the fact that there never was a bloody piece of evidence to begin with.

Molton said, "Tarnishing the reputation of police officers in this city is not going to bring these boys back to life. It is not going to find their killers. I wonder what the point of doing that is. Certainly someone trying to cover up knowledge of a crime might act this way."

"Are you accusing me?" Zawicki demanded.

"No. Just making an observation."

Two uniformed officers brought in a fourteen-year-old girl named Justine and her parents, Mr. and Mrs. LaPorte. All three looked a little bewildered. Molton stood up, introduced himself, and all the other official personnel. Turner got three more chairs from the conference room.

Molton said, "Miss LaPorte, we want to thank you for coming forward." She wore a bright green winter coat that nearly reached to her ankles. She kept her hands in the pockets.

She said, "I'm the biggest fan of these guys. I can't believe any of them are dead. It just can't be." Tears. Great gushing gouts of them. Her parents leaned close to her until she controlled herself.

"Honey," her father said, "just tell them what you know."

She snuffled a bit more then began. "Well, like I was at the vigil. Dad was in the car. It was really cold out. Some of us wanted to call for pizza to be delivered. Dad said that wouldn't be right. So he called, and we were going to go pick it up. When we got to Chicago Avenue and Rush Street, I thought I saw Jason Devane. I rolled down the window and called his name. He didn't turn around. I know they're trained not to, so that fans can't trick them into giving themselves away."

"Are you sure it was him?" Molton asked.

"It had to be. He was tall and thin. He had a Game Boy in his hand. Everybody knows that Jason always had a Game Boy with him. It's his trademark."

"Was he with someone?" Molton asked.

"No, by himself."

"Did you get a look at his face?" Molton asked.

"Oh, yeah. It was him."

"How long did you see him?"

"Just a couple seconds, but I know I'm not wrong."

Mr. LaPorte said, "I drove around the block, but the traffic was a mess. I hit every light. When we got back, he was gone."

"What time was this?" Molton asked.

"About six," Mr. LaPorte said.

Justine said, "It was dark, but I knew it was him."

Fenwick said, "Are you sure? He wasn't wearing his coat with the band's logo on it." A simple test to see how reliable a witness she was.

"I would have seen the logo. I would have remembered it. I have two sweatshirts and four T-shirts with the logo on them all. But I didn't need to see the logo to recognize him. It was him all right."

"There," Zawicki said. "Finally, something concrete."

"I heard the appeal on the news," Justine said. "I just had to call right away."

They thanked her and her parents before they left.

Molton said, "The problem with this is twofold. One, it can be proven that Mr. Devane was, in fact, wearing a coat with the band's logo on it. Two, because of your announcement every crackpot and fool in the country is going to be calling. We will get hundreds, probably thousands of calls upon which thousands of man-hours will be wasted when we need to be examining real leads right here."

Zawicki said, "I am going to do what I feel is necessary and right to do. You will have my schedule later in the day." He and his lawyers walked out.

The remaining city officials looked at each other. "It's a

mess," Molton said. He pointed to Turner and Fenwick. "I know you need sleep. Work for as long as you can now. I'll deal with the public pressure."

Stacks of pink message slips covered half of their combined desks. Tips. From the public. The vast majority of the time stunningly useless.

Fenwick said, "What do you want to bet ninety percent of these don't even come from Chicago, and they'll claim to be eyewitnesses?"

"No bets," Turner said. His phone rang. "If that's a tip," Fenwick said, "threaten to shoot them."

It was Mickey Pendyce. "This is really odd," he said. "No one is interested in the Blundlefitz story. Everybody wants tears and hysteria. Nobody wants to know about underwear."

"Isn't that the first question teenage girls want to know about?" Turner asked.

"Yeah, but these are national media. And the local media are swamped, and Blundlefitz is kind of a presence around town. *Hot Trends* is seen as really cool. I'll keep doing what I can."

Turner reported this to Fenwick.

"Our leverage is leaving us," Fenwick said.

"We need to talk to the guys in the band," Turner said, "especially Clendenen. I need to get Ms. Haupmin on the phone."

The operator at the Plaza Mart Inn connected him to her room. A male voice answered. Turner asked for Haupmin.

"Ms. Haupmin is not available."

Turner identified himself then said, "Ms. Haupmin needs to make herself available to the police."

"I am her lawyer. She will meet with you with me present or not at all."

"She's not a suspect."

"I told you the conditions."

Turner hung up. He told Fenwick, "Haupmin's lawyered up. I'd bet the mortgage the guy I just talked to works for Zawicki's firm. First she's willing to blab anything, to make wild accusations, to confront him in public, and now she's got a lawyer keeping us at a distance. Zawicki's gotten to her."

"Gotta be," Fenwick said. "If Zawicki was keeping secrets, why'd he open up Sunday night?"

Turner said, "We had him cornered for the moment. Perhaps he was emotionally vulnerable. Maybe he thought he still had deniability. He thought he'd been caught, but then he started getting in touch with people and knew he could orchestrate a cover-up. Now he's got lawyers and publicists arrayed against us. He's got the remaining members of the band hidden, Haupmin neutralized."

"Blundlefitz," Fenwick said. "Let's pay us a little visit to this great voice of the gossip elite."

They called the magazine. Blundlefitz was in. The magazine's headquarters were on the fifth floor of a building just south of the corner of Fullerton and Clark. Fenwick parked illegally in a bus stop. You had to have a special sticker to park in this neighborhood day or night. Even then it was nearly impossible to find a spot. Half the time the bus stops were crammed with illegally parked cars.

The offices were more spartan than Turner expected. A shabby old couch in a small entryway. The receptionist, one man sitting at a computer, a phone with five lines next to him. Piles of the magazine's latest issues covered much of the floor in the anteroom area. The person at the entrance pressed a button and told Blundlefitz he had visitors.

When the reporter saw the detectives, he gave them a thin smile. A short little man in a goatee accompanied

Blundlefitz. He held out his hand. "I'm Marshall Rolt, the publisher and editor-in-chief of *Hot Trends*. You must be the detectives investigating the murders. Please come in." Rolt was a fleshy man, maybe five-three with poundage on him that resembled a munchkin football linebacker gone to seed. He wore a pair of too large jeans, a white shirt, and a dark blue tie. He led them to a conference room. Turner assumed the offices must go back the length of the building. He saw only two other people working at computer terminals. Turner knew from Ian's stories that most of the work on these smaller newspapers was done by stringers.

The conference table was well-worn Formica. The chairs didn't match. Clearly, the magazine's money was not invested in amenities. There was an instant coffeemaker and a microwave oven. Each had a little sign on it reminding those who used them to clean up after themselves.

Rolt said, "I'm sure we can come to some kind of understanding."

Fenwick said, "Your guy came to us Sunday morning with information that Jonathan Zawicki was screwing all the guys in the band. By late Sunday evening, he and Zawicki were orchestrating a campaign to blame the police and cover up any mention of sexual activity."

Rolt said, "Randy has explained everything to me. We at the magazine are interested in journalistic integrity."

"Telling lies and switching stories is integrity?" Fenwick asked.

Rolt said, "We want to get to the truth. We're willing to help put a murderer behind bars. We also don't want to see innocent people suffer."

"You know Jonathan Zawicki is innocent?" Fenwick asked.

"We're going to follow wherever truth leads," Rolt replied.

189

"Your reporter took underwear from a dead young man," Fenwick said. "Don't you think that's a little unusual?"

"Randy was eager to get a story."

"Are you listening to yourself?" Fenwick asked. "To each of our questions, you've responded with illogic, nonsense, or non sequiturs."

Turner wished this was the first time in his career—not the ten zillionth—that he'd met such blind recalcitrance.

Rolt said, "We are not the enemy of the police here. We're a small magazine with a small staff. The music industry does pay for a lot of the ads in our paper, but that does not mean we are shills for them. We give honest reviews and do factual reporting. No one here knows anything about the murders. They are awful and tragic. We're going to have a memorial edition."

"Are you exploiting these murders?" Fenwick asked.

"We're reporting the news," Rolt said, "giving our readers what they're interested in."

"I care that these young men are dead," Blundlefitz said. "Is there a manual on how people are supposed to react? I know there are hundreds of crying teenagers out in the cold. I feel bad for them, but I have no personal stake in it. I didn't know them. I'm interested in the news."

"Can you tell us what the latest is on the investigation?" Rolt asked. "Your replies would be strictly off-the-record."

To his credit Fenwick did not guffaw. He said, "We can't discuss an open case. Perhaps Mr. Blundlefitz can check with Mr. Zawicki's people and get some information for you."

"I've done that," the reporter said, "and I'll continue to do it."

"Mr. Blundlefitz," Turner asked, "why did you change your point of view?"

"I follow where the news leads, where the truth is. You

gentlemen humiliated me. You tricked me. I should have brought the lawyers with me. My ego got in the way. That won't happen again."

"You told us you had some notes from a meeting that talked about the band breaking up," Turner said. "Where are those notes?"

Rolt said, "If he has such notes, that would be privileged information."

"You can't bully me now," Blundlefitz said. "Maybe there were no notes."

"Maybe you're an asshole," Fenwick said.

Rolt said, "Really, is it necessary to call names?"

"Do you have Dexter's diary?" Turner asked.

"He kept a diary?" Blundlefitz asked. "I'd love to read it."

Turner got no sense whether this counter-question was a cover-up or a genuine expression of his lack of knowledge.

"Who have you been talking to?" Fenwick asked.

"I don't have to respond to that," Blundlefitz said. "The police have a terrible record."

"The media have written lots of stories about police corruption," Turner said, "and I'm not going to say that improper behavior doesn't happen, or that mistakes aren't made, but how does that apply to this? Aren't you having an extreme reaction?"

Fenwick said, "He just wants to investigate so they sell more magazines, and he gets the glory for himself."

Rolt said, "We are very interested in cooperating with the police and in finding the murderer. At the same time we are not going to violate journalistic integrity."

They got absolutely nowhere with them.

Turner and Fenwick walked down the wide hallway to the front. A man in his mid twenties left an office and followed them out to the elevator. He called, "I've got an interview," to the receptionist, who barely nodded. After the elevator car arrived and all three of them entered, the new person said, "You didn't get far with them, did you?"

"Who are you?" Fenwick asked.

"Ned Lummy. I work at the paper. I hate Randall Blundlefitz. I think Marshall Rolt is a shit."

"Why do you still work there?" Fenwick asked.

"I like getting a paycheck. Cheers me up every week. Finding a job and not being a stringer at one of these papers isn't easy. I think I might be able to give you some information."

The elevator door opened on the ground floor.

"Where can we go to talk?" Lummy asked. "I don't want to be seen around here with you guys if I can help it. It's too cold out just to walk."

"Our car," Turner said. "We can drive over to Lincoln Park. It certainly won't be crowded at this time of the year, especially in this cold."

They sat fifty yards from Lake Shore Drive. The heater did its best to keep them from freezing, its best being barely adequate.

Lummy said, "You guys have a crummy car. Can you turn the heat up?"

"Not if we want the engine to keep working," Fenwick said.

Lummy sat in the back. The two detectives each leaned an elbow on top of the seat back and looked at him. Lummy rubbed his hands together, blew on them, then put his gloves back on. "I hate Blundlefitz. He lords it over everybody as if that crummy rag we work for is actually a real magazine. He's a big nobody in a tiny pond. The receptionist called and told me the cops were here. It could only be about one thing. Did he really steal underwear from that dead kid?"

"Yeah," Fenwick said.

"Sick. I know why he switched from anti-Zawicki to pro."

The detectives leaned forward.

"Blundlefitz hates boy bands. He has never given one of them a good review, but he likes being close to celebrity, so he always hangs around the concerts. Zawicki has promised him access to every group at Riveting Records."

"Who told you this?" Fenwick asked.

"Blundlefitz isn't making a secret of it, at least not at the office. He's bragging. And he's really mad at you."

"We were told he talked to the magazine's lawyers," Turner said.

"Ha! Lawyers? There's only one. The guy consults for us because he's a buddy of Rolt's. He's really a corporate lawyer. He knows little about constitutional or any other kind of law. Blundlefitz uses him to make bluffs, but half the time when he says he's talked to him, he hasn't."

Turner realized that Blundlefitz must have talked to Zawicki's lawyers sometime Sunday, presumably at the afternoon meeting.

"Would Blundlefitz help keep the identity of the killer secret?" Turner asked.

"I don't think he knows who did it, but he thinks he's going to solve the murder. Rolt's pushing him to. I've never seen Blundlefitz's fat ass move quicker. He has called in every marker he has. They think if they find out who the killer is before the police, they'll make themselves into celebrities and catapult the magazine into national prominence. Ha! As if. Although Blundlefitz did get permission from Zawicki to talk to everybody connected to the band."

"What's the background on Blundlefitz?" Turner asked

"He's been into music since he was a kid. He even had a band when he was a freshman in college. Called the Left-handed Masturbators. Everybody wants a name to get people's attention. Their music might not be any good, but at least someone will notice."

"Was their music any good?" Fenwick asked.

"I never heard them. Blundlefitz claimed they were great, but everybody says that."

"How come they never made a name for themselves, or at least, why did he drop out of the band?"

"He never said. No one else around the office ever heard of the band that I know of. Ninety-nine-point-nine percent of the bands that start up go nowhere. I assumed their story was the same as most bands. They don't make it for any number of reasons. They don't want to put in the time. They find out what a struggle it is. Egos go out of control. Maybe people get bored. Or maybe it's as simple as they aren't any good. People quit bands and walk away for no reason. Some don't want to commit as much as others. Lots of ordinary reasons."

Lummy didn't know anything else. They dropped him off a block from the paper to lower the risk of him being seen getting out of their car.

"I don't get it," Fenwick said. "Blundlefitz gets access and we don't."

"Several possibilities," Turner said. "Zawicki doesn't think Blundlefitz will ever find out, or he thinks that if Blundlefitz does find out, he can control that information or do something about it. Use it to his own advantage. Remember, his main goal is profits. He can still sell a lot of CDs. Right now, I think this is more about control than cover-up. That could change real fast."

⬩ 18 ⬩

They drank coffee, ate food, and indulged in witty cop banter
at Harriet's Rat Food Special Drive-in. Cops flocked to the
place. It was in the warehouse district west of the *Tribune*
plant on Chicago Avenue. No sign identified it as a place
open to the public. All the parking in the area was illegal.
Although it was called a drive-in there was in fact no place to
drive in. If you weren't a marked or unmarked cop car, you
got towed within minutes. The name was to scare away civilians who might stumble on the listing for restaurants in the
phone book. The foyer was painted flat black and unlit. This
was the one sure place in the city cops would not be dis-
turbed by accidental walk-ins.

   After Turner and Fenwick ate, they drove to a warehouse
on the near west side about half a mile from the Loop. It was
the home of Lost Chicago Records, the business of Jeremiah
Boissec, the man who Mickey Pendyce said might be able to
tell them more about Jonathan Zawicki. The building looked
like it should be the next one to be rehabilitated or bull-
dozed in the march of the Loop's economic renaissance

westward. It was a one-story disaster waiting to collapse. The roof sagged. The exterior of all the windows had metal bars which didn't look solid enough to keep out flies in summer. Instead of glass panes, warped boards covered all the windows. Shards of shattered glass littered the pavement. The sidewalk was cracked and broken. The black painted door rattled on its hinges as they opened it. The grime in the entryway could have served any twenty other buildings for a month. The receptionist chewed his gum and read a book, while lounging back on a chair which had two broken arms both held together with black electrical tape.

Fenwick said, "We're looking for Jeremiah Boissec."

"You found him." Boissec was short, squat, and ugly. Warts on his nose, ear hair an inch long, nose hairs unclipped. "You the cops Mickey said were coming around?"

They showed him ID.

Boissec said, "Your buddy Zawicki is nuts." He led them to an office. The difference between the decor back here and out front was a large metal desk doing its best to add rust to the grime surrounding it.

The detectives settled themselves on metal chairs that could have been from the era before World War I. The grit on them almost certainly was.

"What's your history with Zawicki?" Turner asked.

"I was vice-president in charge of creativity at Riveting Records. I developed new talent. I helped find new bands. I succeeded. I was on my way up in the industry. Then I crossed the son of a bitch. He said I'd never work in that town again." Boissec shook his head. "I chose not to believe him. That was a mistake. He was quite right. I never worked in that town again. That was four years ago. I scrounged for a job for a couple years. Finally, I came back to Chicago. I develop talent here, manage a few acts." He swept his arm around the office. "Hell of a place, huh? I do failure very well. I almost got a band on local cable once. Not a terrific track record. I used to be great, the best."

"Is Zawicki still holding you back?" Fenwick asked.

"I'm off his radar screen."

"What got you fired?" Turner asked.

"I objected to his method of recruiting members of groups."

Fenwick said, "You didn't like it that he required the boy band members to service him?"

"Boy bands? Ha! Zawicki did not discriminate. He made the women service him, too. He wasn't choosy. He required half the people who worked for him to let him screw them. I didn't have to because I am fat and ugly. I was lucky. I had talent. I got hired for my brains. And while I don't want to seem like I'm defending him, he wasn't the only executive in Hollywood screwing those who wanted a job. Actors, musicians, you name it, they want to be famous, they got to pay the price. No, everybody isn't getting fucked to be famous, just almost everybody."

"I find that hard to believe," Fenwick said.

"Maybe I'm exaggerating, but I don't think by much. Some Hollywood executives must be honorable. You'd think at least one of them. While I was out there, I never met him or her."

"Were you honorable?" Turner asked.

"More than some, less than others."

Fenwick asked, "But how can he hope to silence a scandal of this proportion? People who turned him down, who didn't make it. Employees he's dropped or fired."

"How many actors or actresses have you heard accusing their producer, director, manager, agent, or anyone else of sexual harassment?"

"None," Fenwick admitted.

"Precisely," Boissec said. "Ain't gonna happen. And in a boy band? They have enough problems with their sexual reputation as it is. Everybody thinks they're gay."

"We know," Fenwick said.

"But there's been a murder," Turner said. "Why doesn't that trump all of this?"

"Only the murderer cares about that. Everybody else cares about fame, money, and their career. Plus Zawicki is very careful, very rich, very powerful, has lots of good lawyers, and there ain't gonna be any proof. No tapes. No smoking gun. He is not a fool. Zawicki is still concerned about the bottom line. Two deaths in two days is enough to scare the piss out of anybody. One death and Zawicki can make a fortune—sympathy, nostalgia, sex, and intrigue, what could be a bigger draw? Two deaths? That gets dicey. My guess is Zawicki is planning with his creative team even as we speak on how to spin it or exploit it. If he can do either, he will."

"He sounds like evil incarnate," Fenwick said.

"Nah, he's a greedy Hollywood executive. Lots of people do think that's synonymous with evil incarnate. He's not acting out of character. If you're one of the people who think consistency is a virtue and that as long as he's consistent to what he believes in, then he's a saint. Follow that logic to its conclusion and we'd all worship ants." He shrugged. "Zawicki's type is endemic and not just in Hollywood. It's just more obvious and prominent in Hollywood. He's also more honest than some. At least he doesn't try to hide what a shit he is. I think on some level, it does bother him that these guys are dead. Nevertheless, I'm not sure he's expressed a genuine emotion in a long time. That's pathetic, but it's not as sad as these poor guys getting killed." He paused. "Don't get me wrong. I'm not trying to build sympathy for the guy. I hate him. But he's not an inhuman monster, not completely."

"But he's got everybody covering for him about this sex thing."

"He's not hiding what he is from them, just from the frenzied media hordes and secondarily from you."

"But he admitted it to us," Fenwick protested.

"Doesn't matter. He knows as good government servants you can't call a press conference and give this to the media. And if you have contacts in the media to try and get the story out, he has more and better contacts. He's a pro with a media machine behind him. Can you match that?"

Turner knew they couldn't. They might not be out of their league, but they certainly were playing in the other guy's ballpark.

"Would he kill one of the band members himself?" Fenwick asked.

"He wouldn't have a reason to. At least I can't think of one. They were making him tons of money."

"Would he murder someone who was going to tell or have someone murdered?"

Boissec considered for a moment. "Definitely maybe. Even if I said yes, it would be only an opinion. I hate him."

"Would you kill one of these guys?"

"I wasn't at the concert. I would not have been allowed backstage. I haven't seen any of them since I was fired."

"Anyone among the entourage who might have a grudge?" Fenwick asked.

"I knew some of them. This was four years ago, just as Boys4u was getting big. A lot of these people would turn on each other pretty damn fast if they thought it would advance their careers. Hinkmeyer's a hack, been around since day one in those silly hats. Eudace, the agent, comes in second to Zawicki in the evil incarnate competition. On the other hand, Pastern really cares for those kids. I sometimes wonder if he wasn't a little closer than just a guard."

"What do you mean?" Turner asked.

"Maybe he was getting a little on the side himself. I have no proof of that. He always seemed like a straight guy. Just a twitch I guess. Murial Arane, the choreographer, was a wild woman. She fought with everybody, but she was the very best. She had those guys doing moves they never thought they could. She was incredibly talented. I think Roger resented how good she was. He thought he was pretty hot shit. They had a brief fling just after the band signed their first contract with Riveting Records. I don't think they were actively hostile to each other until that Haupmin woman came around. All of sudden, Roger wanted Murial fired."

"You're sure?" Turner asked.

"It's what I heard. I may be dead in Hollywood, but I still know a few people. And I hear rumors. I put two and two together. Sometimes I get the right answer. Sometimes not. And my news could be way out of date. I don't have a hot line into Zawicki's office."

"Anybody else who you think is suspicious?"

"Nobody struck me as a murderer when I was there. A few I wouldn't have minded if bad things happened to, but that's normal in any job."

"Would any of the three living band members have killed the other two?" Turner asked. Turner knew the remaining members were under guard, and it would have been difficult for them to have killed Jason Devane. Still, slip-ups could happen. It was unlikely, but he couldn't completely discount the possibility.

Boissec thought for a moment. "I doubt it. Danny has a big ego, but then they all do. I guess I mean he's more brash about his ego. He thinks he's funny. I'd laugh to build his ego. Ivan struck me as a sincere kid, mature, sensible. Dexter is not tightly wrapped, very needy. I heard he had a hell of a family. I never met them."

Boissec knew no more. They left.

In the car Turner said, "We need to talk to the choreographer now."

"Heading for the Hotel Chicago as we speak."

"I've been thinking about our last question," Turner said. "Could one of the three that are left have killed the others?"

"Sure it's possible. We just have to figure out why, come up with evidence and a confession."

"Buck, Buck, Buck. That's so like you. Evidence and confessions. You probably want DNA, too."

"You know me."

While they drove, Turner tried not to think about how tired he was and how much sleep he needed. Celebrities did get treated differently. The poor schlubs who had to deal with them in any capacity never got enough sleep.

They found Murial Arane in her room. She said, "I can't believe that Zawicki is trying to shut us up. I think we need to help the police."

"We appreciate your being willing to talk to us," Turner said. "We've heard some odd things."

"I'll answer anything I can. I want to help."

Fenwick said, "We were told you had an affair with Roger Stendar."

"I had sex with Roger, yes. I had sex with all of them at one time or another over the past several years."

"Oh," Fenwick said.

"It was kind of exciting, but it wasn't a big deal."

"To them or to you?" Fenwick asked.

"Both."

"At the time did the others know you were doing it with the others?" Fenwick said.

"I don't know what they discussed. They were really not very good in bed, not very experienced. Danny orgasmed in less than a minute. They're little more than boys after all. They all had fragile little egos. I had to teach Dexter so many things. He was the best of them actually. He listened and learned. He wanted to do right. He wanted to be a great lover. He had the most potential. He gave his all."

"This didn't cause dissension?" Fenwick asked.

"It didn't cause murder. It was more casual. Roger was the first. This was just after they were officially a band. One night we stayed late working together. We were sweaty. He was hot looking in his skimpy little shorts. So we did it. I wasn't like Zawicki, forcing them to have sex. Believe me, they wanted it."

"You knew about Zawicki?" Fenwick asked.

"Nobody told me, but I'm not blind."

"Were they trophies for you?" Fenwick asked.

She gave him a sour look. "I suppose you could look at it that way. I haven't had sex with everyone I've choreographed, but yes, I've had sex with lots of them. Yes, women, too. Does that bother you?"

Turner said, "Only if it has something to do with the murder. Does it?"

"No. It couldn't possibly. It was just sex. None of the guys got jealous. There was no reason to be jealous."

Fenwick said, "Maybe they wanted Roger out of the way so they could be closer to you."

She snorted. "That's absurd. Roger was nearly five years ago. I don't even know how many of the others knew about him. I didn't think it was a big deal."

"Maybe one of them thought it was a big deal," Turner said.

"If they did, they never said so to me."

Fenwick asked, "Did Ms. Haupmin want you out of the way?"

"That no-talent bitch. All she had to do was move a little,

202

shimmy, shake, tap her foot, anything. I told her whatever she did, I could get the backup boys to follow along. I finally had to choreograph them separately. She's an incompetent moron. She could barely walk and chew gum at the same time. She was stupider than half the bimbos in Hollywood, and believe me, I've met a lot of stupid bimbos in Hollywood."

"Would she have any reason to kill Roger or Jason?" Fenwick asked.

"Roger was her meal ticket. Not a chance. Jason was an amiable cipher. Why bother?"

"Were these guys friends?" Turner asked. "Were there fights?"

"They got along, mostly. I suppose Dexter would get annoyed at being teased once in a while, but nothing ever got out of hand."

"How good of a security guard was Mr. Pastern?" Turner asked.

"With a band this popular, there are always stalker problems. The guys were taught what to do and what not to do. Every threat was reported no matter how small. Nobody ever got close to these guys. Pastern was tough, but he was never mean. He never had to punch anybody. He had a way about him."

Fenwick asked, "Was he exploiting them the way Zawicki was?"

She considered him carefully. "I can't imagine it. He cared for these boys. So did I. I would do anything that I could to help you find the killer."

Fenwick said, "We heard there were plans to fire Mr. Pastern before the deaths."

"Maybe if they had gotten rid of him the boys would still be alive." She sniffed and dabbed at her eyes, then resumed, "After every rumor, he got a raise. I never believed they'd fire him."

She claimed not to have talked to Devane or Stendar since before the concert began. Turner and Fenwick left.

In the lobby of the Hotel Chicago they saw the older couple who had stood next to Dexter Clendenen at the press conference. Turner tapped Fenwick and pointed. "Dexter's parents." They strolled over, introduced themselves, and showed ID. The four of them sat in a small alcove in a corner of the lobby.

Mr. and Mrs. Clendenen were in their late forties or early fifties. Mr. Clendenen wore a maroon sweater, jeans, and heavy work boots. Tall and lean, his ponytail matched his wife's. Only the mustache part of his goatee matched her facial hair. She wore a beige sweater, jeans too tight on her slightly bulging frame, and walking shoes.

"We're afraid of the reporters," Mrs. Clendenen said. "They don't seem to want to let us alone."

"Where are they?" Fenwick asked.

"Mr. Zawicki is having a luncheon press conference." *Smart,* Turner thought. Feed their stomachs and feed their appetite for salacious news at the same time. What could be better?

"Where's Dexter?" Turner asked.

"We're so worried about him," Mrs. Clendenen said. "Mr. Zawicki insisted he attend the press conference. I don't think Dex is in any shape to go anywhere. He should be resting."

"He's not some pansy," Mr. Clendenen said. "Let the boy be for once."

Turner said, "He was at my home for a while yesterday morning. He was sitting on the floor, rocking back and forth, and banging his head against a wall."

"What did you do to him that made him do that?" Mr. Clendenen asked.

"There isn't enough psychological ill health I could inflict on anyone in the short time I had with your son to cause him to do that. His actions are the result of years of abuse. You know Mr. Zawicki required sexual favors of him?"

"Dex says that's not true," Mrs. Clendenen said.

"Dex isn't some fag," Mr. Clendenen said. "Even if he did get picked on when he was a kid and called names and wouldn't fight back. I know he's not a fag."

"Gay," Turner said. "The word is *gay*."

"You a fag?" Clendenen asked. "You don't look like one."

Fenwick asked, "How often did you force yourself on your son?"

Mrs. Clendenen gasped. Mr. Clendenen stood up. "You son of a bitch. Are you saying we abused him?"

The detectives rose as well.

"Just asking," Fenwick said.

Turner said, "I'm saying something is wrong when a young man sits against a wall, rocks back and forth, and bangs his head repeatedly against the plaster."

"It's not our fault," Mr. Clendenen said.

"Whose would it be?" Fenwick asked.

Mr. Clendenen turned very red and began breathing heavily. He put his nose three inches from Fenwick's. To do this he had to stand on tiptoe. Turner stifled a grin at the odd sight. Fenwick neither flinched nor blinked. He had at least six inches and nearly one hundred pounds on his nemesis.

Mr. Clendenen said, "If you didn't have that badge, you wouldn't be so tough."

Without removing his gaze from Clendenen, Fenwick unclipped his badge and handed it to Turner.

Mr. Clendenen took a step back. His eyes shifted between Turner and Fenwick. "There's two of you," he muttered.

Turner knew it helped cowards to have an excuse not to try and back up their own bluffs.

Mrs. Clendenen stood next to her husband and said, "Clem, stop it." Her husband took another step back. She continued, "We never did anything to Dex. He's a normal boy."

Turner said, "The attack seemed to be triggered when he touched a condom."

"You have condoms in your home?" Mr. Clendenen asked.

Turner said, "We need to focus on your son's breakdown. What led up to him having a reaction to the condom is the problem, not the condom itself."

Mrs. Clendenen said, "I have no idea why he would react that way."

"Zawicki told us not to talk to you," Mr. Clendenen said. "He told us you'd make all kinds of accusations."

"We're trying to find out who killed Roger Stendar and Jason Devane," Turner said.

"So why did you need to ask about our private lives?" Mrs. Clendenen asked.

"Something in these boys' pasts might have triggered the killings. We don't know what that could be unless we ask."

Mr. Clendenen said, "This has nothing to do with our son. I never touched him. That's an insult. Just because I don't wear some suit like that Zawicki doesn't mean I'm a child molester. I didn't kill nobody. I wasn't in town. I've never been to one of these concerts. I don't want to go."

"Have you been?" Turner asked Mrs. Clendenen.

Mrs. Clendenen said, "Oh, yes. They had a mother-son event at a concert one time in Los Angeles. It was so nice. Everybody was so kind. When we got the news about Dexter, we decided to fly right out. Mr. Zawicki paid for our fare."

Mr. Clendenen said, "Is our son in danger? We don't really want a policeman hanging around outside his door."

"Can you ensure his safety?" Fenwick asked.

"No one's been able to," Mr. Clendenen said. "These people are going to get their asses sued when this is all over. They were supposed to protect the kid."

"He didn't die," Turner pointed out. "If he did die, how would suing help?"

"Someone's got to be responsible," Mr. Clendenen said. "They're the ones who've been putting all this pressure on him."

Fenwick said, "It must've been great when Dexter helped you guys out financially after the band made it big."

"He was a good boy," Mrs. Clendenen said. "I always wanted a nice house."

Mr. Clendenen said, "Zawicki says you guys don't know shit."

Fenwick said, "I'm more interested in what you can tell me. Dexter told us he came back to his hometown and they had a parade for him."

"They did," Mrs. Clendenen said. "They had a band and the local fire department put on a display. He even sang a song at the Elks Club." She spoke with genuine pride. Tears welled in her eyes. Her little boy made it big. Turner felt a little sorry for her.

"Did any of the band members show up with him?" Fenwick asked.

"Oh, no, they each go their separate ways," she said.

"He didn't hang around with them when they weren't on tour?" Fenwick asked.

"He hung around with girls," Mr. Clendenen said. "Living in that house with those guys was enough."

"How did he get along with the others?" Fenwick asked.

"He was always excited when he called home," Mrs. Clendenen said. "Even when they were overseas, Dexter called every Sunday night. He always told me about the crowds, and the fun they were having together. He didn't have a lot of friends growing up."

Mr. Clendenen said, "Band and chorus and singing lessons. Nobody I ever knew had singing lessons."

Mrs. Clendenen said, "It paid off, didn't it?" The first evidence of defiance in standing up to her husband. "But now he had friends. With the band he was doing things with people. He'd talk about the exotic restaurants they'd go to together, the sights they'd see. As they got more famous, he'd send things. Now we live in the nicest place in town."

"Yeah," Clendenen said, "those uppity snobs and their country club, they don't try and take advantage no more. Dexter could buy and sell their country club."

Turner's guess was that those who sucked up to money didn't change from small towns to large. Money substituting for ego strength. Not unusual, Turner thought. Cash allowing them to feel superior, cash necessary for them to feel superior.

"We'd like to talk to Dexter," Turner said.

Mrs. Clendenen said, "Mr. Zawicki keeps saying Dexter has to have a lawyer with him when he talks to the police. Why is that, if he didn't do anything wrong? You don't think Dexter did these things?"

"We're hoping he can give us information," Fenwick said.

"Well, I don't know," Mrs. Clendenen said.

Mr. Clendenen said, "All this fancy talk with lawyers and executives. I think they're all fairies." He glanced at Turner, said, "Sorry," in his most unapologetic tone, and continued. "They're just using our kid. We'd take him home, but he refuses to leave."

"I'm worried about him," Mrs. Clendenen said.

"I have a psychologist friend," Turner said. "He came to

my house and helped Dexter. We got him to the hospital. Maybe I could ask him to come by."

Mrs. Clendenen looked uncertain. Mr. Clendenen said, "We don't need more people to talk to. We don't need no psychologist interfering. We got too many people talking. We don't need no more talk. We need to get out of here with Dexter. He needs to be away from all this shit. I'm going to talk to Zawicki again. To hell with his lawyers."

◣ 19 ◢

Back in the car the dispatcher called. Turner answered. "Detective Turner is supposed to call a Mrs. Talucci."

Turner used his cell phone. Mrs. Talucci said, "It would be good if you could come over now. Bring Fenwick with you. I've got another one of your band members here."

Turner was exhausted. He wished he was going to the neighborhood and his home to go to bed. He doubted if that would be for a while yet.

They took Lake Shore Drive to Roosevelt Road, west to Halsted then over to Taylor Street.

Mrs. Talucci answered the door. "This one kept banging on your door. I brought him over." There was very little in the neighborhood that got past Mrs. Talucci. She led the detectives into the kitchen. "They don't feed any of these kids." It was Ivan Pappas. He was hunched over a bowl of meatballs and Italian sausage smothered in Mrs. Talucci's special red sauce and topped with more Parmesan cheese than a herd of cows could make in a year. A small television was turned to the local news station. It too had all-dead-Boys4u all the time.

"Dexter told me where he went," Pappas said. "I had to get away. I wanted to see you. He told me about the neighbor lady." He pointed to the television. "I don't think they've missed me yet. It hasn't been reported. Or they haven't told the press, just like they held back the news on Jason."

The detectives sat down. Mrs. Talucci stood with her back to the sink. Turner didn't ask her to leave. If the members of the band were using her house as a refuge, he wasn't about to tell her to get out.

"What happened?" Turner asked.

"Danny and I have both been threatened. We got notes. We got phone calls. Nobody is even supposed to know where we are. Nobody is supposed to be able to get through the switchboard, but they did. Danny and I talked about what to do. We couldn't agree. We're really scared, and we don't know who to trust. Danny went to take his note to Zawicki. I don't trust Zawicki. I don't know why Danny does."

Turner asked, "Did Dexter get the same threats?"

"They wouldn't let us in to see him," Pappas said. "This whole things makes no sense. We're in trouble, and the police are the enemy? That's crazy. This isn't some silly Hollywood intrigue where everybody but the people in the cast know what's going on. This isn't some stupid teenage slasher movie. This is real. I've been on a hell of a ride to the top. I guess it's over. I don't care about that right now. I don't know if I ever will again. Roger and Jason are dead, that's awful. I've never felt this bad. It's like I'm empty. Roger and Jason were the songwriters. I never could write about what I feel, and I sure don't feel like singing about it." He paused, then whispered, "Even more, I don't want to be next. I care what happened to the guys. I really do. But it's awful to think that I might be next. Does that make me a terrible person?"

"Fear is a normal response," Turner said. "It's okay to be concerned for yourself."

212

Pappas said, "Zawicki seems to be more concerned with lawyers and cash. Even Jordan is so distraught that he's hardly any help. We used to be able to talk to him. He was always pretty normal. The rest of this is crazy. They can't seem to protect us."

"Did you recognize the voice on the phone?" Turner asked.

"No. It was muffled, distorted. Almost like a computer voice."

"Could you tell if it was male or female?" Turner asked.

"It was so indistinct."

"Where did you find the notes?" Turner asked.

"Mine was under the pillow on the bed I was using in our new suite. Danny's was in his shaving kit. There's no guard on the door when we aren't there. Maybe if they can get in to leave those notes, they'd stay in there until we got back then kill us. Maybe we've just been lucky. Maybe someone's trying to kill the whole band. They don't care who they get first or last."

"That would explain the sabotage at the concert hall," Turner said, "if someone wanted you all dead. But who would? Is somebody that angry?"

"We never did anything to anybody. It's not our fault we're bigger than the other boy bands. Nobody's angry. But somebody got in our room. How?"

Good question, Turner thought.

Pappas said, "We've dealt with stalkers, and they never get close. This isn't some teenybopper stalker who wants to squeal and touch us. This is murder. It's gotta be somebody we know. It's gotta be somebody who was in that suite. This is not the time to be trusting any of them. Danny is crazy to take this to Zawicki. I don't want to go back there. It's dangerous. I don't think Zawicki would care if we all died."

Pappas's insight that the killer was probably someone in

their inner circle made sense to Turner. He asked, "Who's been allowed in the suite?"

"You might as well ask who hasn't been in. Zawicki hauled everybody over from the Plaza Mart for a meeting. Even though the new suite they've got us in was as big as Zawicki's, it was crowded. He even let Sherri Haupmin in."

"She a big problem for you?" Turner asked.

"She was a pain in the ass. She wasn't as good for Roger as she thought. She played around with other guys besides Roger."

"In the band?" Turner asked.

"Yeah."

"Who?"

"Me for one. But I meant outside the band. I got no proof, but I think she might have talked to Zawicki on the side."

"Do you think he did more than talk?" Fenwick asked.

"Yeah, but I wasn't about to tell Roger that, especially after I boffed his girlfriend." He glanced at Mrs. Talucci. She had her arms folded on her chest. She gave him a simple nod.

"How'd you wind up having sex with her?" Turner asked.

"She came onto me one night. I guess she thought she needed me for an ally in her campaign to be one of the opening acts. Like I cared."

"But Roger never found out about the two of you?"

"Not that he ever told me. There was never any big confrontation. Haupmin got to be the opening act. Maybe she thought I helped. I didn't. I didn't try and stop her, either."

"Maybe that was enough," Turner said.

"She make it with all the guys?" Fenwick asked.

"I don't know."

Fenwick said, "What I don't get, if Zawicki was screwing you, why not do something about it? You're rich. Break it off. Sue him."

Pappas looked flabbergasted. "I wouldn't dare. You don't know the power he has. It only happened to me once. I could handle once. I didn't know what he was doing to the other guys. I didn't want to know."

"Was anyone not connected to the band in the suite?" Turner asked.

"That reporter, Blundlefitz. He's creepy. He's got all-access all the time. He's been around constantly. He asks us questions."

"What kind of questions?"

"Sick shit, like, when do we masturbate and stuff. He says he's trying to help solve the murder, but I just think he's a perv."

"Do you have the note?" Turner asked.

Pappas reached in his winter coat which was hanging on his chair and took out a plain white sheet of paper which had been folded in four.

Turner said, "Was it folded and wrinkled when you found it?"

"No, I just stuck it in my coat."

"Did you show it to anybody?"

"Only Danny. Then I took off."

"Who did you tell where you were going?"

"Danny. I told Jordan I planned to go to the police, but I didn't say specifically here.

"How did you get away?" Fenwick asked.

"Jordan offered to go with me if I'd wait. I was afraid he was going to tell Zawicki. Jordan's a good guy. But I'm not sure who to trust anymore. I decided not to wait."

"That was stupid," Fenwick said.

"What? I came here."

Turner said, "You don't know who the killer is. You don't know if the killer is after the rest of you. Whoever sent the note probably knows your movements. It makes sense to conclude that someone you know is threatening you. It could be the killer or it could be someone trying to take advantage and scare you."

"That's sick."

"Right now," Turner said, "I think you're right not to trust anyone."

"But Jordan's our guard."

"He shouldn't have let you out of his sight," Fenwick said.

"It wasn't his fault. I snuck out when the room-service guys were setting up. Zawicki was having another big meeting. People were in and out. I was careful."

"What about the cop in the corridor?" Fenwick asked.

"He was an older guy. I don't think he knew who I was. Aren't they there to keep people away from us? Are they supposed to follow us around?"

"You weren't supposed to leave," Fenwick said.

Turner used the tips of his fingers to hold the paper. He doubted if they'd find any useful prints, but he didn't want to ruin whatever minuscule chance there might still be. In the middle of the paper were the words, "Die, you sick fag."

"When did you find this?" Turner asked.

"Everybody was up late. Danny and I were in with Hinkmeyer and Jordan until almost seven in the morning."

"Why?" Fenwick asked.

"Why? We just wanted to talk. They're as close to normal people as we know in that crowd."

"Are your parents coming to town?" Turner asked. He thought of normal, and he thought of family connections.

"Mine aren't. They just want me to get home. They'll go to the funerals and stuff out in California. Danny and I are really scared. Why would somebody want to kill any of us or all of us? What did we ever do but sing and dance and entertain people? We're not trying to hurt anybody."

216

Turner didn't have an answer to these questions yet.

"Have you talked to Dexter at all?" Turner asked.

"For a few seconds at the press conference. He's gone nuts. He hates his parents, and they showed up. Nobody gets to see Dexter in the suite. I think Zawicki had some quack doctor in. They've got Dexter on all kinds of drugs."

"Has Dexter been doing drugs and booze?" Turner asked.

"We're not a heavy metal act. Nobody's an addict. Sure, we all drink, but we're of age. We like to party."

"What does 'like to party' mean?" Fenwick asked. "You mean you like naked orgies with cheerleading squads from several universities and everybody there ingests enough drugs to start a pharmacy, or does it mean you like to go to parties, the way I mean it?"

"Maybe somewhere in between, but definitely no hard drugs. No heroin or cocaine. I haven't seen anybody using anything. We've talked about what we did in the past. Most of us did a little dope in high school and that was it."

Fenwick asked, "What's the deal with all of you denying you had sex with Zawicki after we know all about it?"

"Man, he threatened us. He's got power. He can talk any-body in the industry into anything. He got to Dexter first. Dexter is scared of his own shadow half the time. Whatever they've got him doped up on is powerful. The guy was zonked when he was at that press conference. We were told to just keep our mouths shut. Zawicki can be intimidating. We've got contracts and all, and I think I understand them, but hey, this is like crazy. I don't have some economics degree. Danny's not really much help. He's as scared as I am. I got undressed for bed and pulled the covers back. I kind of fluffed the pillow. I felt this note. Who's trying to kill us? Why do the lawyers say it's important for us not to talk to the police without them present?"

"But you're here," Turner said.

"Yeah."

Turner said, "Murial Arane claimed all of the guys in the band had sex with her."

"All of us?"

"Yes."

"I knew about Roger and myself, of course. Everybody?"

"Yeah."

"Murial was mostly okay. She made us look good. We had strengths and weaknesses. Dancing, I mean. She helped us with them. The sex with her just kind of happened one night after practice about three years ago. She's hot. She's got this tight pink outfit that shows her . . . Well, anyway. We did it. I was in love for a couple weeks. She was real nice. She let me down easy. She's ten years older than I. She taught me some stuff. I was a little naïve."

"Any of the guys get jealous about the others having relations with her?"

"Not that I know about. One time somehow Roger and I got around to talking about having sex with her. You know how guys are. We were commenting on how fine she looked. She's got a great ass." He glanced at Mrs. Talucci. "Sorry."

Mrs. Talucci said, "It's okay. I might be old, but I still appreciate a good ass myself. If I dropped seventy years, and I thought skinny runts were nice looking, your butt wouldn't be half bad." She gave him a slight smile. Ivan managed a weak grimace.

He turned back to the cops. "Roger and I were talking guy stuff, you know. And Roger said it was a great ass to touch, and I agreed and we talked about it."

"But not with any of the other guys?" Turner asked.

"No."

"Nobody was smitten with her?" Turner asked.

"We didn't get smitten a lot. We had a lot of choices of girls. Murial was good to us, not a lover."

"Do you remember Jeremiah Boissec?"

"Sure. Jerry was pretty okay. He was the one who finally put us all together as a group. He believed in us before anybody else. He'd come to our gigs before we were under contract. When no one else would come, he'd be there. Danny and I sang in a bar in Temecula, California one night. Three people showed up, and Jerry. That was about the lowest. He was loyal from the first. He worked hard to get us bookings. One time we played some bar in Blythe, California for a week. We filled the place. It was our first success. He was there every night. He got canned. He still around?"

Fenwick said, "He said he thought maybe Jordan Pastern was getting it on with guys in the group."

"Jordan? Nah. He never came on to me. Nobody ever said anything about him doing it with them. He's got a wife and a couple kids. They live in the Valley. He's always been good to us."

"None of you discussed doing it with Mr. Zawicki," Turner pointed out.

"Yeah, but that was perverted. Jordan was just a nice guy. Even when one of us got a little out of line, he was always nice. He never yelled. He never tried to hurt anybody."

"Did someone else try to hurt you?"

"No, I guess I meant he didn't try to be mean. He didn't have a big ego like the rest of us. I don't think he'd hurt me, but I don't trust any of them anymore. Where am I going to stay?"

"Galyak might have told and Pastern might have guessed."

"I told Jordan I was going to the police, but not here."

"They're not stupid. They know Dexter came to my house."

Mrs. Talucci said, "He can stay here. I'll call someone and

have the house watched. He'll be perfectly safe. You both need sleep." Mrs. Talucci's powers in the neighborhood were legendary. No one ever knew if she had some mob connections from her life back seventy or eighty years ago, or if her husband had been important to the mob, or if she was just a revered old lady, or if there was some other secret to her powers. Turner never asked. Mrs. Talucci never told. For whatever reason, whenever Mrs. Talucci said something would be so, it was so.

"Can I stay here?" Pappas asked.

The boy was still a suspect in a murder investigation. Turner didn't want to leave him here without guards present. Even with Mrs. Talucci's grandnieces armed with shotguns and her legendary neighborhood prowess, he wasn't eager to leave Ivan alone with them.

Mrs. Talucci said, "You think I didn't check him as thoroughly as I did the Clendenen boy?"

Paul said, "I know you did."

Turner called the commander and okayed the operation. He arranged to have a patrol car out front. Mrs. Talucci patted his arm when he told her this. "That's all right, dear. They won't be in the way. Tell them not to park directly in front of either of our houses. We don't want them to draw attention to us."

He knew Mrs. Talucci. She'd be out with little care packages of cookies and cakes and other goodies. At the least hot chocolate or hot coffee in this weather.

Turner trudged home. It was nearly one in the afternoon. He slept.

20

Loud banging on his front door woke Paul out of a deep sleep. He leapt out of bed. He threw on some shoes, jeans, and a sweatshirt and hurried downstairs. Brian would be at practice until six. Jeff had a chess club meeting until five and would, in the normal course of events, stop at Mrs. Talucci's. Ben would be at his auto shop until after seven. The bitter cold seeped through the storm door. A hatless man in a winter overcoat had Blundlefitz in an arm lock.

The man said, "This guy was lurking outside. He's not supposed to be."

"Thanks," Turner said. "Come in," he said to Blundlefitz.

"You want me to stay?" the young man asked.

"No." Paul thought he recognized the man from church. Maybe he read at the lectern once in a while. Did mob thugs go to church? Turner supposed they could if they wanted to. He let Blundlefitz go and the reporter entered.

Blundlefitz was pissed. He stomped his feet on the entryway rug. "What is the meaning of this? I am not to be manhandled." He shrugged his shoulders, pulled on his sleeves, and twisted his neck.

"Neighborhood watch," Turner said. He shut the door and led the reporter into the living room.

"Neighborhood bullshit. That was some mob hit man. He was strong. He tried to hurt me."

Turner smiled. He did not offer Blundlefitz a seat. "What do you want?"

"We know one of the guys in the band is here."

"And what would you like me to do with that piece of information?"

"He needs to be back at the hotel."

"And they sent you to rescue him?"

"When we found out he was gone, a search was started. I talked to Dexter. I know about you and your neighbor."

"You took a guess. You in fact don't know where he is."

"If he was gone, you'd be out looking for him. A third member of the band missing? You wouldn't be getting any sleep."

"What is it with you?" Turner asked. "You're more a caricature than a person. Why don't you ask sensible questions? You're at my house. Why not ask what's the latest I have on the murders? Why not ask if I know one of the guys in the band is missing? Why be aggressive to start with?"

"You guys fucked with me the other night. You're the enemy."

"I always try to get along with the press," Turner said.

"You're not going to get a free ride from me."

"See?" Turner said. "You're hostile again and you're resorting to clichés. Do you write the same way?"

"Who are you to criticize?"

"There aren't good critics and bad critics and standards by which they can be judged?"

222

"I'm going to solve this murder. You are all going to look like fools."

"Do you take pointless aggression lessons?" Turner asked.

"If he's not here, I know he's next door. If you don't cooperate with me, I'll tell the world where he is. I'll have CNN out front and half the teenagers in the city camped out on the streets around here."

"And what good will that do?" Turner asked. "How will that help you or the police solve the murder? It might make you feel better to put the boy in danger, but why do that? Who does that help?"

Blundlefitz actually paused at this and looked thoughtful.

Turner said, "My question is, why are you sucking up to Zawicki? We heard you got a nice deal on access, but why sell out? He can't have that much power in Chicago. Why would he even care what kind of access you have? What's in it for him to have you on his side?"

"You sound as snide as your partner."

"I'm just asking questions. This doesn't add up. Only if you're an egotistical moron who has abandoned all common sense."

"I want what's best for the remaining members of the band."

"Who Zawicki's people have been unable to protect. It isn't the fault of the police that there have been two deaths and that one of the remaining members of the band has had a breakdown."

"Why did Dexter come here in the first place?"

"I suspect he thought he might be safe here. Have you asked yourself the question, why he wouldn't feel safe with Zawicki's people? They've got security. They've got people he's used to. Why would he come to strangers?"

"The kid's confused."

"Give it a little more thought. Don't you think something is odd here?"

"Yeah. You're gay and you've got these hot young men coming to the house. Maybe you're trying to get into their pants."

"I didn't steal their underwear."

The doorbell rang. The young man Turner had seen with Blundlefitz and another who could have been his twin flanked Mrs. Talucci. She smiled at Paul and said, "These young men would like to talk to Mr. Randall Blundlefitz." The three of them entered the house.

Turner smiled. "I'm not sure he'll want to go with them."

"They can be very convincing."

Blundlefitz joined Turner in the entryway. "Hey. What is this?"

"The neighborhood watch," said the young man who'd brought Blundlefitz to the door. "We need to talk."

"I'm not going anywhere with them." Silence from the young men. They might have been itinerant preachers come to the house, except they looked far more muscular than your average doorbell ringer. Turner presumed there were weapons under those heavy coats.

"I'll call the police," Blundlefitz said.

"I am the police," Turner said.

Blundlefitz looked at the four of them. "Is this a joke?" he asked.

"I don't hear anyone laughing," Turner said. After letting silence build for a while, Turner said, "I would go with them quietly. You'll be fine. What harm could come from two such fine young men who arrived here accompanying a sweet little old lady?"

"Have you seen one of those?" Mrs. Talucci asked. She

and Paul laughed. Blundlefitz and the young men didn't seem amused.

"You'll be safe," Paul said. "You can talk in the kitchen. If something goes wrong, shout."

The two men surrounded Blundlefitz and led him into the back of the house.

"How's the kid?" Paul asked.

"He took a little nap then ate some white chocolate gelato. I've got Arabella at the front door with a shotgun. Arabella likes that gun all too much. One of the other girls is at the back door." She hooked a thumb toward the kitchen. "I didn't want a hassle from this fool. *Hot Trends* magazine, ha! What a joke. Blundlefitz hasn't written a sensible review ever."

"You read rock reviews in *Hot Trends* magazine?"

"Of course. Why not?" She gave his arm a grandmotherly pat. "Even you need to be reminded at times that I'm not nearly dead yet."

Blundlefitz and his escort were gone less than five minutes. When they returned, Blundlefitz said, "Fine. Intimidate the press. Your career is over, Detective Turner."

He marched out of the house.

The first young man said, "He won't be back to the neighborhood. I didn't have instructions about making him leave you alone."

"It's fine," Paul said. "I'll handle him if I have to."

The two of them left. Mrs. Talucci said, "You haven't had enough sleep."

"No, and I'm not going to for a while. This case has got to get solved."

"Has to be someone in the entourage or one of the members of the band," Mrs. Talucci said. "How can it not be?"

Paul agreed with her. Mrs. Talucci left. Paul called Fenwick. Madge said, "He's been up for half an hour. He's going in early tonight. Are you and Ben still coming to dinner next Sunday?"

"Yes."

Fenwick picked up the phone. Turner told him about Blundlefitz's visit.

"We gotta talk to Zawicki," Fenwick said. "Let's get him and his lawyers back down to the commander's office."

Turner called Molton and told him about Blundlefitz's visit and their plan to talk to Zawicki again. Molton said, "I just had a press conference. I've got several more meetings, but I agree. Zawicki's got to answer some questions."

Paul stopped next door. Jeff was ensconced in front of Mrs. Talucci's computer along with Ivan Pappas. Jeff was showing him a trick he had learned with a PowerPoint presentation. Paul hugged his son. Made sure Pappas was secure for the moment. He drove to Ben's garage. The evening customers were in picking up their cars after the day's work. Ben kissed Paul hello. They didn't wait to hide their kiss in Ben's private office. Ben owned the shop. He worked on more exotic cars than anyone in town. His shop had the reputation as the best in the city.

"I'm going in early," Paul told him.

"I'll take care of the boys."

"Thanks. There's another guest at Mrs. Talucci's. I think he needs to stay there. She's got friends keeping watch. I've got a patrol car out front."

"You think he's a killer?"

"I don't know. Mrs. Talucci's got her private army on guard so I'm not worried about her."

After telling Ben he loved him and Ben repeating the same back to him, he left.

Turner spent the first hour he was at work looking at the video of the concert. He got no indication of a gun being fired or anything being wrong. The members of the band sang, danced, chatted with the audience, and each other. They seemed to be happy and energetic. Certainly no indication of murder was present. No one in the audience had come forth with a tape.

Commander Molton surveyed the large conference room. There were fifteen chairs. Jonathan Zawicki and two lawyers stood at the far end away from the cops.

Molton said, "I like it when we round up all the suspects. I've always wanted to dramatically reveal who did it in front of an audience."

"You never have?" Fenwick asked.

"Nobody else I know outside a Hollywood studio does that very much."

"I do it all the time," Fenwick said. "You should stick with me."

"Glamour and glory, Buck Fenwick's stock in trade along with stupid jokes."

"Hey, I've been getting better, although what I should do when this whole crowd gets here is tell them the story of Doris and Sam, the two clams."

"No," Turner and Molton said simultaneously. Turner continued, "We want them sane. That would be cruel and unusual punishment. I've heard you tell it six times."

"Five."

"Six. I keep very accurate count. You always leave out the first time."

The room was now nearly filled. Present were Jordan Pastern, Ralph Eudace, Aaron Davis, Danny Galyak, Ethel Hinkmeyer, Frances Strikal, Murial Arane, and Sherri Haupmin. Blundlefitz had been summoned but had not arrived. A phalanx of cops had helped all of them run the gauntlet of the press crammed into the first floor of the station.

When Dexter entered the room, Turner walked up to him

and put his hand on the boy's elbow. Dexter pulled his arm away as if he'd been scorched. "Get away from me," he hissed. The lawyers rushed to his side. Turner retreated.

"What the hell was that all about?" Fenwick asked.

"He's whacked," Turner said.

Zawicki said, "What are we waiting for? Let's get started." Everybody who wasn't a cop immediately sat down. Zawicki looked at the three police officials. "What?" he demanded.

Molton said, "We were hoping Randall Blundlefitz would join us."

"Who cares?" Zawicki said. "We have places to be."

Molton said, "Thank you all for coming. I'll want my detectives to take over the questioning."

Zawicki said, "I hope we're going to get some answers. It's been nearly forty-eight hours since the first murder. Someone must know something."

Molton said, "No one's going to know anything more unless you shut up."

Turner and Fenwick had seldom heard Molton be this sharp with a member of the public. Molton had long since perfected the administrator's art of placating civilians without giving out valuable information. Molton said, "Mr. Zawicki, we're trying to solve the murders. The more speeches you make, the longer we're going to be here. It would help if you would let the detectives go about their business."

Turner said, "As far as we can tell so far, many of you had some secrets. Ms. Arane and Mr. Zawicki had sex with each of the members of the band."

"I'll have you sued for slander," Zawicki said. He pointed at Arane. "You're fired."

"You need me more than I need you," Arane snapped.

Turner continued, "Ms. Haupmin was having sex with more than just Roger."

Haupmin glared at Zawicki. "You can't fire me."

Turner said, "Mr. Pastern, did you have any relations with these boys?"

"I did not. Who told you such a thing? I've tried to be cooperative. How can you ask such a thing? I've got a wife and kids."

"We check out everything we're told. We ask," Turner said. "We got a rumor. I checked with you. The answer is no. I've appreciated all your help. We can't stop asking questions of all the people who are helpful."

"I don't like it. I guess." He subsided.

"Mr. Zawicki," Turner said. "The main thing I don't understand about you is why all the lawyers? We're all trying to solve the murder. You insist on having lawyers present when the police are asking questions, yet you give a reporter from a small local magazine total access. Why?"

Zawicki said, "It's good to have the press on your side. You've just mentioned sex several times. Are you saying that sex is at the heart of solving the mystery? Roger's murder took place in the locker room, where he was not having sex. Jason was murdered out in the cold where it was unlikely he was having sex."

"We're trying to find out the dynamics of all these relationships," Turner said. "A killer could be trying to murder everyone in the band. The most logical reason would be to get back at you. Kill the band and you lose a source of income, but you've already pointed out that you're going to make millions from these deaths. How does anyone else benefit? Someone with a secret? If so, what secret? What knowledge were these two harboring that led to their demise? Does someone else have the same information? If so, are they in danger?" Turner spoke directly to Pastern. "Mr. Pastern, you knew Ivan wanted to leave. You let him go."

"I didn't *let* him. I told him I'd go with him to the police if he just waited. We figured he went to you, but we couldn't get an answer at your place. We didn't leave a message on the machine. We didn't know where you were. Dexter told us about the neighbor lady, but we got absolutely no information there. Everything I've done so far has not worked for protecting these boys. We made it through six months of touring in seventeen different countries and it comes to this. In forty-eight hours, it's all gone. I will miss those boys."

Turner asked Zawicki, "When were you going to report to the police the threats these guys received early this morning?"

"I didn't know about them until Danny told me. I had everybody in. I questioned all of them. Before the notes appeared, I had a lot of people in that suite. People were back and forth through interconnecting doors to my room and half the damn floor for all I know. Once you're in the suite, things aren't locked. We didn't think we had to."

Turner said, "Either the killer was in the suite with the rest of you, or someone is playing a very sick joke."

"None of us is a killer," Zawicki said.

Eudace doing his best as Greek chorus said, "We're still quite worried about the role of the police in all this."

Hinkmeyer said, "It's almost as bad to think one of us is capable of placing such a note in their belongings. None of the guys are going to be safe until this thing is solved. Can't you do something?"

Turner and Fenwick went through the chart of who was where when. For nearly an hour they checked statements. They got varying degrees of hostility, but no one refused to cooperate. The lawyers offered few objections. When they were finished, everyone present had given some sort of alibi. Some were less perfect than others. The detectives hadn't pinned down a time for Jason's murder exactly, but anyone of them could have committed one or the other murders. No one could have done both murders—at least according to the stories they'd told.

As everyone was preparing to leave, Dexter Clendenen stood up. He said, "More people are going to die." Then he collapsed. Turner rushed to him. The kid was breathing hard. Turner didn't think the kid had banged his head on the way down. He couldn't revive him.

⌐ 21 ⌐

The crowd had been gone for about an hour. Dex had been taken under police guard to a hospital. Turner and Fenwick had spent most of the time since they'd left catching up on the paperwork involved in the case.

In the report from the evidence techs they saw that there were no fingerprints on the gun in the locker room. The underwear from Blundlefitz had cum stains presumably produced by the original owner. The pills were for pain. Turner called Pastern. The security man told them that Roger had twisted his ankle and gone to the doctor. He only took a few of the pills, felt better, didn't take the rest, and just never got rid of any extras. Turner confirmed that one prescription was for thirty pills and there were twenty-seven left in the container. The other was for twenty-five with ten left. "Why'd he have two prescriptions?" Turner asked.

"The first one didn't have much of an effect."

A quick perusal of the rest of the reports showed no further help from the evidence techs. They had Devane's phone records. He'd called his parents the night of the murder and no one else.

The photos from Blundlefitz's one-time-use camera had been developed. They showed the bed in each room. All completely made. The suitcases, bed stands, and closets were featured in others. Nothing struck Turner as a clue.

Hinkmeyer had sent over a list of stalkers and crazed fans. None were known to reside in the Chicago area. There was no evidence that any of them had been in town.

They had the lab results from the water bottles. The one with the incorrect label had a small quantity of bleach in it and no fingerprints on the outside.

Turner called the lab. "Would the amount of bleach in it have been enough to kill someone?"

"It wasn't much. I'd want to get the victim medical attention, but they probably wouldn't die."

"How about a delayed reaction that would make him suicidal?"

"Never heard of bleach causing that."

"How about something else in it that could cause that?"

"Haven't found anything. Don't think there was. I'll perform a few more tests to be sure."

The report on the currents in Monroe harbor confirmed his supposition. The wind had been blowing so strong that it was the likely reason that the body had shown up on the east shore of the lake. The currents in the harbor were minimal because it was sheltered.

Another report from the beat cops who worked the pier said no one on the boats or the pier reported seeing anything suspicious. With the cold there hadn't been a lot of people out strolling.

Turner called the ME who said, "Gunshot killed him. Dead before he was in the water. At the most fifteen minutes between when he got hit and when he was dumped in the lake. Your boy was also anally penetrated within an hour of his death. Got no semen, but a violated rectum."

"You got an approximate time of death?"

"Anywhere from six to nine hours before you found him."

Turner gave Fenwick the news then called his friend Ian. The reporter said, "I cannot get a lick of information. The recording industry is not my milieu. I talked to Mickey Pendyce again. He can't get anybody to talk. Your buddy Zawicki has true power and these people are afraid."

Molton arrived at their desks. He said, "These people are going to have to be allowed to leave town eventually. We cannot hold them here forever."

"One of them is a killer," Fenwick said.

"You're sure?" Molton asked.

"We got no indication that it's somebody outside the entourage."

"Any luck on the gun?" Molton asked.

Fenwick pointed to a stack of reports. "The bullets came from the same gun. There are several zillion of the same caliber in the metropolitan area. Not much help there yet."

Dan O'Leary called from downstairs. "You'd better hurry. You've got another dead one at the All-Chicago Sports Arena."

"Another band member?" Turner asked.

"Nope, that reporter with the stupid name, Blundlefitz."

Turner and Fenwick rushed over. Beat cops met them at the main entrance. The cold held strong as did the vigil outside. The television crews trained their cameras on Turner and Fenwick. Most reporters now recognized them instantly. Fame peripheral to the rich and famous.

"Are there developments in the case?" several of them called from out in the cold. Turner and Fenwick hurried past them without making any comments.

McWilliams led them inside and through the concrete entryway to the center of the arena. The vast interior felt colder than before. All the abilities of man gathered together to make a modern cavern that provided little warmth without forty thousand people in it. All the lights had been turned on. The elaborate set remained in place. Blundlefitz knelt in the center of the stage. A rope tied around his waist led to the highest platform. Turner and Fenwick approached carefully and walked around the body. A small pool of blood surrounded Blundlefitz. His winter coat, which was still buttoned all the way up the front, had dark stains on the back. His head bent forward at the neck. The rope held him up. There was a bullet hole in the back of his head.

"Execution style," Turner said, "like the others. We've got one killer, and he or she is very systematic."

Fenwick asked, "Why Blundlefitz? He's not a member of the band."

"Most logical deduction," Turner said, "is that he was investigating and he was getting close to the killer, knew too much, and had to die." He paused.

"Or he was a moronic asshole and there was a whole line of people ready to kill him in a grotesque way. Start with every band member he's ever savaged and work up from there."

"Want to bet our boy Blundlefitz did not get screwed?" Fenwick asked.

"His clothes weren't disarranged. The ME can tell us for sure."

"Who found the body?" Fenwick asked.

Two members of the permanent crew looked pale and shaken. Both claimed they'd simply been checking for anything small enough to move without the union crew. They vouched for each other.

"Where's his notebook?" Turner asked. He put on his plastic gloves then carefully inched open Blundlefitz's lapel. He reached into the inside pocket and took out a pad of paper. All the pages were blank. He showed it to Fenwick. "Pages have been torn out."

The ME and the evidence techs showed up. They got together with the detectives after they finished their work.

The ME said, "Hasn't been dead long. The blood isn't dry. It's cool in here. He bled a lot so it would take a while to congeal."

"Shot here?"

"No sign that he was dragged. No blood spatters. No prints in the blood. No smearing. All those heavy clothes caught most of it. The backs of his sweater, shirt, T-shirt, long winter underwear, coat, and ass of his pants are damp."

"Anybody else's blood?"

"Not that we can see."

"Shot first or tied up first?"

The evidence tech said, "Shot on the spot. Probably didn't know the killer was behind him. Wasn't hit from up close, but I can't tell from exactly how far away."

"He wouldn't turn his back on a killer."

"Not if he knew he was there."

"Must have been sneaking up."

"A meeting?"

"Why meet a killer here?" Fenwick asked.

"Why meet with someone you think is a killer anywhere?" Turner asked.

"He was out for glory," Fenwick said. "He was going to solve this himself."

"All the suspects were with us until two hours ago," Turner said. "The killer could have left that meeting and have had plenty of time to get over here and do this. Or he had just committed another murder and sat calmly through that meeting."

The ME said, "I'll get you an approximate time of death as soon as I can."

"Why tie him up?" Fenwick asked.

"Dramatic effect?" Turner asked.

Fenwick said, "The killer had time or was sending someone a message or the killer is a raving loon or the killer had some extra rope and was practicing knots."

"Jesus," the ME said, "cop banter. Everybody hates it but you."

"I live for cop banter," Fenwick averred. "I think it's funny."

The ME said, "Not to me and most of the rest of us."

Turner and Fenwick inspected the immediate area of the killing. Beat cops were detailed to examine the rest of the interior. The detectives didn't hold out much hope that they would find anything. They took their time climbing the platform to the other end of the rope. None of the janitors or guards on duty had seen or heard anything. One of them said that he had noticed various strands of rope lying about. Several beat cops were dispatched to talk to members of the crowd to see if anyone had seen people entering or leaving the building. They got a preliminary report back before they left that no one had.

"How'd Blundlefitz and his killer get in and out with the security?" Fenwick asked.

Aaron Davis the equipment manager, Pastern, Hinkmeyer, and Eudace had joined them. Davis said, "Almost everybody in the band crew was here earlier. No one wanted to be left alone. Paranoia has gotten the better of us. A huge clump of people connected with the band tromped over here before the meeting at the police station. Many stayed while your meeting went on. A few came back after. They finally had permission to start boxing things up. They were starting with all the stuff in the locker room, lots of personal things. It takes a while to pack up one hundred eleven semi-trailer trucks. The union guys from the arena would dismantle the stage tomorrow morning. There was no need for anybody to come up here. They had lots of stuff to get."

Pastern said, "As long as the guys were protected, I didn't care who was in here."

Hinkmeyer said, "Mr. Blundlefitz had permission to be here."

Pastern said, "I wasn't supposed to be guarding Blundlefitz. I had no responsibility for him. I didn't even know he was here. I was guarding the guys."

None of them and no other members of the entourage admitted to seeing Blundlefitz. None of them had heard a shot. Zawicki and other members of the inner circle were beginning to appear in large numbers as the detectives prepared to leave. Zawicki, Pastern, et al. claimed they had alibis. In the presence of lawyers the detectives took statements from the major players, then set the uniformed cops to interview the others.

Turner and Fenwick visited stadium security. Frances Strikal, the stadium representative was present.

"How can this happen?" Strikal demanded.

The nameplate on the uniformed guard read SMITH. He was old, grizzled, but alert. "How the hell should I know?" Smith said. "They told me to let the band in to begin taking things down. There were a million people in here. There were all kinds of people on these screens." He pointed to the numerous monitors. "The band people were supposed to have their own security. I don't know who all of them are. Talk to them. I didn't see or hear anything. There's no camera on the main stage. We watch entrances and exits. We've got one on every hallway." He pointed to the rows and rows of monitors.

Turner examined the picture on each of them. Several

were pointed at the crowd outside. "Can somebody get in here without being seen?"

"Not possible."

Turner asked, "Where's the picture of the special parking for athletes and performers?"

"We don't need a security camera for that entrance. They have their own security. No one can get in there except the performers. They have a special code."

They took Blundlefitz's address from his driver's license and drove over.

Blundlefitz lived in the middle of the block across from the Salvation Army Headquarters on the first street south of Addison. He owned an entire house. As Turner and Fenwick experimented with the keys they'd taken from Blundlefitz's pocket, a man got out of a car parked near the intersection and hurried toward them. It was Ned Lummy, the reporter from *Hot Trends* magazine. He rushed up the stairs.

"What's going on?" Lummy asked.

"What are you doing here?" Fenwick asked.

"I got a call from Blundlefitz early this evening. He told me to meet him here at midnight."

"Did he say why?" Turner asked.

"Nope."

"He make that kind of request often?"

"No."

"Why honor it?"

"Rolt called. He's supposed to be here, too."

"Exactly what time did he call?" Turner asked.

"About six."

"You need to wait in your car," Fenwick said.

"Is something wrong?" Lummy asked.

"Blundlefitz is dead," Fenwick said.

"What?"

"Shot at the All-Chicago Sports Arena."

"Another killing? What is going on?"

"If you could wait in your car," Turner said. "We'd like to talk to you in a little while."

Lummy retreated to his vehicle.

They entered the house. Once out of the cold, Turner said, "My guess is Blundlefitz was going to have a planning meeting. He knew who the killer was or thought he did."

"What he knew or thought he knew got him killed," Fenwick said. "There's no point in the whole arena scenario unless it's connected to these killings."

"I don't know, killing a critic in and of itself might not be seen as a bad thing. My guess is he's got a whole lot of enemies who'd be happy to see him dead."

"Great, a list of all the enemies a critic has. I'm not in the mood to write a phone book."

"Blundlefitz disliked all the boy bands," Turner said. "I wonder if that was an honest appraisal, or he was getting even for something."

"Or he was just a jerk."

"Always possible."

Fenwick asked, "If he hated boy bands, why steal those guys' underwear?"

"Pappas or Galyak said he was a perv. Maybe he had a thing for underwear. I bet there are lots of people gay and straight who are into underwear and who aren't pervs."

Fenwick said, "I prefer equal opportunity sexual dysfunction."

"Why?" Turner asked.

"I get to dislike more people that way."

The downstairs of the house had a large entryway, steps on the right leading up to the second floor. A hall straight

241

ahead led to a kitchen. An opening to the left revealed a living room with a dining room behind it. The downstairs was clean and spartan: a pricey antique vase in one corner of the living room, brass pole lamps in two other corners, a brown velvet couch, not much else.

The kitchen drawers and cabinets revealed kitchen drawer and cabinet stuff. The basement was unfinished with a pile of dirty clothes sitting in a hamper next to a washer and a dryer that looked less than a year old. They found boxes of old mementoes stacked against one wall. They inspected several.

In one they found yearbooks from high school and junior high. Turner flipped the pages of several of these. "Funny," he said.

"What?"

"There's nothing written in these. I thought everybody had their yearbooks written in."

"Maybe he was unpopular as a kid. Wouldn't come as a surprise to me."

"Maybe he became a critic to get even with the world."

They found box after box of Blundlefitz's own columns; the entire newspaper on the day something of his appeared with the clipping of the day's article encased in plastic on top of it. Upstairs they examined a bedroom cramped because of the king-size bed that dominated it, a walk-in closet with clothes neatly lined up, and an office.

"Just what I was looking for," Fenwick said. "A room of a dead person's soon to be oozing clues."

Fenwick started with the file drawers. Turner switched on the computer. He hit the MY DOCUMENTS icon and got hundreds of articles listed by title and date. He found the most recent ones: reviews of numerous bands, groups, and solo acts. Each article had a listing under a title. The same title was also listed with the letter N after it, listed again with the letter F after it, and a fourth time with the title and a letter R. After calling up only a few files, Turner realized the N must mean notes for the article, F for future things to go into the article, and the R for research for an article. In the few lettered categories Turner looked into he found extensive material. Whatever his strengths or weaknesses as a critic might have been, Blundlefitz certainly did his homework. In one file Turner found articles about a group that was coming to Chicago. He found tour dates and corresponding articles or reviews from each city the band had performed in. He checked Blundlefitz's reviews against a few of the others. Turner wondered if perhaps Blundlefitz might have plagiarized other critics. A few minutes' perusal revealed no hint of such a thing. Positive or negative, in Blundlefitz's reviews hardly an adjective existed without a superlative ending. His ability to find the smallest fault and make it a major failing seemed uncanny. Generally he packed his venom into the space of one or two paragraphs for any given group. Turner could examine more of these at his leisure, but Blundlefitz sure looked like the queen of the hatchet job. Turner wasn't familiar with rock or many other kinds of critics around the country, but a great many of Blundlefitz's remarks that Turner glanced at seemed gratuitously cruel.

Turner checked all the information he'd gotten on Boys4u. He discovered a vast array of information that Turner suspected a teenage girl might love, but which had no interest for him. Blundlefitz had pictures and complete files on all of the band members.

In separate files they also found extensive notes with backgrounds on all the major players: Zawicki, Pastern, Ralph Eudace, Aaron Davis, Ethel Hinkmeyer, Frances Strikal, Murial Arane, and Sherri Haupmin.

Turner found a blank disk and downloaded the file and then printed out two copies of the entire thing. He and Fenwick sat and read the bios.

"Most of these people wanted to be in bands," Turner said when they finished. "None of them had any success, which bears out the idea that most bands don't make it. I think I knew that before somebody explained it to me. I don't see anything in these backgrounds that would make any of them a murderer. Although Pastern and Eudace were in a band named Damn Skippy in college."

"Is that one that Zawicki turned down?" Fenwick asked.

"Let's ask. If it is, did Eudace or Pastern refuse to put out for Zawicki?"

"Could Blundlefitz have killed the two band members?" Fenwick asked.

"If so, he was investigating himself. It would take a very self-possessed killer to be playing that game."

"When's the last entry?"

"Six in the morning today." He glanced at his watch. "Yesterday now. If he found something from six A.M. until he was killed, he never recorded it."

After checking all the files that looked promising, Turner announced, "I think this is all we're going to be able to find. We can get the computer guys down here to go over this in case there's something hidden."

"No porn," Fenwick said. "No tapes. No magazines. No hidden underwear souvenirs. I always get disappointed when there's no porn involved in a dead person's life."

"You keeping a list?"

"No. Just hoping for something salacious. You figured if he kept underwear, we'd find some more of those kinds of things."

Turner said, "Maybe he didn't really plan to take the kid's stuff. Maybe it was just an impulse."

244

"Or maybe he was a fucking moron."

Fenwick knelt down over the last file cabinet drawer and reached far in back. "I got something." He pulled out a thick, pink notebook. Fenwick flipped it open. "It's Dexter's diary." The two of them clustered around it.

The doorbell rang.

▴22▴

Turner stuffed the diary into his regulation blue notebook and followed Fenwick downstairs. Rolt and Lummy were at the door. The detectives let them in. Everybody sat down in the living room.

Turner said, "We understood you both got phone calls tonight."

"Yes," Rolt said. "Randall called just after six. He said we had to talk. He said to meet him here at midnight. He wouldn't tell me what it was about."

"Me, neither," Lummy said.

"I can understand why he'd want Mr. Rolt here," Fenwick said, "but why Mr. Lummy as well?"

"I don't know," Lummy said. "Maybe because I'm the only permanent reporter on staff, just like he's the only permanent reviewer on staff."

Rolt said, "Sometimes he craved an audience. He liked to show off."

"Did he say he'd found the killer?"

"No," Rolt said, "just that we had to be here, that it was important news."

Fenwick asked, "And you just showed up when he summoned you to his home late at night? Had he done this before?"

"Well, no," Rolt said. "He did say it had something to do with the murders, but he didn't say if he knew who the killer was. I asked what was going on. He said our reputations were going to be made."

"How come you got down here an hour after Mr. Lummy?"

"On my way here, I got a call on my cell phone from a reporter at the All-Chicago Sports Arena. Word was out that they found his body. I hurried there, but I couldn't find out a thing. Ned called me on my cell phone and said you were both here so I came by."

They heard a commotion in the street. Vans from two local television networks pulled up outside.

"Great," Fenwick said. "More circuses."

Rolt said, "You're only going to get more of that until you solve this."

"How could he afford this place?" Fenwick asked.

"He wasn't being paid by the music industry, if that's what you're implying," Rolt said.

"Just asking a question," Fenwick said.

"He was cheap," Lummy said. "If you went out for drinks, he'd ask for water. If you were out for lunch, he'd order the smallest, least expensive thing on the menu. If you were out in a group, he was the one who always underpaid. I can't tell you how many times he said 'I only had a salad so I don't owe as much.' "

"That's nickel and dime stuff," Fenwick said. "This place is probably worth half a million. How could he afford this place on the salary at a two-bit magazine?"

"We are not two-bit," Rolt said. "We make a very handsome profit. We sell plenty of ads. Blundlefitz was part owner, a minority shareholder. He was also a freelancer. He wrote many articles. He's had more articles in the *Trib* magazine section than any other author for the past three years. He's had numerous articles in the *New York Times* and other prestigious media outlets. He may have been frugal, but I think that was from habit."

"Who were his enemies?" Fenwick asked.

"He got bluster from bands he didn't like. No personal enemies."

"His reviews didn't sound impersonal."

"I'm sure you can check to see if any of the members of any of the groups he gave rotten reviews to are in town, but really, are people going to be that angry over style?"

Fenwick said, "You never know."

"Every critic has people who dislike them," Rolt said. "You don't become enemies over a review. There are no permanent animosities."

"I wonder if the people who have been savaged feel as magnanimous as you just put it," Turner said. "I bet there's lots of hurt egos and desire to get revenge."

"Everybody's got an ego," Rolt said, "but everybody understands how the game is played."

Turner said, "Tromping on someone's dreams could be devastating. I read a few things of Mr. Blundlefitz's. I'd say he did a lot of trampling."

"His criticism was on the cutting edge."

"What the hell does that mean?" Fenwick asked. "He wrote criticism differently from anyone else in history? Did he reverse the order of syllables in words he was using? What?"

"Detective, you've given public performances for which you've been criticized," Rolt said.

Fenwick ignored the insight. "Anybody specific recently

that he pissed off? Or maybe someone who called to complain?"

"No one. Randall was a professional. He knew the rules. In this case he was after a story. He thought he could bring justice to the case."

"He was getting justice from Jonathan Zawicki?" Turner asked.

"He was getting respect from Jonathan Zawicki. He was treated well."

"I'll have to find out who gave him sucking-up lessons," Fenwick said. "I'll take the class."

"Why was respect from Zawicki so important?" Turner asked.

"Randall was kind of a mess. He needed the approval he never got."

"He could have given reams of approval," Fenwick said.

"He felt the need to be honest," Rolt said.

Fenwick said, "There's a difference between honesty and savagery."

Turner said, "He said nothing to either of you about why he wanted to see you?"

Head shakes no. Rolt and Lummy left.

Before Turner and Fenwick headed out they examined Dexter Clendenen's diary.

"How'd Blundlefitz get this?" Turner asked.

"He had more access than anyone."

The diary was hand-written in pencil, different colored pens, markers, and at times in what looked like lipstick.

The handwriting was blocky and childish. Turner noted that spelling had obviously not been Clendenen's strong point. Some entries were dated. Others were not. A great deal of it was nearly illiterate drivel about places he'd seen in new cities and itemized lists of everything that was in their hotel rooms.

Interspersed throughout Clendenen had detailed all the times he'd had sex. The diary mixed pornography and banality. He wrote about sex with guys with an emphasis on how big or long a guy's dick had been and how he'd always tried to find bigger and longer guys. At least half the entries didn't mention any name. He also detailed the first time he was screwed by each member of the band and by Zawicki. Either he didn't include all the other times or he'd been done once by Galyak, Devane, Pappas, and numerous times by Roger Stendar. Nowhere did he talk about enjoying what was happening to him during sex. A scientific accounting rather than a pleasure diary.

Clendenen penned occasional entries about wanting to be hugged and held, that he enjoyed the times most when Roger would hold him. The detectives didn't recognize most of the names in the diary. Clendenen had obviously found as many guys in different cities as the others had found women.

At various intervals he talked about growing up. This section was heavily laced with sexual adventures which included sucking off the quarterback of the high school football team. Dexter listed among his conquests numerous movie stars, or people who he claimed were movie stars and listed them only by their first names, such as Tom. Tom Cruise who spent his life denying he was gay? Tom Hanks? Tom Thumb? Tom Postern? Had to be a lot of actors in Hollywood named Tom.

"Size mattered," Turner said, "at least to him."

Also included was a long string of complaints against both parents. These ranged from allegations of indifference to accusations of physical abuse. They found a long list of reports relating incidents of being picked on—from memories of kindergarten to violence on his last day of high school. Nothing indicated who might have wanted to kill the members of the band.

Turner and Fenwick drove to the offices of *Hot Trends* magazine. Rolt let them in. Blundlefitz's office was neater than an anal retentive's who had swallowed an entire bottle of speed. They checked his computer. Turner scanned a number of the files. They seemed to match what the reporter had at home. It looked like Blundlefitz kept back-ups of all his work. His hard-copy files had every article he had ever written in chronological, alphabetical, and subject order. On the computer there were duplicates of all these.

"Man had a system and he kept up," Fenwick said. "I hate that. And that is not cop banter. That's only a sarcastic crack."

"What makes it banter?" Turner asked.

"You have to play the straight man."

"A role for which I am not well suited."

At the police's request, Rolt had summoned the other employees. It was the middle of the night, but it was the best place for the detectives to start. They got nothing from them.

Turner's pager went off. They were wanted back at the All-Chicago Sports Arena. This dispatcher didn't know who the caller was, but the message said that it was urgent.

The cavernous interior was dark. They found a security guard eating lunch in front of a bank of monitors. "Aren't you supposed to keep people out?" Fenwick asked.

"You're the cops. I knew it was you."

Fenwick said, "We got a call that we were needed here."

"I ain't heard nothing."

"Somebody from the band is in here," Turner guessed. "You better turn the lights on. We've got to look this place over."

"A whole crowd from the band was in and out of here all night. They got started on the takedown, but the union guys won't be here until morning. Rules are pretty strict. Far as I know, they took a lot of personal stuff, small stuff. Some of the band guys were here when they found that critic. With another dead body, your guys told them they had to leave all the rest of their stuff."

Turner, Fenwick, and the guard walked around the entire backstage and ground floor area. They heard their footsteps and the hum of electric fixtures, nothing else.

At center stage in the middle of the remnants of the Blundlefitz crime scene, they found a smashed and broken cell phone. Turner looked up at the high platform. "What is that?" He pointed at the tip of what looked like a yellow rag. Fenwick and the guard shrugged.

Fenwick said, "I already made that climb once. Until I lose fifty pounds, I think only one of us has to go up there and get that."

Turner began to ascend. As his foot touched the first platform, a voice called from above, "Don't come any higher."

Turner shaded his eyes from the glaring ceiling lights. "Who's there?" he called.

Dexter Clendenen's face appeared over the edge of the highest platform. He held a yellow T-shirt emblazoned with the band's logo. "Don't come up here."

Turner forbore ascending further. He called up. "Dexter, what's going on?"

"I'm going to jump. I'm going to splatter myself on center stage."

"Why?" Turner asked.

"It's my only option. I can't take the pain anymore."

"Did you kill the other guys in the band?"

"No."

Turner heard distant pounding on one of the doors. "Go

see who that is," Fenwick ordered. The security guard hurried away.

Turner took several steps on the platform. Whatever Dexter's motivation might be, and despite the disclaimer of a moment before, Turner wasn't eager to be up on a high platform fifty feet above the ground with a possible killer.

Dexter said nothing. He too seemed to have been distracted by the knocking.

Turner sat down on the steps leading to the next level. He felt the heat from the lights. He said, "Dexter, what pain is it that's so powerful? If you tell me, maybe I can help."

"Nobody can help me."

"There's lots of people who would like to," Turner said.

"I don't want lots of people. I wanted you. That's why I called and left the message. I knew you'd come."

"Why me?"

"You're gay. So am I."

"Being gay isn't a reason to kill yourself," Turner said.

"I know. That's not why I'm doing it."

"Then why?"

"It hurts too much to do this stuff. It takes too much. I don't have any friends. No one cares about me. Not really. You care because you're a cop assigned to this case. All those fans care because they want to be part of the life of someone famous. Nobody really listens to me. Nobody really wants me. Nobody cares if I live or die."

"I do." Dexter gazed down and Turner looked over at this new voice. Jordan Pastern stood center stage with the security guard. Pastern called, "I care, Dexter."

"You're like the others. Taking advantage."

"How'd I take advantage?" Pastern asked.

"You know."

Clendenen wrapped his body around one of the fiberglass poles which no longer had the protective strings attached. He swayed for several seconds, lost his balance, and toppled back onto the platform. Turner pelted upward. Pastern rushed for the stairs. Fenwick told the security guard to call for backup, including an ambulance, and then lumbered after the other two.

Turner got to the third level before Dexter's voice rang out, "Stop!" Turner looked up. Dexter's face appeared at the top of the stairs at the fifth level about twenty feet above him. Pastern was about ten feet below Turner.

Turner lowered his voice and spoke down to Pastern. "Do you know what this is about?"

"I can hear you," Dexter said.

"No idea," Pastern said.

"How'd you know to come here?" Turner asked.

"Yeah," Dexter said. "I didn't tell no one."

Pastern said, "I've been listening to Dexter all day. I've been worried. He kept talking about finishing everything off. I was worried that he was the killer. Everybody took cabs or vans back to the hotel. They were supposed to stay together. Dexter told me he was going with Mr. Zawicki. He lied. When we got back to the hotel, I went to check on everyone and to double the security. We ordered everybody to get permission to go anywhere. It was a madhouse. I went to look for Dexter. He was gone. The last anybody saw of him was here."

Clendenen said in a voice they could barely hear, "Zawicki is never going to fuck me again."

"You don't have to kill yourself to stop that from happening," Turner said.

"Killing myself will make him sorry for what he did," Dexter said.

Pastern said, "Jonathan Zawicki has never been sorry for anything he's done. He never will be. You know that Dexter. You've seen how he works."

"You still work for him, and you're going to be fired."

"I work for you guys. Let me come up there."

"No. You stay down. Paul can come up to the next level." Dexter sat with his feet dangling over the edge of the platform. He leaned his head over to gaze at the three adults.

The security guard reentered the hall with a small crowd of paramedics, beat cops, Dexter's parents, Zawicki, Hinkmeyer, and others Turner didn't recognize.

"Get the fuck away!" Clendenen yelled. He scrambled onto the metal strut leading from the center of the platform to the roof. Turner remembered that what appeared from a distance to be a smooth construct actually had foot- and handholds at regularly spaced intervals. Clendenen ascended about ten feet. The kid was higher up now, but if he jumped from that position, he'd almost certainly land on the fifth platform. Almost certainly landing safely wasn't good enough for Turner in this situation. The kid could easily tumble over into nothingness after his jump.

"Dexter, come down from there," called a new voice from below.

Everybody on the platforms looked down. It was Clendenen's mother who had called. His father was with her. Along with several others, she began to ascend. Clendenen responded by climbing higher onto the strut.

"I think you should stop," Turner called down.

"Why? He's my son."

Turner said, "He's climbing higher." Everybody looked up. Clendenen was now nearly fifty feet above the platform.

Pastern called up, "I care, Dexter. Please, let me come up to the top platform. Please come down."

"I want everybody but Detective Turner to leave."

"I won't go," Mrs. Clendenen said.

Dexter leaned out from the strut. He held on with one hand and one foot. He swung back and forth. "I'm not afraid of heights," he called. "Not anymore, but I don't know how much longer I want to do this. Whee!" He swung out again.

Turner said, "Let's do as he says."

Zawicki called up from below, "Everybody come down from there. The detective is right. They know how to handle this. If it's going to help bring him down, let's let him do it."

Turner wasn't surprised Zawicki hadn't rushed up with the rest of the crowd to try to save the kid. At the same time, he wished he had as much faith in his ability to save Dexter as the words indicated.

Pastern retreated, Fenwick with him. They joined the mother and the crowd. At the exit, she turned and called, "I love you, Dexter."

Finally Turner and the kid were alone. Turner climbed up to the fifth platform and sat down with his back against one of the fiberglass corner poles. Dexter's tatty brown backpack sat near the center pole. Turner removed his coat, hat, and gloves and placed them on the platform. He looked up at Dexter. The kid wore tight black jeans, white athletic socks, and black running shoes. The boy had climbed down to about twenty feet above the platform. Turner did not relish the idea of scrambling that high up to bring the boy down. He could see that Dexter was crying.

Dexter murmured, "I'm really scared." Turner saw that the kid's eyes were closed. Now he clutched the strut as if it was his only lifeline, which it was. "I don't think I can move from here."

"I can get you down," Turner said. "Or we could have some specially trained people come and help you down."

"I just want you."

"Why?"

"I liked it when you carried me."

"I can carry you again, but I'm not sure I could do it on that strut or on this platform or on the stairs down." Turner wasn't afraid of heights, but he wasn't stupid, either. Carrying a hundred-twenty-pound adult around your shoulders was not the smart way to descend from such a height. He said, "I don't want to risk dropping you. If you want me to hold you, that would be okay. I don't have to carry you for me to hold you." Turner thought the training all cops get in how to deal with possible suicides was okay. Speak softly and confidently and don't make any sudden moves. Not this high up he wasn't going to. He realized the accuracy of what they'd told him about the conflicted feelings he was having about whether what he was saying was what would save Dexter. He was also furious with Dexter for even putting him in this position, high above the stage.

Dexter said, "I always figure unless I'm psychologically needy, I can't get what I want."

"You don't need to blackmail me into giving you a hug."

"I already did. You're here."

"Were you faking the other day at my house? Doing all that banging, just to get me to hold you, to carry you?"

"I don't know."

"Why did touching that condom cause you to begin banging your head against the wall?"

"I was forced to suck on a classmate's dick when I was in eighth grade. He wore a condom. It made me gag. I'm pretty fucked up. It's like I can't do anything just because I want to or need to. It's like I've always got to have an excuse. Nobody's going to meet my needs unless I blackmail them into doing it."

"When you come down, we will hug, if you want. We can talk for as long as you want. I'd like it if you came down." Turner's neck was also getting a crick from constantly having to look up to talk to the kid. He tried to maintain as much eye contact as he could. After he dropped his head for several moments, then looked back up, Dexter had taken several steps down. From this distance his bare torso revealed tattoos: roses, lightning, a Pegasus. The ones on his wrist that Turner had seen the edges of in their first interview turned out to be musical notes.

"How'd you get in here?"

"I came in through the secure entrance. All of us were given the star code. It was some kind of security thing."

Turner said, "I thought you were petrified of heights."

"I'd like to die like this. That's what I was always afraid of. That I'd let go. That I'd fly off. That I wouldn't be able to hold on."

"Down here you can hold onto me."

Clendenen shut his eyes. He lowered each leg slowly until it firmly rested on the next rung down. Turner knew there were cops watching. He saw several people easing along the struts near the ceiling high above. He didn't think they'd be able to do much good. They couldn't possibly rappel down faster than gravity would bring the kid down to earth. He knew Fenwick would keep anyone from taking any precipitate action. He didn't know what Dexter would do if the kid became aware of them.

It took fifteen minutes for Clendenen to descend the twenty feet. When he had both feet on the platform, Turner stood up. Clendenen could still dash to one of the sides and hurl himself off. Clendenen took a stop toward Turner.

Turner spoke softly, "It's okay, Dexter." He also kept his back up against one of the fiberglass end poles, his feet firmly planted, and his muscles tensed. Clendenen could also make a rush toward him to attempt to throw him off or to get them both to fly off together into the vast nothing between their perch and the floor far below.

Clendenen closed his eyes. Turner took a step toward him. Turner was now closer to the boy than the boy was to the edge or to the strut. He didn't know if the boy had noticed. Turner wasn't about to do something rash. He waited. Eyes still closed, Clendenen paced toward him in minuscule increments. When he did reach Turner, the boy crushed him in an embrace. Turner held the kid. If anything the boy was thinner than just a day or so ago. He wondered if the kid had eaten anything since Sunday morning at Mrs. Talucci's. He felt annoyed when the boy swiveled his hip to place his crotch, now bulging prominently, against his own. Dexter began to slide to the floor.

Turner held him up by his armpits. Clendenen placed his hands on Turner's ass. Turner took the boy's arms firmly and held them away. Clendenen met his gaze.

"No," Turner said. "You met Ben. I love him. I will help you, but I will not be part of seducing you or being seduced. I will not be part of using you or being used by you."

"I could try to kill myself again."

"Real or fake attempts at psychological blackmail are not going to work." Clendenen tried to move his hands. Turner kept a firm grip on them.

Clendenen said, "You wouldn't hurt me."

Turner said, "If I wanted to, I could cuff you to the center strut. I'd rather not."

"Will you hold me some more?"

"You need more help than my holding you."

"I feel safe with you."

"I want you to feel safe."

"Roger wasn't. Jason wasn't."

Turner waited. He assumed a confession was coming. It didn't. Clendenen shut his eyes and leaned forward to kiss him. Turner gripped Clendenen as tightly as ever and said, "No."

Clendenen leaned hard against him. He felt the kid's weight. He eased the two of them onto the platform. He held the young man and let him snuggle close.

Clendenen muttered, "They all fucked me. I let them. I

liked it. It made me feel part of the group. For a few minutes I didn't feel alone."

"We found your diary."

"Some of the stuff I made up. Some I left out. The first time we went on an overnight trip. We were in Fresno. Roger was the first. He was nice. The others were rough. Sometimes we did it all together in a hotel room."

"Everybody watched?"

"Sometimes."

"Did you kill them?"

"No. I let them fuck me because I wanted the pain to go away. It hurts being the most unpopular kid in school. I wanted them to like me."

"Did they use condoms? If they were screwing with others, you could have gotten any number of diseases."

"I've been tested. I'm fine."

The kid snuggled his head into Turner's chest. Physical closeness was the only safety the kid wanted. Turner appreciated all degrees of touching, from a good hug to a night and day of passionate lovemaking, as much as anyone, but this seemed to be all the kid understood.

"I'd like to stay like this forever," Clendenen said.

"We have to find out who killed the three of them," Turner said.

"I don't care. They're dead. Most of the time I want to be dead." He wrenched himself from Turner's embrace. He leapt to one of the end poles, teetered on the platform edge for several seconds, let go, yodeled in triumph, and set his arms like a diver.

It was the yodel and the diver crap that gave Turner time to lunge after him. He caught the kid's ankle. There were shouts and a loud scream from below. The kid dangled by one leg. With his other hand Turner gripped the kid's calf. He heard pounding on the steps behind him. Within seconds

Pastern and Davis had latched onto the detective. Moments later, several more hands gripped Dexter. They dragged him back.

When they got him safely back into the middle of the platform, Clendenen began to cry. The members of the Riveting Records entourage began surrounding the nearly deceased band member. Turner said, "We need to take him off this platform very carefully. I suggest handcuffs for his feet and arms."

Every single one of the entourage began to protest. His mother and father objected the most firmly.

Fenwick puffed up to the platform with several uniformed cops in tow. To the beat cops Turner said, "Surround Dexter Clendenen. Restrain him. Cuff him if you have to." More uniforms appeared at the top of the steps. Turner said, "I want all the people who are not part of the Chicago Police Department off this platform."

More protests. Dexter kept his eyes closed and his lips pressed tightly together.

The platform groaned. There were nearly twenty people trying to cram onto it. "This thing is unstable," Turner said. Hangers-on began to scramble backward. Beat cops hustled the rest away. Along with Turner, four uniforms and Fenwick remained on top.

"Is this thing going to hold?" Fenwick asked.

The platform swayed slightly then stopped. "I hope so," Turner said. With uniformed cops gripping either elbow and one in front and one behind, they duck-walked Dexter Clendenen down. It took quite some time. When they got to the bottom, Turner looked up at the platform. Workers from the stadium began hurrying up. When the first of them took a step onto the top platform, it groaned and swayed. Workers pelted back down the stairs. Moments later there was a loud crack. The people still on the stairs jumped for their lives. The crowd on the ground scattered. Seconds later the entire structure crashed to the ground.

From the edge of the debris, Turner saw one of the workers from the arena on the ground moaning. He'd broken his leg when he fell. Everyone else had gotten off and out of the way in time.

Clendenen said, "I tried to loosen all the connections." He smiled as he said it.

"Get him out of my sight," Turner said. He was more than fed up with the band member. The adrenaline rush was beginning to wear off. He felt the muscles in his shoulders and arms tremble a little. It had been a supreme effort to hold onto the kid and keep him from plummeting to his death.

Mr. and Mrs. Clendenen left with Dexter.

Turner explained everything Dexter had said to Fenwick and Molton, who had arrived on the scene.

Fenwick said, "He's a raver. Are you okay?"

Turner said, "Nothing a lot of sleep won't cure." The area they were standing in was completely sealed off from anyone but Chicago police. Evidence techs were combing the remains of the platform.

"How the hell could that kid be up on the platform and no one notice?" Fenwick asked. "Where the hell was security?"

The guard was summoned. He said, "They all came in that star entrance. They were in and out all night. How was I supposed to know which of them was going to try and commit suicide?" He shuffled off.

Turner looked at the mess. "Dexter conquered his fear. A triumph of modern psychology. They got him to sing and dance fifty feet in the air, but they couldn't make him happy."

Fenwick said, "Let's arrest him for several crimes."

"I'm not sure destroying their own platform is much of a crime, unless Zawicki wants to press charges."

"Book him for being a psychotic creep who almost got a bunch of people killed," Fenwick said.

One of the beat cops brought over Clendenen's backpack. "This was at the edge of the wreckage."

Turner looked inside. A small-caliber revolver.

Fenwick said, "Son of a bitch."

"My sentiments exactly," Turner said.

On the way out Hinkmeyer came up to them. "The press wants to interview Detective Turner. He saved Dexter's life. He's a hero. I already have CNN, Fox, ABC, NBC, CBS, and all the major print media interested in interviews. We managed to get a picture of Detective Turner holding onto him."

"Go away," Turner said. His innate well of courtesy was just about dry.

Hinkmeyer said, "We'll want pictures of you with Dexter."

"Your boy is in jail at the moment," Molton said. "We may be charging him with a crime."

"Are you sure you want to do that?" she asked.

Pastern joined them. "Thank you for saving him."

◢ 23 ◣

Turner and Fenwick sat back at their desks. Clendenen had been interrogated for over an hour. In the presence of cops and lawyers he had done little but weep and claim he'd never seen the gun.

Back at his desk, Turner called Mrs. Talucci and asked if she was sure there hadn't been a gun in the backpack when she looked through it.

"I don't miss firearms," she said. "I had everything out. A pink notebook, three pencils, a tiny pencil sharpener, a novel, and a T-shirt."

Turner hunted for McWilliams to ask if they'd checked Clendenen's backpack at the stadium when they were searching the first time.

"No," McWilliams said. "We hadn't when we found the gun. There was no reason to search once we had it."

Made sense.

They sent the gun out to be checked for fingerprints. Clendenen was definitely the prime suspect, but they had to be absolutely certain. The killer could have planted the weapon. An incorrect arrest and the media would crucify them.

Turner and Fenwick did detective paperwork for over an hour and weren't nearly done. They downed vats of coffee. Turner picked up the history Blundlefitz had pulled together. He began a chronological record of the connections between each person involved in the case from the early days to the present.

"Look," he said to Fenwick, after he'd been working for half an hour. "All these people are intertwined more incestuously than a backwoods Appalachian family."

Fenwick perused what Turner had done. "They were all in bands at some point?" Turner asked.

"Everybody except the choreographer and she worked with some of them in that capacity, but she never appeared onstage."

"What happened to all their bands?" Turner asked.

"You heard what we've been told. Most don't succeed. They get their success secondhand by working with this band."

"Why did all these people fail?"

"Is it important?" Fenwick asked.

Molton trudged up to their desks. He glanced at the papers in Fenwick's hand. "Anything?"

Fenwick said, "Lots of bands that flopped."

"A band named 'Damn Skippy'?" Molton said.

"Yeah, Blundlefitz wrote a review of them," Turner said.

Molton held out the piece of paper he held in his hand. "This says Jordan Pastern was in that band."

Turner said, "I think somebody else was, too." He hunted through the papers on his desk and pulled out the fifth sheet he looked at. "Yeah, Hinkmeyer sang for the group for a while. According to Blundlefitz's notes they made a small splash in Florida." He found Blundlefitz's review. "He saw them when they came through town with one of those rock conglomerations at a summer all-day band festival." Fenwick and Molton looked over Turner's shoulder. The review was short and vicious. "More pretension than music occurred at the twenty-four-hour all-rock festival in Tinley Park. Perhaps the most pretentious was the least talented group, Damn Skippy."

Molton said, "These people were all connected. Let's get them in here again. They can bring as many of their goddamn lawyers as they want."

While they waited for them, the detectives continued their research. Turner tapped the Internet connection on his computer and typed in "Damn Skippy" in the search line. He found a Web site that was at least six years out of date.

"Don't these things ever die?" Fenwick asked.

"Unless the server company cleans house, they must not," Turner said.

Fenwick said, "Let's go through all the background that Blundlefitz found on these people."

Turner stuck the disk into the computer slot and called up the data. Turner found out that Zawicki had grown up in Laguna Beach, California. That he was the valedictorian of his class but never gave the speech—no reason given. That he'd worked his way up through various companies following the Hollywood rule that if you got fired from one company you moved up to a higher position in the next one. Over time he'd managed groups who'd made him rich and his reputation for making people rich made him powerful. He hadn't had a miss in fifteen years.

Jordan Pastern had been an MP in the military and a cop on the force in Northridge, California, moonlighting in Hollywood as a security guard.

Eudace had been in numerous bands, all of which flopped. He'd been the one who organized each of the bands.

Hinkmeyer, according to Blundlefitz, was the most efficient and well organized of any press person he'd done business with.

Turner called Jeremiah Boissec, Zawicki's former employee. Turner explained the connections they'd been making.

Boissec said, "They were all in bands. They'd go out drinking sometimes, and they'd get all nostalgic about what could have been. I thought it was pretty pathetic."

"Who was most pathetic?"

"The whole crowd. They thought they should have been superstars."

The members of the entourage entered arguing. Pastern, Eudace, Zawicki, and company crowded around the detectives. Some demanded answers. Some began berating Turner and Fenwick.

Fenwick said, "Shut up."

He got several startled, several huffy, and several enraged looks.

Turner said, "We have a great deal more information than we did a little while ago. Mr. Blundlefitz kept excellent files. My guess is, something he discovered led him to believe he knew who the killer was. All of you are deeply interconnected with one another."

"So what?" Eudace said.

"There was a band called Damn Skippy," Turner said.

"Big deal," Zawicki said.

"They went nowhere because the leader didn't put out," Turner said.

"The leader did put out!" Eudace said. "I did put out. I just didn't want to be in a band with those guys anymore. I wanted to be an agent. Jonathan got me started."

"You son of a bitch," Pastern said.

Eudace said, "How do you think you got this job? I felt sorry for you."

Galyak and Pappas were led to a stark interrogation room. Company lawyers were present.

"What happened to Dexter?" Pappas asked.

Fenwick said, "You all fucked Dexter Clendenen."

"What?" Galyak said. "That's not true."

"He says it is."

"He's nuts."

"You saying you never had sex with Dexter?"

Galyak said, "He sucked my dick a couple times in South America. That's not really sex. I was horny. It was no big deal."

Pappas said, "What's going on?"

Fenwick said, "You all fucked Dexter Clendenen."

"All of us?" Pappas asked.

"Yep," Fenwick said.

Pappas said, "He asked me to, begged me."

"Group sex?"

"A couple times Roger and me took turns with him. We were horny. He enjoyed it. Hey, I'm not gay. I don't know about the rest of the guys. I just figured Dexter was probably this closet case. Nobody wanted it to get out that one of us might be gay. That would blow the image with all those teenybop girls."

Fenwick was pissed. "Everybody was having sex. Nobody seemed much interested in anything but making money and fucking. Big egos got in everybody's way but nobody wanted to kill anybody? This whole thing is totally screwed up."

Galyak asked, "Why can't Dexter be the killer? Somebody said he loosened all the bolts on the platform and that's why it fell down. Maybe he did all the rest. He was nuts."

Jonathan Zawicki was the next person they interviewed. He looked pale and shaken. "What the hell is happening?" he asked. This time it didn't sound to Turner like a demand, but more as if Zawicki was generally distraught.

"What were you trying to do with Randall Blundlefitz?" Fenwick asked.

"I was using the fat fool."

"When we first talked to him, he thought you did it."

"Yeah, well, he was stupid and egotistical."

Fenwick said, "If being egotistical is a crime, we'd have to arrest all of you."

"Blundlefitz wanted an 'in' to the industry. He might have been a medium-sized fish in the very small pond of Midwest critics, but he was a member of the local press. We could use him, and we did."

"Did he tell you about his investigation?"

"Not really."

"Do you know who he talked to?"

"I gave him access to everybody."

"What did he ask you?"

"Mostly he asked about everybody's history. I guess he must have thought that the killing had something to do with what had gone on in the industry prior to this."

"And did it?"

"I have no idea."

Fenwick said, "You have lots of people pretty pissed at you."

"So do you."

Fenwick said, "But people I know aren't dying."

"Is that by random chance, luck?"

"These people aren't dying by random chance," Turner said. "Many of your employees were in bands before working for your company."

"Many people in the industry work for a variety of bands

270

and companies before they either hit it big, give up and go back to Keokuk, or take mid-level jobs that keep them close to the action, but not out in the spotlight. Being close to center stage is the most they are ever going to get. My question to you is this: If someone is so angry at me, why don't they kill me? Why bother with the guys in the band, and certainly I wouldn't be terribly discommoded by the death of a minor critic?"

"Getting revenge is often about making someone suffer, not about killing them. If they're dead, the revenge is over. If they're living and suffering, the revenge repeats itself every minute of every hour of every day."

Lawyers pushed. Suspects left. Paperwork ensued. They picked up on the cops' hesitancy to charge Dexter. He was released but told not to leave town.

Around six Mrs. Talucci called. "I've got that Pappas boy here. You should stop by."

Turner hurried home. It was almost time for breakfast. The temperature was nearly twenty below. In the cold and the wind each breath seared as he pulled it in.

Pappas sat in Mrs. Talucci's living room. Mrs. Talucci's grandniece, the prettiest and smartest one, Donna Marie, sat next to Pappas. When Turner and Fenwick arrived, Mrs. Talucci ushered her grandniece out of the room.

Pappas said, "I talked to Dexter. He said something funny that I thought you should know."

"What's that?"

"Jordan Pastern and Roger and Dexter used to have three-way sex scenes."

"Did you have sex with Jordan?"

"No. He never asked. He never tried. I don't know if I would have or not. I suppose I would have. I don't know. Mostly I had women. Sex came so easy, it wasn't a big deal."

"So why tell me about this?"

"It seemed to upset Dexter. I guess what he wanted most was a stable quiet relationship. We were a long way from home for a very long time for a lot of years. It can be very comforting to have people physically close to you that you know."

"Did you need that?"

"I had lots of girls. I'm telling you this because I think Dexter was going to kill himself because of Jordan."

"I don't understand."

"I don't, either. You should go talk to Dexter."

Turner had had just about enough of Dexter and all the members of the band.

They headed back to the Hotel Chicago. Outside Dexter's room, they found a Chicago cop. "Everything quiet?" Turner asked.

The cop nodded. "There was some therapist in there with Clendenen. The head of security and some other band people are in there, too."

Turner and Fenwick entered the suite. Hinkmeyer sat at a desk in the first room with a sheaf of phone messages in front of her. She had a hotel phone in one hand and a cell phone in the other. She gave him a brief wave.

Turner said, "Where's Dexter?"

"I don't know. I haven't seen him."

Ralph Eudace entered. "What's going on?"

"Where's Dexter?" Turner asked.

"I told him to stay here."

"He's supposed to be under guard," Turner said.

"Pastern said he would be safe. Pastern said he would be with him."

"He was with Pastern?" Turner asked. "Where?"

"I don't know."

"Where did Clendenen say he felt safest?" Fenwick asked.

"The tour bus," Turner said. "He said it was a heaven." They detailed other cops to hunt through the hotel rooms. The bus was parked underground. The lights were off. Hinkmeyer gave them the key. Turner and Fenwick entered quietly. Everything was silent as they stood next to the steering wheel. They found made-up beds and scattered clothes and suitcases in both front rooms. Behind the third door, they heard voices. Turner thought he heard Dexter shout, "Stop!" and another voice, "Take it, you cock-sucking little faggot."

Turner pounded on the door and announced himself as the police. Still nothing.

Hinkmeyer joined him. She said, "I heard the noise."

"You got the key to get in here?"

She produced a card. "I'm in charge of accommodations. What's going on?"

Turner inserted the card, turned the handle, and pulled the door open. Clendenen was on his back. Naked. Pastern, his pants around his knees, his shirttail covering his butt, his back to Turner, was thrusting his hips toward Clendenen's ass. Both of Pastern's hands held onto a gun which he had jammed into Clendenen's mouth. The young man was gagging and squealing. There was blood around his mouth. Pastern's head was thrown back, his eyes shut, his breath coming in ragged gasps. His dick was deep up Clendenen's asshole.

Turner pulled out his gun. Pastern gave several more thrusts, gasped deeply, then held still. Clendenen whimpered. Pastern pulled his condomless cock out of Clendenen's butt. Turner grabbed the gun.

Pastern opened his eyes. "What the fuck?"

"My question exactly," Turner said.

Clendenen rushed to Turner and held on as if his life depended on it.

"He was going to kill me." Dexter fainted. Turner picked him up and put him on one of the recliners near the entrance and covered him with a blanket with the band's bright cheery logo emblazoned on the front.

24

The detectives had Pastern handcuffed to the steering wheel of the bus while they talked.

Turner said, "You were in a band in college that was not picked up by Mr. Zawicki."

"We were told we weren't very good," Pastern said. "The problem was none of us would put out. Except that traitor Eudace."

"You were asked?"

"Not explicitly, but I figured it out."

"How'd you get so many twenty-two revolvers?"

"I'm a security guard. I can get as many guns as I want. They aren't illegal. I can bring as many guns into anyplace I want."

"Why'd you kill them?" Turner asked Pastern.

"Zawicki and the band are morons. I should have had that life, but I was getting pleasure from them. Every time I had my dick up their tight little butts, I thought about them being out onstage, with all those little girls and faggot boys wishing they had what I got. I only got Dexter and Stendar, but that was enough."

"Why kill Jason Devane?"

"Devane seemed to be catching on. They aren't all as dumb as everyone thinks they are. That afternoon he said he just had to get out. I offered to go with him to keep him safe. I made sure nobody got told we were going. We walked to a coffee shop. He kept a hat down over his eyes. As he talked, I realized he was figuring out about all the sex. He'd had suspicions. He was going to die anyway so I decided then would be as good a time as any. I fucked him first. Before that he'd only been fucked by Zawicki. I found a nice quiet place to screw him at Navy Pier. He squealed a little with my dick up his butt. I shot him, shoved him into the lake, and came back. I should have been one of them. I should have had their career. Zawicki fucked me and now Zawicki is fucked."

"Not as fucked as you are," Fenwick said.

"Why wait until Chicago?" Turner asked.

"This was the height of their popularity. I'd been planning the killings for a while. Zawicki was going to fire me. They lied when they said they told me. I, however, had found out accidentally. Zawicki keeps far too many notes on everything. I had to act now."

"Why kill Blundlefitz?"

"He'd found the diary. He figured the unknown person who kept being mentioned had to be me. No one else had the access. He guessed, and he was right. I didn't need him as another enemy. He asked to meet me. I went with everyone to the stadium. He showed up. I told him we'd talk at center stage. That part wasn't going to be taken down. I knew center stage didn't have security cameras. The fool figured he was invulnerable."

"You didn't fuck him?" Fenwick asked.

"God, no."

"Why the sabotage?"

"Diversions. There was enough to cause all kinds of suspicion or take up a lot of the cops' time. None of it was enough to kill anybody. If I got lucky with one of the shots in the auditorium, then it was all for the best. I killed Blundlefitz before you dragged us all down here for that dog-and-pony show with all the likely suspects."

"Somebody could have walked in."

"Then I'd have waited, but it worked and getting him at center stage was a stroke of luck."

"How'd Blundlefitz get Dexter's diary?"

"Mostly Dexter kept it with him. He was so zonked out on drugs, Blundlefitz probably took it while he was in the hospital. He had all-access all the time. I tossed the gun that I used on Blundlefitz into Dexter's backpack after we left here when you had all the suspects together. I knew I could put suspicion on him."

Turner asked, "Why'd you screw them?"

Pastern gave a short laugh that sounded more like a bark. "Roger Stendar was straight, but after a concert he loved getting fucked. I obliged. He'd just put himself out in front of huge crowds. I guess he need affirmation. I was in a band. I understand the rush and then the letdown when it's over. He needed touch."

"If he was straight, why not get a woman? A lot of them were throwing themselves at him."

"Maybe he was gayer than he thought."

"How'd you get rid of the gun?"

"No one was going to walk in, so I walked out through the sauna, tossed it, and hurried back the same way. Then stationed myself at the entrance to the reception."

◣ 25 ◢

Paul stopped at Mrs. Talucci's later that night. Ivan Pappas sat at the table in Mrs. Talucci's house. He was next to her grandniece, Donna Marie. He was very nicely dressed in a suit and tie. Mrs. Talucci presided at the head of the table. It was Donna Marie's birthday. Paul, Ben, and their sons were present, as were numerous relations of Mrs. Talucci. A fuss was not being made over Ivan Pappas. He had very properly asked if he could pay court on Donna Marie who had giggled and said yes.

Much later, Paul crawled into bed next to Ben. He could hear faint music from Brian's radio. He knew when the timer clicked off that his son was asleep. The boy always clicked it for ten more minutes if he was awake.

Ben murmured, "At dinner Jeff announced he wanted to be part of a rock band."

"As an adult?"

"I believe he was on the Internet with his friends trying to form a group within the next five minutes or so."

"What instrument is he going to play?"

"I don't think they got that far in the details. It's being in a band that seems to be the operative thing."

"I may swear off music for the rest of my life," Paul said.

Ben pulled him close. "As long as you don't swear off other things."